D1319313

FROM MACHO TO MARIPOSA

FROM MACHO TO MARIPOSA

NEW GAY LATINO FICTION

EDITED BY
CHARLES RICE-GONZÁLEZ
& CHARLIE VÁZQUEZ

Tincture
an IMPRINT OF LETHE PRESS

Published in 2011 by Tincture, an imprint of
LETHE PRESS, INC.
118 Heritage Avenue • Maple Shade, NJ 08052-3018
www.lethepressbooks.com • lethepress@aol.com
ISBN: 1-59021-241-X
ISBN-13: 978-1-59021-241-7

These stories are works of fiction. Names, characters, places, and
incidents are products of the authors' imaginations or are used
fictitiously.

Set in Bell MT, LD Eleanor Rae, and Lithos.
Cover and interior design: Alex Jeffers.
Cover image: Joan Crisol Guisado.

LIBRARY OF CONGRESS CATALOGING-IN-PUBLICATION DATA
From macho to mariposa : new gay Latino fiction / edited by Charles
Rice-González & Charlie Vázquez.
    p. cm.
 ISBN-13: 978-1-59021-241-7 (pbk. : alk. paper)
 ISBN-10: 1-59021-241-X (pbk. : alk. paper)
 1. American fiction--Hispanic American authors. 2. Gays' writings,
American. 3. Hispanic American gays--Fiction. 4. Homosexuality--
Fiction. I. Rice-González, Charles. II. Vázquez, Charlie, 1971-
 PS647.H58F76 2011
 813'.0108920664--dc22
                            2011012823

Introduction from the Editors

CHARLES RICE-GONZÁLEZ

In 2007, I met with Jaime Manrique. I suggested that he do another queer, Latino anthology. He had edited *Bésame Mucho: New Gay Latino Fiction* with Jesse Dorris which came out in June 1999. That same year Jaime Cortez edited *Virgins, Guerrillas, and Locas: Gay Latinos Writing about Love* which came out in October, and Erasmo Guerra's non-fiction anthology *Latin Lovers: True Stories of Latin Men in Love* came out in November (Guerra's book included non-Latinos). Then, in 2008, Emanuel Xavier edited *Mariposas: A Modern Anthology of Queer Latino Poetry*, but no gay Latino fiction anthologies since 1999. I figured with Jaime Manrique's reputation and connections he could land a publisher. "Jaime, it's about time, don't you think?" I was pushing him because I wanted to be in it.

"No!" His deep baritone voice boomed in his small West Village apartment. "I'm working on a book. I'm too busy, and besides who's going to be in it? You, me and Rigoberto González?"

I pleaded that there were other queer Latino writers out there even though I had yet to meet Charlie Vázquez, Justin Torres and many other writers who are included in this anthology. I was in my MFA program at Goddard at the time and I had this vision of queer Latino writers, like me, in MFA programs all over the country and writers writing in their rooms and cafes. I had also been to a few writer conferences where I'd met other queer Latino writers.

Jaime didn't relent.

In 2009, Steve Berman from Lethe Press called me. He liked my story that he published in *Best Gay Stories 2008* and he had an idea to do a queer Latino anthology and wanted to know if I'd be interested in editing it for a new imprint that he was going to start called Tincture to publish work by queer writers of color.

Me? I thought. I had been trying to get someone else to edit one and I didn't think that I could do it. We met in the Seven Bar and Grill near Penn Station in New York City on a snowy day in early 2009. I was still unsure, but he was confident that I could do it. Then, I thought, *Who else?* I had the passion and commitment to see this project through and I was interested in developing a community of queer writers. Then, I got excited at the thought of putting out a call and seeing who was out there. The anthology became an act of activism. I put out the call—drafted releases, set up a Facebook page, made flyers—and set out to find as many gay Latino writers as possible.

By the deadline for the call, which was in January 2010, I had received over 60 submissions from all across the country and even a couple from outside the United States. There were even a couple of submissions by women. I asked Steve about doing a queer Latina anthology and he said that he was open to it, but he wanted a woman to edit it.

In May 2010, I brought on Charlie Vázquez to co-edit the manuscript with me. I had met Charlie in June 2008 at the reading for *Los otros cuerpos: Antología de temática gay, lésbica y queer desde Puerto Rico y su diáspora*. He'd just started his PANIC! reading series at the Nowhere Bar. After he invited me to read at PANIC! in January 2009, we connected and I felt like I'd found a kindred spirit—a writer who took the development of his own work seriously and who was interested in creating a community of queer writers. When we started working on this anthology our one rule was that any story in the collection was one that we both agreed should be included. The first part was easy. I sent him all the stories that qualified in accordance with the call, then we ranked our choices with a yes or no. The ones where we agreed upon favorably or unfavorably were clear. That middle group we discussed.

It was a rough road getting to this final group because, I wish I could have published every single writer and secondly because although I asked for the stories to be ready for publication several really wonderful manuscripts had fallen into that middle group and some were a few drafts away from being ready. Charlie and I made a decision to connect with some of the writers, give feedback, so that they could do another draft. With some writers I worked on two, three, even four drafts of a story before Charlie and I accepted them or in some cases still didn't.

Speaking to other editors, I learned that we went beyond the call of duty, but it was important to get as many voices into the collection.

What you have in your hand is a collection of 29 writers—all male and Latino identified, from 10 different states and Puerto Rico. The writers' Latinidads are Chicano/Xiqan@ and Mexican, Puerto Rican, Dominican, Cuban, Salvadoran, Chilean and Brazilian. And for nearly half, this is the first time their fiction is published.

What I like to think about when I read these works is that these stories are what this group of writers is sharing with the world. From timeless issues like unrequited love to empowered youth for whom being queer is not a question, from tough, swaggering machos, owning their love of men to gentlemen with the emphasis on the gentle.

There are tales of revenge, modern day parables, and stories navigating relationships—having them, getting them, working them out. From border towns to the streets of L.A. and the Bronx, to the lush mountains of Puerto Rico, to metropolitan cities of the Dominican Republic, to a disco in Silver Lake and a panadería in Kansas, the stories, experiences and worlds are varied and connected.

Charles Rice-González
Bronx, New York
February 2011

CHARLIE VÁZQUEZ

Returning to my native New York City in 2006 from my seventeen-year "exile" in Portland, Oregon and Baja California Norte was one of the hardest decisions I've ever had to make—yet one that has rewarded me with an increased sense of community and belonging. Not only did I want to reconnect with my family in the Bronx where I grew up, I wanted to meet other queer Latino writers and get involved in (what I hoped to be) a necessary lit-

x

erary and political movement—as we queer hispanohablan-tes often encounter significant difficulties while navigating between our vibrant and passionate Latino cultures and the complex sphere of the LGBT/queer movement, which inher-its much of the discriminations and opinions of mainstream American culture, desirable and otherwise.

The first angel I befriended on this rather spiritual journey was the groundbreaking New York poet and writer Emanuel Xavier, whom I met through our mutual writer friend Trebor Healey, who was in town for an event at The Center in the West Village in 2006. Emanuel's kindness of spirit and gen-erosity were clear from the onset of our friendship and it's been a great fortune to get to know and work with him (we even launched our books together at a June 2010 Barnes and Noble dual book-signing on the Upper West Side, as we also share the same publisher, Rebel Satori Press).

The watershed moment for me, however, was the reading that took place at the Clemente Soto Vélez Cultural Center for a book of Puerto Rican letters called *Los otros cuerpos: Antología de temática gay, lésbica, bisexual y queer desde Puerto Rico y su diáspora* (Editorial Tiempo Nuevo, 2007) a volume edited and published on the island which featured Arnaldo Cruz-Malavé, Angel Antonio, David Caleb Acevedo, Larry La Fountain, Luzma Umpierre, Frances Negrón-Muntaner, Robert Vázquez-Pacheco, and this book's co-editor, dynamo Charles Rice-González, (whom I would meet for the first time), all in one handsome Spanish volume.

When Charles asked me to co-edit this collection with him in spring 2010 I thought, we've hit the jackpot! Much new tierra needed to be covered since the eminent Jaime Manrique edited *Bésame Mucho* in 1999 for Painted Leaf Press—an anthology which included now-established voic-es such as Rigoberto González and the aforementioned Emanuel Xavier. But a whole new generation of gay/queer

Latino writers had surfaced since then and their stories and identities had yet to be exposed—this would be a way of making that happen. Furthermore, the outreach potential of the internet and social media would more easily put us in contact with people outside the stateside Latino "loop" of California, Illinois, Florida, Texas, and New York.

In addition, this journey required a much more severe degree of temperance than I had foreseen; many of the stories you're about to read tread into very intense psychological landscapes, many of which gave me sunny joy, many of which caused me profound sadness. But the spectrum of experiences and emotions that haunt our mortal days are what give life its dimension, and for us gay/queer Latinos, these experiences often embody striking similarities and common ground. One of these commonalities is the cellular longing for that ultimate loving, male energy; brother energy, father energy: los machos, los diositos de nuestros sueños—the men and boys of our never-ending fantasies. Add to that equality, intimacy, friendship, respect, freedom, justice, dreams, love...in other words, editing these stories with Charles was often haunting.

I'd had considerable experience with editing text as a writer, but the politics inherent to the crossroads of English and Spanish—or Spanglish/code-switching—would require absolute redefining of textual style. Like many young English-focused writers, I learned my basic editing skills through Strunk and White's *The Elements of Style* handbook back in the mid-1990s, when I began composing my first novel, *Buzz and Israel* (Fireking, 2004). And if I recall correctly, this starchy and aging handbook urged to never use foreign language words when writing in English—and if you must include them to italicize them. This is what I had done and encountered for many years as a writer and literature addict.

While working on Karen Jaime's piece for *The Best of PANIC!* (Fireking, 2010) reading series anthology (she's a poet and Performance Studies major at New York University), I was pleased to discover that she didn't italicize Spanish unless the need was the same as for English, such as with the names of books. Her explanation was that using italics "others" a language—distinguishes it from English—which doesn't necessarily reduce it, but marginalizes it. Sets it apart. Well, this doesn't work for bilingual Latinos, so I took Karen's philosophy to heart and discussed this with Charles, who also agreed that our nation's unofficial second language—which preceded English here by over a hundred years and is spoken by over 35 million people in the U.S. by 2009 Census Bureau estimates—deserved equality here.

Ahead of you is a miniature galaxy of queer Latino ecstasy, fantasy, tenderness, violence, desire, heartbreak, wonder, hope…a cross-section sampling of our wildly diverse and tempestuously passionate lives; the experiences that affect us so deeply that we put them to the page to share with others. I hope that this book will serve as a catalyst to connect individuals and groups, even if virtually (writers: connect with us/each other via social media!). I'm forever grateful to Charles Rice-González and Lethe Press for including me on this colorful odyssey and hope that you'll enjoy reading it as much as we did organizándolo. ¡Wepa!

Charlie Vázquez
Brooklyn, New York
February, 2011

Table of Contents

INTRODUCTION • VII
• *Charles Rice-González & Charlie Vázquez*

HUERFANITA (LITTLE ORPHAN GIRL) • 1
• *David Andrew Talamantes*

ON THE LINE • 9
• *Benny Vásquez*

JÚNIOR, REGGAETÓN TROPICAL • 17
• *Lawrence La Fountain-Stokes*

THAT CHILLY NIGHT IN OLD SAN JUAN • 25
• *Bronco Castro*

YERMO • 29
• *Charlie Vázquez*

A DOOMED GAY MARRIAGE • 43
• *Rigoberto González*

GOOD BLOOD • 47
• *Alex G. Romero*

SILLY BOY • 53
• *Booh Edouardo*

BABY, BEAUTIFUL • 67
• *C. Adán Cabrera*

FAIRY TALE • 81
• *Justin Torres*

PREGNANT BOY • 85
• *Chuy Sánchez*

JAVIER • 95
• *Edwin Sánchez*

THE TEAM • 103
• *Johnathan Cedano*

DARK SIDE OF THE FLAME • 113
• *Danny González*

BABY, I'M SCARED OF YOU (FROM **MIXTAPE**) · 121
• *Ricardo Bracho*

ESTE DULCE FRÍO · 127
• *Miguel Ángel Ángeles*

THE FERMI PARADOX · 131
Ben Francisco

ANTOLOGÍA · 147
• *Anthony Haro*

MY HERO ABEL · 155
• *Jesus Suarez*

THUNDERCLAP · 165
• *David Caleb Acevedo*

EMPANADAS · 173
• *Miguel M. Morales*

REQUIEM SERTANEJO · 177
• *Rick J. Santos*

MIDNIGHT WATERS · 185
• *Jimmy Lam*

CENTENARIO (NOVEL EXCERPT) · 189
• *Alfonso Ramírez*

EDEN LOST (NOVEL EXCERPT) · 201
• *W. Brandon Lacy Campos*

FABRIZIO (NOVEL EXCERPT) · 217
• *Guillermo Reyes*

MICHAEL MOVES TO FAILE STREET · 225
• *Charles Rice-González*

THE UNHEARD BORDER STORY · 245
• *Bryan Pacheco*

ORCHARD BEACH, SECTION NINE · 265
• *Robert Vázquez-Pacheco*

ABOUT THE AUTHORS · 269

XVI

Huerfanita (Little Orphan Girl)

DAVID ANDREW TALAMANTES

Pablito's seventh birthday fell on a Saturday that year, making it easier for Senaida to throw him a birthday party. The guests would be mostly family, perhaps a few girls from his class, but none of the boys would be interested—Pablo had asked for a pink party. He wanted his favorite color everywhere: the cake, plates, utensils, balloons, napkins, streamers, even the traditional seven-coned piñata. Though Senaida wanted to give Pablo his birthday party as he imagined it, a tormenting image loomed so strongly in her head that she returned the lively pink party décor to the shelves and replaced it with everyday white.

The piñata remained at the store as well.

She had awoken the night before with her neck drenched in sweat and her hands balled into fists. Beto, next to her, reeked of booze. A vile stench emanated from his glistening brown skin and drooling mouth as he snored hoarsely. In the dream she had seen Pablito in his pajamas, gripping a wooden stick. From the rooftop of the house, a larger-than-life-size Beto laughed while holding fiery flaming ropes and controlling a devil-shaped piñata.

Little Pablo swung at the animated demon (more an evil marionette than a party favor) that was filled with dulces. The devil effigy held machetes in each hand. When Pablito attempted an attack, it pulled back and countercharged like a maniacal ram, slicing a bloody wound into Pablito's arm, knocking him to the ground.

"¡Huerfanita estúpida!" Beto taunted from above, throwing an empty beer bottle that shattered near his barefooted son.

The demonio swooped from above, his right machete flying like a matador's banderilla into Pablo's sternum. The boy collapsed and a choke of blood spewed from Pablito's lips like the spray-flames of fireworks. Senaida pulled herself out of the dream, making the sign of the cross over her body before placing her head back down on the pillow.

Senaida had been offered to Beto by her father Ramón, a retired police chief who had remained an influential and silent leader in the Ciudad Juárez Police Department—they were not married. Beto had become Ramón's mechanic earlier that year and worked on underground projects very few knew about. Ramón moved Senaida into Beto's home two days after Filomena, Beto's wife and Pablo's biological mother, disappeared. Pretty young ladies often vanished in Juárez, and Filomena's body was found in the Chihuahuan Desert three weeks later, her face barely identifiable.

Senaida feared her own death when Beto was drunk, or even around, because she knew the truth about Filomena in her soul; she knew her father and Beto were wicked and heartless men and she wanted to protect Pablo however she could.

As a child she had had a little brother named Mateo who met his death at the age of six after Ramón caught him wearing Senaida's favorite pink bathing suit. She screamed but was unable to protect him, as her uniformed father shook and pummeled the tiny six-year-old senseless. Hearing Beto's antagonism of Pablito reminded her too much of her little brother's fate, and though she had witnessed Beto's physical abuse upon his son, God had never sent her such a graphic and horrifying dream before.

The countless gashes, bruises, and black eyes Beto had given Pablo during the year she lived with them were like childhood war wounds that healed, leaving little scarring, but always a little less of the boy's bright personality. She loved Pablo like a son, the way he was, whoever he'd become. She accepted the fact that neither a baseball player nor a fighter would he ever be.

Beto referred to his only child as "la huerfanita"—the little orphan girl. The name surfaced when Filomena disappeared. Beto claimed she was always whoring around and that Pablo couldn't be his son because the boy was lighter-skinned and Beto's seed could never have brought forth such a pansy flower of a child. Senaida hated this nickname but said nothing since her place in his home was not one of voice or opinion—just work and occasional sex.

Beto's part-time mechanic job mainly supported his alcoholism, but he saw himself as the breadwinner, even though he never paid bills or bought groceries; that was left to Senaida, who sometimes took money from his wallet to pay for these things.

Senaida made and sold burritos from an insulated ice-chest she'd purchased at a dollar store in downtown El Paso. She'd often cook her guisados late, achieving a slow simmer overnight. She charged two dollars per burrito and three for the refried bean and chile relleno version, the most popular. She

3

often returned home several times a day to restock her icechest, only to head back out and make ends meet. The week previous to Pablito's birthday had been good and her sisters agreed to help potluck the event.

Pablo wanted to be a Madonna dancer. He first heard "Vogue" on the kitchen radio while eating his Choco Krispies before school one day. Senaida tapped her foot to the beat while dipping fat long green chiles in egg foam, frying them until they floated.

Pablo placed his spoon in the bowl and threw his arms toward the cracked ceiling. He stood on his chair, and in unison, his arms fell outward, drawing magical mariposa wings at his sides. As his hands landed on his hips, he began bobbing to the snap-beat of the song, stepping right and left in perfect rhythm.

Senaida turned around, surprised. She smiled at him as he cat-walked toward her like a runway model, vibrant and brighter than she had ever seen him before. They joined hands and danced for a few seconds, until several golden brown rellenos popped up to the surface of the grease like dead fish in a pond. The bus honked and Senaida kissed Pablito on the cheek, hugging him like she never had before—he deserved it and she needed it.

The mood on the day of the party was fairly relaxed; Senaida had huge pots of frijoles and arroz cooking, and her sister Lucia brought trays of salpicón and cold-cuts from Carlos's Carnicería. Carlos, Lucia's boyfriend, kept her happy, and as long as she did the same, Lucia had all the free meat she wanted.

Her youngest sister Yoya purchased a few dozen mini bolillos and a cake from the Pastelería Carmen at the Rincón de Cortéz Mercado. She had ordered a white cake with white frosting, and after a half-hour phone conversation with

4

Senaida, decided that Pablito deserved pink roses adorning it.

"Maldito cabrón, Beto," she always told Senaida.

The most wonderful part of Pablito's birthday was receiving his birthday outfit—in a large white dress box. Senaida purchased a white linen sport-suit with a white t-shirt decorated with abstract splashes of pink and splotches of black, brushstrokes of silver sparkle and sporadic aqua dots.

Pablo tossed the multicolored tissue paper on the floor and his eyes widened as if he'd discovered a seaweed-covered treasure chest. The most beautiful and luxurious clothing he'd ever seen (or owned) awaited, folded before him. Speechless, he ran to his bedroom with an elongated grin and newfound vibrancy in his sprint.

He emerged a youthful pop star, throwing his arms around Senaida's waist, squeezing her with surprising strength. Never had he owned such flashy clothes, the perfect outfit for his special day. His primas Anita, Ivonne, and Regina, danced to Madonna, Cyndi Lauper, and Michael Jackson for hours on the makeshift dance-floor. Pablo, feeling like his dream would one day come true, joined them with impeccable rhythm.

Beto stayed in the garage while the celebration unfolded, being kept company by a case of Tecate and a plastic jug of tequila. He peeked out on occasion, frowning in disgust, cursing Filomena, Senaida—all the women in general. "No es mi hijo," he grumbled.

"¡Huerfanita, venga!" Beto yelled from the garage two hours later, propping himself up against the workbench. The guests had gone home. He had finished his case of beer and most of the tequila and had managed to stumble to the liquor store to purchase a few forties of Carta Blanca. Though he was two bucks short the clerk didn't mind; there would be

5

many opportunities to swindle back his cash—and more—in the upcoming weeks.

"¡Huerfanita!" he yelled again.

Pablo had been watching his favorite telenovela (*Matar sin sentimiento*); his body stiffened at the sound of Beto's voice. He removed his white suit coat, placing it gently on his bed as he walked outside, nervous that perhaps his dancing had warranted a beating. He reached the garage and peered in.

"¡Rápidamente! I'm going to teach you how to be un hombre macho, not a pinche muchachita..."

"Okay," Pablo complied, entering the garage and shrinking into his thin frame like a dwarf mouse in the presence of a barn cat.

"Answer me! ¡Con huevos!"

"Okay," Pablo said louder, still sounding squeaky.

"¡Otra vez!" Beto raised his hand threateningly before Pablo's face.

"Okay!"

Beto looked at his son and laughed; he grabbed his forehead with clawed-out fingers and pushed him backward into a stumble. "The tires need to be rotated."

Beto brought the jug of tequila to his lips and swigged it; clear drops fell from his chin onto his stained tank-top. He chased it with the nearest bottle of warm Carta Blanca and drew his arm across his mouth, wiping the remains.

He stumbled to the car and dropped to his knees, further dirtying his unwashed jeans on the unpaved garage floor he had passed out on the night before (Senaida had left him there so she could rest before the party).

Beto removed the hubcaps with the dexterity of a man fifty years his junior. Pablo glanced nervously around the garage, a place he had never dared venture into. He noticed Beto's tire-jack near the vehicle's rear and several tires resting on one another a few feet from the car.

"Now we have to get it off the ground," Beto grumbled. "You stay there. I don't want you fucking anything up."

Beto placed the contraption underneath the rear end of the vehicle, with more than half of the jack peering out. Pablo watched with strange fascination as his father inserted a metal rod into the jack and began pumping it, the vehicle ascending. When the car's rear was sufficiently lifted, Beto stepped on a pedal and the car stayed in place.

Beto then pushed on the side of the El Camino; the car moved from side to side, but the jack held. He removed both rear tires, pausing to suck down a couple shots of tequila.

"Only men drink tequila...toma un pisto." He passed the bottle to Pablo, raising a backhand near his face.

Pablo brought the bottle to his lips and tilted it, allowing several ounces of the acidic silver liquid to wash down his throat. The liquor opened his nasal passages and his face contorted into a wrinkled mess, as the heat burned his esophagus like drain cleaner.

Beto, shocked by Pablo's huge swig, laughed heartily. "Maybe one day you'll be a man—but probably not."

Pablo tried his best to hold it down, swallowing mouthfuls of tainted saliva until his mouth felt dry and the vomiting sensation dissipated. He felt dizzy, unclear, like he was dreaming, like he was in the telenovela he had just been watching.

Beto sat on the ground at the tail end of the El Camino and pushed himself underneath. "I have to check the tailpipe first," he mumbled. "Get the tires up...con fuerza."

Pablo did as he was told, his head aching and feeling light. He wrapped his hands around the tire, disliking the dirty feeling the black rubber left on him. Then he looked down at his pants—the tire's zigzag pattern was stamped on the inside of his knee and had ruined his beautiful birthday gift. He felt angry and stood the tire up so it could roll.

"Grab me a screwdriver."

What's a screwdriver, Pablo wondered.

"The flathead with the red handle. ¡Pinche huerfanita!" Beto added with venom, as if hearing Pablo's unvoiced question.

Pablo studied his father's legs as they peeked out from underneath the brown El Camino. While glancing at the jack's lever and safety, he noticed that the vehicle bounced each time Beto shifted his weight.

"¿El rojo?" Pablo asked with a voice as masculine as he could muster. His small hands gripped each side of the tire's walls and the rubber rested awkwardly between his legs, like an oversized bowling ball. "I got it," he said, inching closer.

"¡Rápido maricón! I can't move." Beto held his hand out, awaiting the tool.

And just like at the ring toss game at the San Ignacio Church bazaar, Pablito lifted the tire and released it from his grip. The donut hole of the tire landed on the jack's pole rigging, loosening it from the grip of the jack's holding mechanism. A running sound of clicks, as if a chain-link curtain was collapsing to the ground, filled the garage, followed by Beto's muffled screaming.

Pablo watched his father's legs dance a corrida, shaking and convulsing, as the weight of the vehicle crushed his skull and ribs, his shoulders and pelvis. He watched until Beto's legs came to a lazy and tired halt.

Pablo swallowed a gulp of air and cocked an eyebrow; Beto's legs were as still and stiff as those of the Wicked Witch of the East under Dorothy's house. Life would be better. He waited another minute, just to be sure, and yelled out, "Senaida!"

On the Line

BENNY VÁSQUEZ

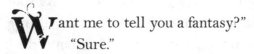ant me to tell you a fantasy?"

"Sure."

"Okay, lie down. Close your eyes and listen to my voice."

I felt my skin tingle, my heart race, and my ears open. As my breath grew heavier, I waited on every word he had to say. Every syllable was like a kiss covering an inch of my body. He continued to tease me with his voice, having me imagine a girl (it was always a girl) kissing the tip of my dick. As the word *dick* flowed from his mouth, he rubbed his rough and slightly wet fingertip along the outline of my lips.

"Do you like it?"

My eyes closed, I nodded my head. With every word, my body came closer to an explosion of sorts. My husky-sized shorts were getting tighter as my hard-on grew. He laughed

and knocked on my dick, as he jokingly said it had transformed into *a wooden door.*

"Wow, you're almost ready, huh?"

"Yeah."

"Now imagine her pulling you there, waiting for you to
put it in her pus—"

We heard footsteps and his words were cut short, interrupted by a loud scream.

"¡Oye, ven a comer—se va enfriar la comida!"

I opened my eyes. "Okay! Let me just finish this game…"

The footsteps soon became faint and I knew that my mother was on her way back to the kitchen. As the room became
quiet again, Danny and I looked at each other and laughed.
He put his head on my shoulder and I rubbed his soft, curly,
blond hair as we got up.

"You better go ahead. No quiero que mami me vea así."

He looked down at me, nodded, and laughed. I turned
around and heard him run into the kitchen. As soon as he
had left, I finished the fantasy and lingered till my husky
shorts returned to their normal size. I ran into the kitchen
and saw Danny laughing with my mom, who was telling one
of her stories.

Mami was a home attendant and always came back with
crazy stories about her viejos. This time she was talking
about one of the viejos who always farted and blamed it on
his talking parakeet. We listened to her story, giggled, and
waited on her every funny word.

I looked at Danny. He was always good at distracting mami.
Whenever we played the fantasy game he would make sure I
couldn't walk; he'd knock on my wooden door and leave me
by myself. He was like a guard. Always protecting me and
preventing my mother from walking in on me while I jerked
off. Danny always had my back.

I met Danny when I was fifteen; he was sixteen.

"Hey Emilio, this is Danny—my new boyfriend," Martha had said.

That bitch gets all the cuties I thought as I shook Danny's hand and looked into his eyes. When I did, I saw reflections of my own.

As Martha left us to become acquainted, I caught myself staring at him. It felt just like the time I watched Alex P. Keaton running around in his sweater-vest.

We began talking and I became increasingly nervous, feeling as if every word I was saying was coming from somewhere else. Looking at his face and seeing his soft blond goatee and thick red lips made me feel lost. We talked for ten minutes or more; it was as though some homeboy had invaded my body—I tried acting as straight as possible.

We bonded on our Boricua connection, hip hop, and surprisingly, our love for "The Breakfast Club." Danny would look at me and lick his lips ever so innocently as this was happening. Every sentence that escaped his mouth ended with his tongue slowly traveling the creases of his lips.

"Danny, come here!" Martha screamed from across the room.

He smiled and said, "Let's hang out soon."

I nodded and waited for him to walk away.

I noticed how his body moved in his clothes; his step had a swagger all its own. As each step brought him closer to Martha, I fixated on the space between his fitted Yankees cap and white hoodie. I stared at his curly hair, which was fighting to escape, falling ever so softly on his neck. It was at that moment that I wished I could become the pants that hugged his hips, the sweater that ran down his back, and the cap that caressed his hair.

I chatted with Danny the next day; there wasn't a day that went by over the following year that we didn't talk. Our conversations were always full of laughter, sexual innuen-

11

dos, and the trials and tribulations of being teens. From the daily annoyances caused by our parents to his explicit sexual encounters with Martha, I hung on his every word.

"So, Lio?" he asked, using a name that only he called me.

"What's up?"

"You don't ever think about getting laid?" Danny quietly waited for my answer.

I breathed heavily on the other end of the line. "Yeah, but no girl really likes me. I still think about it, though."

"What do you think about?"

I thought about what I would've wanted Danny to do to me had I been a girl. I held the phone tightly, tapping my fingers on the kitchen table—hoping it would lead me to an answer.

"I think about kissing a girl and letting her kiss me all over and touching my…"

"Dick?" he added.

"Yes." I became warmer and my breath got heavier.

"Lio?"

"Yeah?"

"Are you hard?"

Nervously, I admitted, "Yeah."

It was then that he asked the words he would continue to ask over and over again. "Want me to tell you a fantasy?"

"Yeah."

Danny began to tell me his fantasy while I pleasured myself at the kitchen table. After I released quietly we laughed and said we'd talk the next day. I hung up, wondering whether Danny had been doing what I'd been doing on his end of the line. Or had I been on my own?

Every time I thought of Danny, I fell deeper and deeper in love with him. Whenever he slept over and was near me, I felt complete. Whether we stayed up talking or playing video games, I treasured each moment I had with him.

I would wish that he'd give me a good night kiss whenever we got ready for bed and that the fantasy we always talked about would somehow become a reality. Instead, we slept side by side so that our hands would touch. He would grab my hand, link his fingers with mine, and quietly fall asleep.

As he slept I would look at him and wish I could caress the soft hairs on his chest, touch the space between his thighs, and feel his beard against my lips. There were many times when he would catch me looking at him and he'd smile. Squeezing my hand tighter, he would release a flow of energy that would travel through every vein in my body. I would look at him, close my eyes, and fall asleep.

When I woke up in the morning to the smell of mami cooking eggs and bacon, I was surprised that our hands were still intertwined and that our bond hadn't broken. Danny and I slept like this countless times.

Even after his breakup with Martha, I felt that he remained connected to me. I always looked forward to our Friday night hangouts, the occasional fantasies, and his hand in mine. He became like a second son to my parents and was always in our house. His admiration for my mother's cooking always won her heart and his talk of the Yankees kept my dad interested. I had never watched a Yankee game with my father—that is—until Danny initiated it. For a minute it felt as though my life with Danny was never going to come to an end and that I would always sleep next to him.

Although my mother loved Danny, there came a time when I noticed she would stare at us for too long. I would catch her and she'd turn away and pretend she was looking at something else. She'd come into my room unannounced when Danny was over. Her funny stories turned into awkward questions. Questions like, when were we going to bring our girlfriends around? Asking why Martha and Danny broke

13

up and condemning my "sick" gay cousin. Things she would never ask when I was alone.

"No quiero a Danny in this house," she warned one day.

The words came so quickly that I felt them take the wind out of me. I looked at her with confusion, trying to hide the heat that was escaping my body. It was as if the room had grown silent and all that could be heard was my heartbeat.

"¿Me oístes?" *Did you hear me?*

Mami's voice became serious and she came closer. I had seen that look on her face before; a mixture of anger and hurt that radiated from her eyes. I walked backwards to the door. I could still feel the breeze that entered through the crevices between the wooden door of the apartment and the wall. I wondered if Danny was still on the other side.

"Why?" I asked softly, like a child. It was as if my favorite toy had been snatched away without warning.

"Porque yo mando aquí. I don't want you hanging out with him." Her voice intensified and her hand went up.

Her hand, a weapon I was familiar with, was about to come near me when I heard my father ask, "¿Qué pasa?"

Mami told my father what she had warned me about. Papi looked at me, then at the floor, and walked away. No words, no reaction. He left me stranded.

Mami put her hand down and went back to cleaning the kitchen. She was breathing heavily and her eyes were focused on the blue liquid dripping from her soap-filled sponge. She wouldn't look at me. Had she, she would've noticed that her only son had tears in his eyes.

I leaned on the door, wishing I could walk through it and run away. After standing there for what seemed like an eternity, my mother turned around and came toward me. She grabbed me tightly by the arm, took me to my room, and threw me on the bed.

14

"¡Suciera del diablo!" She ordered me to strip the sheets off my bed, standing over me like a predator attacking prey, until I stripped my bed clean. The pillows and mattress were raw and empty. My hands trembled as I handed her the sheets. She looked me straight in the eyes. With a bead of sweat falling past her brow, she shook her head violently—she wouldn't even touch them.

She grabbed my arm again. I could see the indentation on my skin; it burned, it hurt. When we walked past my dad, I heard the sounds of fans screaming and someone yelling homerun. My dad, with his cerveza in hand, continued watching TV and ignored what was happening.

My mother dragged me to the kitchen and demanded I throw the sheets away. I had to restrain myself from crying and kicking the shit out of her. I had never experienced such a mixture of fear, sadness, and anger. I looked at the sheets that had known Danny's warmth and tossed them in the garbage—in the mixture of dirty cans, paper, and wasted food. My mother was satisfied and demanded I go to my room. I ran and lay on my bare bed, which felt cold and dirty. I cried until I fell asleep, holding my own hands.

15

I never heard from Danny again.

Whenever the phone rang, I would run to it, but my mother would pick up first and yell that I wasn't home. This happened constantly over a two-week period. It took me a while to gain the courage to call him. I lived with the fear that my mother would know who I was calling and didn't want to deal with the repercussions.

One afternoon, on my way home from school, I decided to try to reach Danny on a payphone. Emotions washed over me when I heard his voice; I felt every hair on my body stand. Although I was excited to hear the voice on the other end, it was cold and distant. The answers to my questions were full of one-syllable words which didn't leave for much discussion.

It wasn't Danny—it wasn't him at all. Abruptly the voice said, "I have to go, check you later." And then a dial tone.

I hung up and leaned against the phone booth. I closed my eyes and flashes of Danny lit up in my head. From holding his hand, feeling his touch, hearing his voice and feeling loved—I was worried that I would never feel him again. I opened my eyes, looked at my watch, and realized I was late for dinner.

I wiped my tears and walked down the block. As I did, I looked back at the phone booth and stopped myself from calling and yelling at him. I wanted to tell him so many things, but knew that I wouldn't be able to form sentences. I ran the other way instead.

When I got home I was overwhelmed by the smell of sofrito and garlic that was emanating from the stove. I looked at my mother; she looked at me too and asked for a kiss. I gave her the bendición and a quick peck on her cheek. She smiled, told me she loved me and to get ready pa' comer.

As I walked to my empty room, it became clear that all of my fantasies had been taken away at once. I sat on my bed and heard the phone ring. My heart jumped as I ran to it, hoping it was him. My mom picked up first and said hello; I heard her asking my dad to pick up some soda from the store. I took a deep breath, sat down, this time knowing that my first love had disappeared forever.

Júnior, Reggaetón Tropical

LAWRENCE LA FOUNTAIN-STOKES

to Raquel Z. Rivera

Because there's no faggots in reggaetón, there's no faggots, no ass lickers, no got a big fat cock stuck in your ass if you don't jump, jump motherfucker! Jump! Jump! Cause not jumping you're a faggot, motherfucker, and I'm no fudgepacker, baby, I'm the MAN! Gangster, aight? He says to you or me and I and a flag, a big motherfucking flag, a flag of flag of flags of bitches and hos and stripes and red and blue, red and blue y no es la pecosa, no Betsy Ross fucker, it's Caribe, Caribe, flag de Cuba y Puerto Rico, repeat, repeat, repeat, repeat, repeat, repeat, repeat cause the rhythm, how you say the rhythm, Júnior? Tell your momma, tell her, tell her everything, tell her, slap, slap, slap, you slapping, motherfucker? No, she slapping me, bitch nigger.

Then the girl sings lindo, lindo, lindo, but you don't come hear the girl, but the girl's aight, she aight, aight, aight, dancing, shaking like a dog, singing, racatá, you a girl (sorta), girl-like or something, bling bling jamming, racatá, shining in your face, the noize, the noize blasting in your head real loud, racatá, come see the boyz, bad boyz, bad bad bad boyz, you a boy? Sorta, you're a Júnior reggaetón boy in Orlando, Florida, stuck en este calor, whatcha doing here? Why you move here with them dads and moms, they got tired of the island, got tired and moved me over here, but you just wait, I know it, next thing you know we'll be packing and back pa' la isla, pa' la isla empacando con el Cangri, con el Nicky, con el Tego, but whatcha doing now?

"Going to college, Central Florida."

"You like it?"

"It's aight."

"Whatcha driving?"

"La vieja gave me her Beamer, negro con Beamer, pa' que veas."

"What is it that she do?"

"Lawyer, motherfucker."

"And you be talking like a gutterboy?"

"Hell yeah, brotha."

"A Boricua with a Beamer, fancy that. And your braids?"

"Bueno they all think I'm from Jamaica, anyways. Boricua's racist, man."

"You Haitian, nigger!"

"Haitian my ass, motherfucker!"

"You want it up the ass, batty bwoy?"

"Shut up, ass wipe, you nothing more than a down low thug."

"Ah ha," he consents, with a big smile.

All on the corner, while Nicky Jam sings away, remembering Pitbull's moves, Daddy Yankee's cool threads, Wisin y Yandel's bling.

"Can you understand what they're saying?"

"Shut up!"

And then you look at the sky, and a star falls in your nappy hair, and the music rings and your body is not yours anymore, your body belongs to the music and to the swing, a child of night, moving that body while your lips repeat bellaquear, and you dream of licking Wisin and Yandel right up, moving that tongue up and down, licking their toes right through their sneakers, biting their pant legs, T-shirt bellaqueando to the swing, moving and you're all together anyways, everyone pressing all together squeezing to the rhythm 'til you touch a guy and he turns around and punches you in the face.

"Júnior, what happened to your face, honey?"

"Nothing, ma."

"Where'd you go last night? Don't tell me you went to another one of those god-forsaken reggaething events!"

"It's reggaetón, ma."

"Reggae my ass! Look at your face! Who did that to you?"

"It was an accident, I fell."

"Mmm hhhmmm."

"For real!"

"You think I'm gonna buy that story, Júnior José?"

"Swear to God!"

"No andes blasfemando, Júnior. We're a Catholic family."

"Ma, ¡déjame quieto!"

"Okay, honey, I'm just looking after my baby." (Who's a big queen and thinks I don't know, but mothers always know, don't they?)

"Júnior, is there something you want to tell me?"

"No, ma, let me go back to sleep."

And Júnior falls back on the bed and forgets the pain of his face split in two and dreams of rhythms and boomboxes and speakers and moving bodies swaying in a very, very hot room full of gangsters and gatitas with guns all shooting each other full of muscles and tattoos and bling, moving those little skirts all tight, hair falling to the side, lips so red, luscious, boy kissing girl, dancing like a dog, por atrás, and Júniol looks at Júnior and Júniol looks like Daddy Yankee and Don Dinero and one of the Bambinos, all with más flow.

Júniol? Yes because there's two, well, there's millions, but here, aquí hay dos, Júniol the bad boy of my dreams, of Carolina caseríos (no, Bayamón), the Nuyorican Júniol, el blanquito pero sólo de cara, he might be white but he's from the projects, baby, pure trouble, and Júnior, el nene bueno de urbanización, ¿negro como un teléfono? ¿Como Tego? No, mulato, mulato oscuro con trencitas, a dark café con leche good suburban boy with a lawyer mom and a dad who's an accountant. So what they be doing in Orlando?

"Orlando's the new New York, motherfucker!"

"Orlando Disney World?"

"It's not Calle Ocho, bitch."

But the thing is that you can't tell a Júnior apart from a Júniol, Júnior and Júniol one big bad thing, you hear? Júniol/ Júnior/Júniol/Júnior/Júniol/Júnior, two in one, in love with each other in their own way, because Júniol is really only in love with bling and with his own face in the mirror, one a big reggaetón star singing right up there, right up next to Don Omar and Nore, shaking that ass, shaking it, no that be the girls, yo, but Júniol don't mind, Júniol got enough bullets and blood under his belt, enough to scare all the bad boys, at least for today, all about respect, respect, and pregnant pussies and panties strewn across the stage, pretty boy no es por nada, and Júnior standing in the front row, swaying and screaming back.

"What's that goddamn faggot doing in the front row? Get him outta there."

But no one moves him and then they meet later on and Júnior knows that Júniol really loves him, deep down inside, deep deep down wanting to taste that black chocolate sweat, wanting to take those little eyeglasses off his nerdy black college student face, scratch his whiskers, slap, slap, slap your booty, be good, mama! Slap that man butt and pretend, pretend you be a girl, you're just like a girl, just like a girl, I could be with a girl right now for all I know, you're a girl, you're a girl, Júnior, and that's why I can be with you, okay?

"If you say so, daddy."

"Now we're talking. Tú eres mía, you hear? You're my gasolina."

And you want to give him all you've got, all of it, everything, todito, cause who would believe it, who? Júnior and Júniol all together, squeezing in the back of a car, no, motel, no, behind the building, no, in your house, how did you get him in? In his house, no one there, no one, in Orlando? Or in San Juan, that night you saw him singing at la Krasha, no, Lázer, or was it Dembow? Walking down those streets, four in the morning, wanna drive? Wanna go down to La Perla to score? Wanna drink for the road, a drink for my lips, I'm so fucked up I don't even know what I'm doing, I don't even know who you are, who I am, all I know is that Júniol and Júnior and Júniol and Júnior and Júniol be a mirror, a thing split at birth and ouch, watch out for your chain! That hurts! Sorry baby, my bling, and he smiles, proud, proud, his bling pressing against his chest and hairs all torn together, medals, big old baseball caps flying, pants flying, sneakers flying, T-shirts flying, athletic jackets flying, sweatpants flying, and licking down the groin, whatcha got, whatcha want, my dog, you a dog, dog, dog, dog, dog, dog, god, god, god, god, good, good boy, doing godlike things with a blunt the size of a cock, you so stoned outta your mind you don't even know what side is up, and it's all good (in the dark).

"Wanna get together tomorrow?"

"But I don't know you tomorrow, I don't know you today, Júnior."

That's what he says, anyway.

"Don't call me. I can't be seen with you, joe. I don't want you ringing me up. Actually, erase my number from your phone."

And he gets dressed all backwards and gets the hell outta there as fast as a bat flying out of hell.

So now what? He be lying, lying! You curse the gods, screaming, motherfucking liar, liar, liar, but it be true? Can it, can it be breaking your heart in a thousand little bits, squashing like a bug, a Júnior doing this to himself, Júniol Júnior hurting so bad it starts to feel good, hurting like bad dark hot tears running down your face? But boys don't cry, boys punch and jump, jump, no fucking cock in my ass, motherfucker, no pussy patos maricones in reggaetón, at least not tonight.

But then, of course, the cell phone rings the next day.

"Yeah?"

"Whatcha up to, motherfucker?"

"Júniol, I thought you weren't gonna call me."

"Yeah, well, you know me. . .whatcha doin', bro?"

"Nothin'."

"Wanna suck my cock?"

"Júniol!"

"I told you real clear, no romance or shit with me. You wanna put out?"

Júnior promptly hung up, but his phone started vibrating in less than it takes to say gasolina.

"I'm sorry, baby, let's try again."

"Okay."

"Hi Júnior, howya doing?"

"Bien."

"Me alegro. Whatcha up to?"

"You already asked me that question."

"How about I pick you up and we go for a nice spin? I have a little present for you."

"What is it?"

"It's a surprise, bambino."

"Okay."

"That's a good boy. I'll be there in fifteen."

And then the Mercedes Lexus Beamer Cadillac 4 x 4 Jeep Hummer SUV bling limo drives up pimped to the max, white red shiny black metallic bed silk rims sound booming, booming, rhythm, aha, bling del castigo, como le corresponde a un buen gangster. But you know how the story's gonna go in this loop of never ending repeat cycles of love, breakup, torture, kiss, fuck, blood, semen, sweat, and tears.

"Perro."

"Get in!"

And so the Hollywood Technicolor video production fast forwards to the end, with a quick tracking shot of cars (one? two? twenty?) moving away in the distance. Love never ends well. Well, almost never.

That Chilly Night in Old San Juan

BRONCO CASTRO

[Frogs are] two legged like us but can't fly either
and were the first vertebrate singers.
— Edward Hoagland, "Earth's Eye"   25

I left the hotel shortly after nine still hating the
thought of dining alone on that balmy anochecer.
And then I saw him, seated on a bench in the cathedral's
plaza: a seemingly lonely, but attractive young man—im-
possibly older than twenty-six—hunched over his laptop.
I crossed the narrow, blue cobblestone street to sit on the
other end of the bench, from where I could watch as he silently read and responded to his e-mails, while I thought of
how to approach him.

Suddenly, without an apology or introduction, I asked him
whether he lived in San Juan or was just on a winter break as I
was. He turned to me, and with a welcoming smile responded
that he lived in La Perla. Incredulous, I asked whether he'd
grown up there (in that forbidding slum—ironically called
"the pearl"—with hypnotic views of the Atlantic, nestled by
squatters in the late nineteenth century between the two co-

lonial fortresses that had protected the islet settlement for centuries).

He explained that he had moved there just a few months earlier, after returning from a sojourn in Madrid where he had been working on directing and producing a screenplay of his. When he ran out of money, he returned to complete the production on the island, and ended up living in La Perla because he did not want to return to his parents' high-rise condo in Hato Rey and thus have to give up la independencia, he said.

Impressed by his determination to be almost destitute for the sake of his art, I asked him about his film. He'd begun to tell me about it, when suddenly I remembered that I was hungry. I interrupted briefly to invite him to dinner—and was relieved and grateful that he accepted.

We talked more about his film as we walked down Calle San Francisco, stopping to look at the menus along the way, finally settling on a nearly empty but fancy place that bordered a callejón, with doors instead of windows, all flung open to let in the night's cool breeze. It had become an unusually breezy evening, and after a couple of cold drinks in us, the breeze even felt cold. When the food arrived, we decided to close the doors to keep the food warm and our conversation private.

As he talked, I watched his youthful eyes and lips move, and suddenly recalled when I, too, sat across from some lonely, older stranger offering me some night of happiness in exchange for my company or affection. I couldn't figure out how, or when, I had become the old man from whose face a lonely, precocious boy still peeped out in search of romance. I do not recall what we talked about, except that it was an intense and long conversation about something important to both of us.

After dinner, I got up to ask for the check, and when I returned I did not see him in the alcove. Seated at the table, I waited awhile for him, thinking that perhaps he had gone to the bathroom, but he did not return.

With the illusion of romance gone, I did not care to speculate about his reasons for leaving me there in the restaurant; instead, I strolled back silently, along Calle Norzagaray, listening to a coquí singing, as if following me, on that chilly madrugada before the *morn purples the east.*

As I stared at the indigo outline of the horizon, I remembered Milton's phrase. Then a chilly breeze embraced me, and I hurried off toward the hotel to sleep before the light reemerged.

Back in my room sadness filled my mind, keeping me awake, so I dressed and left the room again, this time for the still empty and dark hotel terrace, from where I could breathe in the last few hours of crepuscular coolness with which to chill the sadness flowing in my veins.

27

Standing near the edge of the terrace, I could see the city's cathedral with Saint John, Saint Peter and Saint Paul on their pedestals above the entablature. I prayed to the saints for solace, but the only replies I heard were those of the coquí and his kin (still awake at that witching hour!) singing, unseen—enticing me to find them—which I did somewhere in the little plaza where that night had begun… There, to my surprise, I also found the lost young man, enchanted and transformed, among those welcoming me. And on any chilly, breezy night, if you find yourself forlorn on the terrace of the former convent, you too may hear our serenade for you.

Yermo

CHARLIE VÁZQUEZ

Querido Yermo,

You always had the same pinched look on your face when you held up blackening sweet bananas, green plátanos, sticky quenepas, and fuzzy tamarindos, and I always wanted to know why. You shouted their prices in a husky voice that cut through loud stereo speakers; a voice that flew over mountains to swoon hearts in distant villages; a voice that raised skirts like mischievous winds and spoke to the spirits with coarseness.

Your handwritten signs were the most legible in the area, too; young women and maricones often stopped to see what you were selling, but more often to admire your earthly beauty—you who the river gave birth to. You who impregnated me with something I will never part with, something I will never deliver and birth and hold.

Did you know this?

I think you did.

And you were always in the same spot, too—right before the turnoff to the main highway that went to San Juan going east or to Quebradillas and the west coast going the other way. You never wore a hat but always wore the same brown trousers and scuffed black sneakers. Everything you owned smelled like your sweat, everything.

I never saw you take your shirt off, either—even during the prickly and maddening temperatures of high, humid summer. When you had time to yourself between customers you read newspapers, perhaps *El Nuevo Día* or *Primera Hora.*

30

Every time I saw you I thought the same thing—*one of these days I will stop.* And one day I fought my most profound fear of you and I did. It was a Friday, I even remember that. Cutting quickly to the right after a rare break in traffic, I parked my car and walked over to you with my hands in my jeans.

You were alone.

Feeling a little insecure I shot you a friendly smile and said, "Buenas."

"A man with a big black car," you said with a smirk, betraying my false image of you.

"I can never figure out how to stop here."

"You're new to the island, aren't you?" you asked in Spanish, while running your fingernails along your jet-black crew-cut bristle, scraping it like a güiro.

"I'm studying here, taking a break from New York," I informed you, while peering into a green bucket filled with yellow and black bananas, which you were selling five for a dollar. "I'll take ten of those, please," I requested, pointing to them.

You had them bagged and ready to relish in seconds, boasting, "These are the best in Arecibo and quenepas are in season right now." It was then that you scratched your ripened nipple through your t-shirt, while pointing at the pile of sticky berries by my feet. I picked up a bundle of the honeyberries, or quenepas, and set the gluey bunch on top of the bananas. "They look delicious," I mentioned, while breathing in the maddening incense of your scalp.

"Well, those—those are three dollars a bag," you said, confident of their quality and steeper price.

"That's still a deal considering," I admitted, reminding myself that a few dollars was a lot of money to some people— that my Bronx working-class upbringing was perceived as privilege to some islanders, such as yourself perhaps.

"What are you studying?" you asked, catching me off guard.

"Marine biology."

You, the most handsome fruit vendor I had ever seen, put a stiff index finger to your forehead and tapped it a few times, saying, "Everything I learned, I learned on my own." You wanted to challenge me in some uncertain way and your intent was clear in the dark tone of your words.

I wasn't in the mood to tread onto battlefields—not so soon. I wanted to feel warm in your presence, golden, satisfied. "As long as we learn—who cares, right?" I said, smiling.

Your expression became severe. You then offered, "I can give you the tamarindos six for a dollar."

"Then give me two dollars' worth and keep the change," I told you, holding out a ten-dollar bill.

You folded the bill and stuffed it in your pocket. I nodded to gesture that the transaction was over and you grabbed my elbow before I could walk away. Looking me straight in the eyes, you said (almost threatening), "I have to get a ride back with you."

"A ride to where?"

"To bring this stuff back home. It'll be fast," you assured me, organizing your wares in the shrinking shade as if I'd consented.

"And where do you live?"

"Not far, just on the other side of the highway."

"That should be fine," I said, wondering what I was setting myself up for.

When I attempted to help you, you waved me off, insisting, "I have a system."

Once we were moving on the highway you put your sticky hand out and said, "Yermo."

"Carlos," I answered, putting my hand back on the steering wheel as fast as I could. You were hard to read, you know— from friendly to bitter with little or no warning, like no one else I've ever known.

Though there was bitterness about you I basked in your superior sweetness. Or I convinced myself of this and was living in the splendor of the fantasy you were becoming— from a recurring stranger streaking past my window to a sweating man scratching his genitals at my side.

"Yermo, as in Guillermo?" I asked.

"Very good."

"I've spoken Spanish my whole life," I informed you, pushing back, "and I doubt your English is any better than mine."

You nodded with vitriolic thoughts coloring your face, but at the time I couldn't know why. As we came to an intersection, you instructed, "Take a right here."

You enjoyed telling me what to do.

I enjoyed it, too.

As I made the turn you asked, "You aren't married, are you?"

I inspected your sticky fingers without being obvious and answered, "No. Are you?"

"I was before I was sent away, before they made me crazy."

"Where did you go?"

"To the Middle East. For *your* country."

I let out a frustrated sigh.

It was then that I noticed the tattoo on your muscular forearm; it was of a scorpion stinging the edge of an American flag which had been covered with a Puerto Rican one, enough of the vanquished showing as to be recognized. "I'm really sorry to hear that," I added, continuing on a freshly surfaced street.

"Make a right on this road," you said with poison on your tongue.

I turned onto a country road and tried to imagine where it was we were going; it was hard not to wonder if I would become the violent bulls-eye for all of your hatred. Pointing at a crumbling pink house in the middle of a densely overgrown plot of land to our right, you announced, "Right here."

I noticed a rooster and some hens milling around in the yard and parked the car. "It was nice to meet you," I told you.

"It'll be faster if you help me."

"You wouldn't let me help you by the highway so why do you need my help now?" I asked, trying not to sound rude. I pulled my cell phone out and realized that that too was an expensive gadget that could be stolen and sold.

You threw me a dark glare and called me a cabrón maricón before going to the trunk, which I unlatched from my seat with trembling fingers. I was ready to speed my way back to safety as soon as I was clear to do so, as soon as you were far away enough from me to lose you.

You piled your things by the front gate and tapped on the back window demanding, "Come on."

I nodded no.

You persisted, tapping the window with a key.

I turned my phone off and got out. Matching your aggression, I said, "I have an appointment and need to hurry."

Handing me the banana bucket, you said, "Just this." You scooped up the rest of your things and kicked the front gate open demanding, "¡Vamos!"

As chickens scattered I noticed trees and bushes dotted with the same fruit you sold. You grew everything on your property—but was it even yours? I had to wonder where it was you were taking me—me, your most foolish admirer, your sacrifice to murdered island deities, fresh blood for avenging spirits.

You unlocked the crooked front door and kicked it open, revealing a small room filled with glossy weaponry magazines, maps of the continents, and piles of paperbacks (I noticed military mysteries and war hero biographies in English and Spanish). And then I saw what I had dreaded most: a broadsword hanging on a wall, within your arm's reach.

"Nice. House," I commented, frozen by the front door.

You glared at me as if I'd insulted you and snatched the banana bucket from me, stuffing the leftover fruit into a crammed refrigerator humming in a corner.

The house was but a single room; I did not see a kitchen or bathroom and did not ask, as paralysis constricted my limbs, along with the desire to run faster than I ever had. "It was nice meeting you," I said, making my way out.

"You're not going."

"I have to."

"I'm coming with you, wait," you demanded, picking up a knapsack.

"What?"

"You can drop me off," you insisted, patting yourself down, as if feeling for weapons.

We retraced our journey to the country road. Right before the turnoff to the paved street that led to the highway you muttered, "You have to see this—stop."

"See what?"

Pointing to the left, with your index finger in my face, you said, "El río."

I had seen many rivers in my life—trickling and torrential, pristine and polluted—and was not about to go anywhere secluded with you. "I will leave you here and get on with my day," I told you.

"Five minutes," you insisted, "and then you can drop me off by the highway."

"I can't," I told you, trying to contain my frustration.

"You will," you growled, turning the engine off and snatching my keys in a flash that eluded my intervention.

"We can't just leave the car here, we're blocking the road."

You got out, saying, "They can get around us. Ven ya, puñeta."

I followed you down a dirt path through dense vines and trees laden with hornet nests to a green and rocky riverbank. Bugs swarmed my face when we arrived at the river's edge and I sat on a small boulder, annoyed, terrified, nauseated. I was ready to pick up a rock and kill you however I could.

You set your backpack down, commenting, "You're not made for country living, yanqui."

"Why did you bring me here?" I asked, spying a grapefruit-sized rock near my feet—one blow to your head and I would run.

35

Pulling off your sweat-soaked t-shirt, you informed me, "I can wash my clothes in town, but I need to clean my culo and pinga at least once a day." You untied your sneakers and set them aside with your socks tucked into them. "What are you looking at?" you asked threateningly, as I surveyed your jaguar musculature with an awe I could not extinguish.

"Nothing," I said, pretending I hadn't spied the trail of black hair that spiraled around your navel and dipped into the unknown.

"You should go in, the minerals keep the insects away," you said sarcastically, as your trousers and underwear landed on the rock I was going to kill you with.

I stripped while you rolled in the riverbed like a happy beast from the jungle surrounding us, as you patted your armpits and manhood with a small bar of soap you'd taken out of your knapsack. After passing it through the crack of your ass, you held it up and asked, "Do you want this?"

"Sure." I stepped in and caught the soap, before the current claimed it for good. I rubbed it on my skin in soothing circles. And that was when I saw a large school of tiny fish darting toward us, passing around and between your legs and waistline—as if you were a natural river feature. "Look at all those fish!" I exclaimed, surprised by their numbers and speed, as they swarmed around us like a singular organism.

Gazing into the water with your back to me, you mentioned, "They won't hurt you, mister yanqui marine biologist."

I noticed your back and shoulder muscles tensing and realized you were kneading a throbbing erection, which you massaged until you stiffened and sighed. You turned to face me, beckoning me forward with your eyes.

Your body shook and your muscles swelled on your limbs, on your torso—your face distorted and made you look like

36

a mad ogre, as globs of pearly semen squirted onto the river water and passed me in the steady current, just as the fish had moments prior.

Unsure of what to do or say, I made my way to the riverbank and dressed without drying off, setting the soap in your underwear. I took my keys and shook them in the air warning, "Five minutes."

"Cabrón," you growled, while washing away the last of your stringy seed in the pure currents.

You locked the car door, staring beyond the window at nothing, at your thoughts. There was an awkward feeling in the air—maybe you would kill me to silence me over what was now our secret. I could've left you there you know, in that river with your soap and underwear and semen, amidst the hornets and spirits of Borikén to keep you eternal company.

How funny it is that I was ready to kill you before you could do so to me—and now I was begging for you to do something to me. I walked into your trap knowing well what it was; placing myself in front of a speeding train, throwing myself in the path of a bullet—and for what?

You didn't want to admit that you'd pleasured yourself in front of me—that you wanted me to be part of it somehow. I knew this well, for I was once like you. I haven't forgotten and never will. Starting the engine, I said, "The river was beautiful. Thank you."

Without looking at me you said, "You can drop me off at El Teniente."

"What is that?"

"A bar where I used to work—go with me," you beckoned, turning to look at me.

"For what?"

"Because I want you to," you said laughing, revealing a handsome and weathered smile that cut through my heart.

"I had you wrong, hombre," you said, with menace filling your eyes like dark and rising liquid.

When I joined you with our beers you pointed at the pool table and said, "Fifty cents."

Digging into my pocket, I told you, "I don't play well, but I'll play anyway." I took a stick from the rack and inserted the quarters into the slot.

"It's just a game, like life," you said, chalking your tip, grinning fiendishly.

A black man in a bright yellow shirt walked over to us, upon exiting the men's room. He shook hands with you, asking something in a foreign language I did not understand.

You greeted him with childlike enthusiasm and answered him in the same tongue.

The tall and dark man then put his hand out to me and asked, "¿Cómo estás?"

"Bien. Mucho gusto, Carlos." I answered.

"Yoro," he responded, with a large and leathery hand in mine, his bright and luminous smile warming me. Patting our backs and nodding goodnight, the perfumed and handsome giant walked away and exited the cantina.

"Who's that?" I asked, as you plotted my destruction, arranging the balls.

"He's a brujo from Africa. He lives here part of the year."

"What were you saying?"

"Hello, how are you—esa mierda."

"You speak African languages?"

Avoiding my eyes, you said, "I speak Spanish, English, Arabic, French, and Wolof—which is what Yoro speaks."

"Really?"

"I told you I was in the military," you reminded me coldly, as the triangle of colorful balls exploded loudly from your concentrated force, your stiff pool cue bouncing high in the air. "I was *un* trans*lat*or for your Desert Storm," you said, throwing spicy Spanglish at me and sinking a striped ball at the same time.

"Wow," was all I could say.

I wanted to see you smile again.

Switching back to Spanish, you pointed at yourself and said, "You can admit that when you first saw me, Señor Jíbaro, selling fruit by the highway, you assumed I was an idiot."

"I never thought such a thing."

"I would bet money you did—if I had it. No me jodas, mentiroso," you threatened, calling me a liar and sinking five striped balls in a row—fortaleza cannon blasts.

"I just saw a fruit vendor," I corrected you. "You make me sound as if I were some rich asshole who looks down on poor people. I grew up poor, too."

"¡Ay!" you laughed aloud, adding, "with electricity, plumbing, welfare cheese, ice cream, and a televisión."

I stepped up to you, which surprised you. "Don't leave out domestic violence and murder and heroin and rats and thieves and police brutality and disease, bugarrón. I didn't have control over my circumstances any more than you did. *¡Tú* no me jodas!" I threatened back, taking a shot and missing the ball by inches.

"¿Bugarrón?" you asked with the color of murder in your eyes.

"Don't pretend that what happened at the river was any of my doing," I whispered, respecting your esteemed reputation.

"You people are liars, too—what happened to your important appointment? Te lo perdiste."

"What do you mean *you people*? I barely know you."

"People born in the evil empire who think you know everything about everybody."

Restraining myself from knocking you on the head with the heavy end of my pool-stick I admitted, "Yes, there are people like that. ¡Pero yo no soy uno d'ello'!"

People studied us with worried expressions, as our anger swelled and balls sank into pockets with a sniper's precise violence. You dismissed me with a wave of your hand and demanded, "Fifty cents. I won."

I was so distracted and incensed I hadn't realized my defeat. Not one solid ball sunken. I threw two quarters at you and said, "Find someone else to play with." I drank what was left of my beer and set the empty bottle down.

"I insulted you," you admitted, darting over to me, blocking my departure.

"Como quieras, Guillermo."

"Your country ruined my life," you muttered like a child, exposing the root of your circumstances with pain cracking your voice.

"I'm truly sorry to hear that," I remember telling you, "but you have food, health, and beautiful nature to admire. And warm friends who are happy to see you, apparently."

Softening, you asked, "What's that supposed to mean?"

"You have hope. You can use your intelligence to transform your life in ways others cannot."

"Let's go outside for a minute," you beckoned.

"I'm leaving now."

You took my hand gently, surprising me. "Let's go back to the river, Carlos."

"And best of all Guillermo, you're a mind reader."

The house you used to live in was boarded up and abandoned when I went to look for you last and I haven't seen you selling fruit by the turnoff in months. The folks at El Teniente haven't seen you since then, either. I will tear this letter up tomorrow at midnight and give it to your river, to you, to your gods, to the gods that spoke through you when you came on me—to our gods. Ay, Yermo.

Con amor siempre,
arlos

A Doomed Gay Marriage

RIGOBERTO GONZÁLEZ

43

...to the Writer

Three months after moving to New York City, I'm still incredibly lonely, though I am living with my new husband, a journalist. He works long hours at an office in midtown and I, an unemployed poet, stay home to read and compose sonnets. We hold hands during dinner each night, and afterwards I vacate the apartment to wander the city while he does his own reading and writing alone. By the time I come back home, he's already asleep, and I crawl under the sheets next to him, knowing that two people whose paths rarely cross will eventually miss each other completely.

I'm walking alone one afternoon, anonymous and silent through the bustling city streets, unfazed by the speed of other bodies. I cut through the traffic and sit on a bench in

Central Park. This is how I meet him, the widower—a businessman from Thailand.

We meet every day that week, the length of his stay. We talk and laugh and keep each other company. Once we even go to the movies. And twice we share a meal and a bottle of wine. And each night at the conclusion of our date we simply shake hands.

On our final goodbye, he cries because he's returning to his country, a land full of memories of his dead wife. I kiss him and tell him in a shaky voice that I understand. I know what it's like to walk into a room to face the coldness of a blank page.

...to the Cook

On Sunday, my partner the chef and I ride the 6 train to Manhattan's Chinatown. It's our weekly excursion, this search for ingredients prominent in Asian cooking. And with it always the wonderful assault of jade and calligraphy, eel and seaweed, Mandarin and Cantonese. No surprise then to be intrigued by a Chinese fortune-teller speaking through a translator to a Dominican woman. The translator seizes on my interest and grabs my arm. I in turn convince my partner to join in the fun.

The fortune-teller consults his charts, my partner's hands and forehead, and has nothing but glowing things to report: "You are very intelligent. You will live a long life. You will have much luck if you wear a silver ring on your right middle finger."

I roll my eyes at the generic prognostication, but humor the sidewalk encounter by taking my turn on the chair. "You will live a long life," the fortune-teller declares, "if you do not kill yourself."

Startled, I withdraw my hand because I'm good at withdrawing: speech, affection, sex. My partner turns pale, as if he has just identified the scent wafting in the kitchen all this time. *So this explains it,* his face reads.

I want to accuse the translator of mistranslating. Perhaps the word was "overwork": *You will live a long life if you do not overwork yourself.*

"He's got it all wrong," I say to my partner later that night. But he turns his back to me, feigning sleep, pretending he doesn't know that all those times I turned my back to him in bed I was only making believe I was awake.

...to the Musician

The composition sheets stretch across the mattress as if the bed doesn't want to be disturbed. I sit on the floor next to my guitar case, both of us like pets ready to run out the door as soon as it's left open. The window widens on the wall like another mouth wanting to be fed and all it gets is what's leaking down from the moon. I have been tricked like that before when light fills the room but stays empty, when a body cancels out the body lying next to it and no one's left to sing the chorus.

Suddenly a shadow cuts through the window and for a second I believe it's the man who's divorcing me. I want him to recognize this time that without me he's tone-deaf, that only I can play for him with any of the spoons I'm taking with me—my dimple, my big toe, my thumb.

And then the paralyzing truth: *Hey diddle diddle, the cat and the fiddle, and the dish ran away without me.*

...to the Singer

On the first night the singer and I make love as husband and husband, we slip into each other's arms on the living room floor. The gesture is impulsive, and after a few awkward bumps against the couch, the bookshelf, the wall, we squeeze our muscles together until we're like a pile of sandbags, airtight and swollen with pressure. Only our moans can squeak through.

"I'm so glad you found me," he says, though I meant to say it before him—declare him my savior and excuse myself from the burden of making the marriage work. But it's his apartment, so it's his task to guide me, eventually, to our bed.

"I love you," he says. And I'm pleased he says it first and I'll hold on to the order of things for future reference: *It was you who said it. It was you who asked me to move in with you.*

He doesn't turn on the lights and I follow blindly, until we reach the entrance to the bedroom. And then, like the curtain rising at the Metropolitan Opera, the stage is lit, and the bed opens like a lifeboat, a pair of pillows for life preservers.

"Come," he says. I do. Half an hour later, he does too.

In the afterglow I'm struck breathless by the thought of the months ahead: reaching for his cock beneath the sheets at bedtime, waking up next to the man who might bring me breakfast in bed if I don't get up before him to make the coffee and scramble the eggs. And then the anxiety begins: I'll have to keep this performance fresh each night, or else the production closes.

Good Blood

ALEX G. ROMERO

eter drove to the Córdova Cemetery to examine the gravestones of his ancestors, to find out how long he had to live. As he steered the car along the spiraling road he was distracted by a flight of black birds, which appeared to his left. From the direction he was heading the flock seemed to be flying due north, just to his right.

Corneja diestra.

Like El Cid, Peter thought it was a good sign.

When his ears popped from the high altitude he felt a dull pain under his ribcage and he thought about the state of his health. During the last five years he had been plagued with one problem after another. If it wasn't the jaw that locked when he opened wide to eat a hamburger, it was insomnia. It was always something.

The worst had been when the tissue under his tongue had swollen so badly he couldn't eat. When he went to the clinic the doctor asked him if he chewed snuff. Peter shook his head in agony.

"Looks like a stone working its way out. You know—something got in there, like an apple seed or something. It's like a pearl. A grain of sand gets in the oyster and gets bigger from layer after layer of secretions. Same principle. Sucking on some lemons might help," the doctor said. "This is for the infection," he added, handing Peter a hastily written prescription.

Peter spent the next two days in excruciating pain. On the third day he opened his mouth in the mirror and noticed the bone-like protrusion under his tongue. He ended up having to make an opening with a needle to remove the teardrop-shaped stone. It was the first time he'd ever had surgery and he'd performed it on himself.

He had read about other people who had suffered from ill health. The Brontës had been frail and sickly. So had Kafka. And they all died in their prime. This worried Peter, making him feel as though he was working against the clock. He figured he'd want to be prepared for the worst. After all, Ivan Ilyich had died of a floating kidney after a mere blow to the side, so he'd made up his mind to find out his chances of living past thirty. He fantasized about being old and cynical, outliving his ailments.

His ears popped as he caught sight of the rooftops of the village deep in the valley. He had lived there until he was eight years old, herding his father's goats from the time he was old enough to carry a staff made from a branch from the apricot tree that stood in his aunt Cordelia's orchard, the one that was said to be infested with duendes.

It was rumored that mysterious lights could be seen between its knotted branches during certain days of the year.

48

Some said it was just a horde of fireflies, but others were sure it was the work of the Devil. Whatever the cause, it was believed the tree had somehow claimed one of his father's herds.

It was the dusk of a dark day in late summer. Peter and his older sister Rebecca usually took the goats to graze in the nearby hills after supper, but on that day the early evening had looked so stormy that their father told them to take the small herd to the orchard instead.

"Tía Cordelia says she has too many weeds in her arboleda. We can kill two birds with one stone if you take the cabras to eat the weeds," Dad had said, picking his teeth with the end of a matchstick he'd sharpened with a knife he always kept in his pocket.

49

The goats had been grazing on the weeds a short while when Peter was startled by thunder that seemed to be getting louder by the second. It was like the tread of a giant who was steadily approaching the village, threatening to crush it with one footfall.

Then Peter noticed a goat's belly. It had grown like a balloon and the poor creature was moaning and struggling to stand. The others also seemed uncomfortable.

"Look at their panzas!" he called to his sister.

"¡Válgame, Dios! We better take them home," she urged them on with light nudges to their hindquarters.

By the time they got them to the corral two of the goats collapsed. The third soon followed.

"What's the matter?" asked father, running to the stall.

"I don't know," Rebecca said (she was the spokesperson when she and Peter were together). "They just started getting fat."

Dad pulled his knife out of his pocket and made a slit under the tail of each goat. Peter felt the gush of foul, hot air expelled from each animal as his father held it by its hind legs. But it was too late. They soon sprawled with their legs pointing upward and their tongues spilling out of their mouths onto the dust.

Peter didn't connect the event to the apricot tree. It was his grandma Desideria who had attributed the evil to the gnarly old specter. She had been good at explaining things.

Peter had come a long way since those goat-herding days. As his car sputtered up the mountain—as if finding it hard to breathe at that altitude—he saw crosses decorated with plastic flowers dotting the roadside and thought about what his grandma would say about his problems if she were alive. She had known what to do when he suffered from mal de ojo as an infant, when he almost died from dehydration. She took him to a curandero who administered water mouth-to-mouth and cured him.

50

As Peter made it to the summit of the hilly terrain he felt like he was returning from a long exile. If he had truly been exiled, he thought, he would be like El Cid and not shave his beard until allowed to return to his homeland. As it was, he didn't have much hair on his chin—certainly not enough to grow a full beard.

Peter soon reached the spot where he could go to the Protestant side of the cemetery by making a left turn, or the Catholic side by turning right. The sky was a bit overcast as he parked midway between the two and got out of the car.

When he looked up he felt as if he were floating in mist. He had forgotten how close to the earth the clouds and stars were in Córdova. A black bird with a long tail flew by, but he was too caught up in his reverie to notice which direction it went. He only heard the mysterious cry it gave as it passed over him. He recognized the sound; he had heard the cry of the urraca at every burial he'd attended there. The same warbled wailing. His father used to say that if you captured the urraca and cut off its tongue, it would speak with a human voice.

Peter walked to the Catholic side where his father's ancestors were buried. The names and dates on the oldest markers were worn, but he could still make them out. *Such interesting names* he thought. Not like his. Just plain old Peter—although his grandmother always called him Pedrito.

He read the inscription on the first stone. *Matías Morales: 1867-1955.*

"That's eighty-eight years!" Peter shouted out, his chest quivering.

He found the next one. *Jesucita Morales: Nació 1864, Murió 1944.*

"Eighty!" He went to the others and found that all had lived to at least seventy.

Peter was in high spirits when he crossed the road to examine the dates on the markers of his mother's family. Again, the same. Except for his cousin Lucrecia who had died of dehydration shortly after birth they had all lived to a ripe old age. His great-uncle Victor had lived to be a hundred.

"Thank God!" Peter cried. "Good blood means long life!"

The sun was beginning to set as Peter descended toward the village and his mother's house. He no longer felt the pain under his ribs when he saw the shadow of a bird with a long train of tail feathers fly to the left. When he noticed the mysterious lights coming toward him through the swirling dust, the car swerved and Peter thought he felt the tail of the urraca brush against his forehead as it cried *Gracias a Dios*—when he flew through the window and down the arroyo to the valley below.

corneja diestra: In *El Poema del Cid* the hero, Cid Ruy Díaz, is presented with a series of omens after his exile. At the gate of Bivar El Cid and his company witness the flight of the crow to the right (*corneja diestra*). Upon entering Burgos the crow flies to the left (*corneja siniestra*). To El Cid this is a sign that he will one day return to his homeland.

Silly Boy

BOOH EDOUARDO

My legs tremble as they carry me from Jack's bedside in the ER to an empty resident's room. The space is small, unclean, and crowded. Smells permeate the room—antiseptic mixed with moldy food from the garbage can.

A single, unmade hospital bed takes up the majority of the room's space. A small student desk, looking like someone found on a trash pile, slopes in the corner. An equally decrepit metal lamp, clamped onto the back of the desk, juts out from its long narrow arm. My fingers reach for its switch near the bulb; but before I can turn it on, the door of the resident's room closes and the light from the hallway disappears.

Both hands fumble in the dark. My eyes adjust to the lights that shine through the permanently locked window just above the desk. Slowly, my thumb traces the dried raindrops on the glass, the ones on the other side of the pane, an oily imprint on top of dirty tears. My fingers fumble for the lamp's switch, and I blink several times when I click it on because I'm not used to the exposed bulb.

I pull out my wallet from the back pocket of the blue scrubs that I haven't had time to change out of and put it on the desk. The chair grates against the floor as I drag it over. My legs collapse into its lumpy, stained cushion.

Maybe I missed Jack when I had stopped at La Victoria, I think. I had bought some empanadas: espinaca, champiñón, and jamón. Even though we come from opposite directions, he and I use the same route, he going for his evening run, and I walking home.

After I got home, I wanted to shower. I had pulled out my shaving stuff from the medicine cabinet and found Jack's surprise. He had taped a picture on the inside of the door with a note that said, "I don't think this picture is goofy enough. Love, Your Silly Boy," and he had drawn our faces as cartoons with our tongues sticking out. Sometimes he teases me when he thinks I'm too serious.

My fingers had run along the edges of the well-worn photo. Even though Jack and I look and act differently than one another, somehow we belong together. His build is a runner's, long and thin, his eyes, green-blue and hair, gray-blond. My mind had begun to wander as I tried to remember exactly where we were and who took the picture, so I jumped when the phone rang.

Nan, my co-worker and friend who knows Jack, had called me and said that an EMT crew had just arrived with him. I had asked for more information, but she wouldn't tell me anything. Instead, she said to come down to the hospital as soon as possible.

I pull up the chair to the desk. My index finger and thumb gently grasp a tiny scrap of paper that I have carried in my wallet for about ten years. With a gentle tug, it breaks free from other things, old coupons, an expired temporary driver's license, and a list of something that I no longer remember or need. My fingers, whose delicacy have earned me As and a promise at an ER surgery fellowship once my ER residency is complete, fumble with the paper until it rips at its crease. My eyes trace the two names and numbers in the handwriting that I know as well as my own.

As I unhook my ID card from my blue scrubs shirt, I wonder what I will say. I would rather wait until tomorrow but waiting might make things worse. She might ask why I didn't call right away. Jack might want to see her if…when he regains consciousness. My left hand grabs the phone's receiver and my right pecks out my badge number on the key pad so that I can get an outside line. After I hear a dial tone, I enter the phone number.

55

"Hello?"

I hear a Midwestern drawl. "Can I please speak with Mrs. Baker?"

"This is Mrs. Baker."

"Uh, Mrs. Baker, uh, this is José Palafox-Díaz."

"Who?"

"José, you know, Jack's friend—his husband," I say, as my gold wedding band shines under the light bulb and reflects onto the tearstained nighttime window.

"My son's name is John, a good Christian name."

I take a breath. "I'm sorry to give you bad news Mrs. Baker, but…"

"And he's not married to any Juan Valdez."

A loud click echoes in my ear. I try to take a deep breath but not much air enters my lungs. How can I tell her what happened if she won't listen?

If you'd like to make a call, please hang up and dial the number again. This is a recording. If you'd like to make a call, please hang up and dial the number again. This is a recording…

My hand tosses the receiver back into the cradle. I pick up the scrap of paper as delicately as possible, but it crumbles a little more. When I sit next to Jack holding his hand, I must believe that I've done everything possible to help. As I whisper into his ear, I need to tell him honestly that I have contacted his family and that they know and care and want him to get better. My right hand reaches for the receiver again and my left picks out a second set of numbers.

"Hello?" The voice is different than the first.

"May I speak to Joy Jenkins please?" I ask.

"This is Joy."

"I have some news about your brother, Jack."

"I'm sorry. You must have the wrong number."

"Wait. Don't hang up. Are you still there?" I ask, because I no longer hear her breathing.

"Yes," she says.

"I have some news about your brother. You know, your brother who lives in San Francisco."

"Who are you?"

"It's José. Jack's…John's…his friend."

"My mother said your name was Juan—Juan Valdez," she replies. "You must have the wrong number."

"It's not the wrong number. I've known Jack…I mean John, a long time."

"Oh."

"Your brother was hit by a car when he was crossing the street earlier today and he's not likely to survive. Could you let your mother know?"

My ear discerns noises: footsteps, rustling, and voices in the background. As I wait, I stretch my neck from side to side. My vertebrae pop. The phone makes more tapping and rustling noises.

"This is Mr. Jenkins."

"Hello, Mr. Jenkins. This is Dr. José Palafox-Díaz at San Francisco General Hospital's Emergency Room." I don't want to use my official title, but I can't think of any other way to get this call over with.

"Huh? You must have got it all wrong," he says to someone other than me. "It's a Dr. Pala...Palaladeezz."

"No, no she didn't," I stammer.

"He didn't say anything about being John's—he's the doctor. No, he said his name was Dr. Palala...something like that. He's not...stop crying and just get over here. You've got it all mixed up again."

I make out more sobbing and arguing in the background but not the conversation. I hear sounds like children crying. Then a door slams.

"My wife's changing the baby's diapers, so she can't talk. Why are you calling us doctor?"

"Your wife was correct. I am both a doctor and Jack's, John's, friend. I called to tell her that he was hit by a car today and his injuries are...serious."

I wait for some kind of response. I stretch my neck again a couple of times, but my vertebrae don't pop. I clear my throat. "Are you still there?"

"Yeah," he says.

"I thought Joy and her mother might want to visit and maybe..."

"Just so you know, Joy and her mother are entitled to everything John's got. They're his next of kin, not you."

"That's really not the issue," I say, surprising myself with my composure. "I just wanted to know if any of your family would like to see Jack, given the severity of the situation."

"You think that you can pretend to be a doctor and get my wife all upset. You're not going to pull any schemes on us because we're on to you."

"I have to hang up now. Call our home number if you want to find out how Jack's doing."

"You son-of-a-bitch, we've got his phone number and address. And we're getting a lawyer and..."

"Goodbye."

When I hang up, my hand throbs because I have held the receiver so tightly. My throat feels like I've swallowed a rock. No wonder John switched his name to Jack when he left home, I think. I would've changed my name too, so that I could try to forget my past.

Two questions flash in my mind. Why did Jack have to go running this afternoon? And why does he have to look so gay? As soon as I think of them, I hate myself and push the thoughts out of my mind.

I pick up the phone once more and dial the proper codes and numbers. Instead of my call going through, however, the hospital operator gets on the line. She tells me that I can't make an international call through the resident's phone line. When I explain that it's an emergency, she gives me permission to leave a message, but she tells me that she has to stay on the line.

I don't recognize the voice when I am connected to the Hotel Belmar, but I'm not surprised, since I left home more than twelve years ago. The clerk explains that my mother has just finished dinner with a group a tourists and that she's not sure if they have gone sightseeing yet. She promises that as soon as they can locate my mom, she will give her the message.

When I put the phone down, I glance over at the bed and feel the fatigue of working a twenty-four hour shift and the hyper-alert state I entered once Nan called. I shouldn't sleep, I think. I turn toward the desk and look for a distraction. My fingers begin to peel off splinters of the tabletop's laminate.

I can't leave the room because I need to wait for my mom's call. The phone will wake me, so I won't sleep too long. Besides, I told Nan to page me if Jack's condition changes. My feet have kicked off my shoes and my arms have pulled the sweatshirt off before I am conscious of what I am doing. My legs carry me to bed and I fall fast asleep.

In my dream, I stand beside Jack in a private room in the ER. Next to us, the heart machine beeps and the respirator wheezes. The sounds engulf me. The room detaches from the rest of the hospital and floats up to the sky.

We sit among the rain clouds. The structure of the room becomes all glass: floor, walls, and ceiling. Lightning and thunder crash, but the sealed room keeps us warm and dry.

My body detaches from itself. I sit on top of the glass roof and look down at the frozen picture of us in the room. The heavy rain makes me cold. Another clap of thunder rings out next to me and I shudder.

59

The hair on my body transforms into quills of creamy-white and tawny-brown. As the wind picks up and the rain changes to hail, my feathers become longer, fuller, and warmer. My body no longer shivers from the cold.

My arms squeeze my legs into my chest. My legs and feet become claws. My arms sprout into wings. I have become a Red-tailed Hawk.

The wind blows hard and knocks me off the glass roof. My arms open as I tumble downward. I freefall and somersault toward the room and the frozen figures. Just before I hit the glass ceiling, my wings navigate me away from the danger and carry me above the turmoil.

When I fly toward the moon the color and contour of my wings become clearer. Long creamy-red feathers cover my arms and extend outward. Midway down, they turn bright white, the same color as moonlight. At the edges, the tips of my wings become invisible because they are the same color as the clouds.

My wings take me above San Francisco's stormy sky and then out to sea. Hours and hours seem to pass, but I don't get tired. Instead, my journey makes me feel rested. The cool moonlit night turns into warm blueness. Below me is a calm oceanic morning.

A bird calls to me from far away. The sound is primal and familiar so I follow it. It takes me toward the beaches of my youth where white sand meets the sea. Up ahead on a sloping mountain with a long, narrow cobbled passageway, my eyes make out a rectangular lighthouse painted blue against white with a red dome sitting on its top. My claws reach out and I touch down.

My mother, who has become a red-tailed hawk too, sits on top of the unlit lighthouse, flapping her wings. She welcomes me with a nuzzle. Together, we caw about nothing: the weather, the sea, where the fattest bats and fish live, those easiest to hunt.

My mother and I stop talking as Jack approaches. He runs up the cobblestone at the base of the mountain. He wears the same clothes that he did when the car hit him: triathlon tights and a tight, long-sleeved, form-fitting top.

Following close behind Jack are two female and two male inhuman figures. They hover in long, white filmy robes. Corded knots cinch their waists to nothing. Hoods surround their transparent, melted white faces. Their eyes are hollow pits of empty black space.

Jack's arms pump hard and fast to quicken his pace. He raises his knees to the same level as his hips and winds his way up the mountain. At the end of the road on its top, he stops, leans forward and tries to catch his breath.

Jack turns and looks for another way out. His body quivers when he sees me and my mother, and he waves. My large hawk-black eyes blink in rapid succession a few times, and he smiles.

The creatures descend and drag Jack to the edge of the cliff, but he doesn't fight them. Instead, he looks first at the sun and then to the sea. They pick him up high into the air and throw him off the cliff's edge. He floats for a moment. When he falls they follow him.

One of my mother's black eyes stares at me from the side. She caws three times and then flies away. I caw once in response. One of the creatures moves away from the group and follows her.

My wings open and my claws release. I am back in flight. Another creature leaves the group and chases me, but I am not afraid.

Jack freefalls like a windmill, tumbling in the air nearer and nearer to the rocky shoreline. My wings stretch as far as possible and I duck. Jack lands on my back as if seated in bed.

My body adjusts to his weight and we fly over my old world. He sees the hotel where my mother found work after my father died and where we lived until I left for the U.S. We fly past the islands where I spent my youth: Stone, Wolf, Bird, and Deer, where I served drinks to tourists as they shuttled back and forth from island to island, my first real job, the one that helped my mother and me survive.

When we fly back offshore, three of the creatures chase us. My wingspan is so large that I know that I can out-fly them. My claws open up in case I need to use them. I have located two of the creatures directly to either side of me, but I have lost sight of the third one.

From behind and above, the third creature knocks Jack off my back. He falls into the water. I swoop down to pull him to safety, but the creatures grab me. They break the bones in my wings and plunge me into the water.

I look for Jack but cannot find him. As I sink, I am surprised that I am not buoyant, but I don't seem to need to breathe air anymore, either. On the way down, I find Jack. We grab one another as best we can.

My form no longer resembles a Red-tailed Hawk. Jack and I have become ourselves again. When we get to the ocean floor, he falls into his hospital bed, and I plop into a chair. The heart monitor and respirator beep and wheeze although they sound muffled from being underwater.

The beeping gets louder before becoming a constant monotone—the sound it makes when a patient has died. From above the water I can hear my mother's caw, sounding frantic and scared.

My legs push my body away from the chair, but I cannot stand up under the pressure of the water. I fall forward onto the ocean floor, trying to fight the weight of the water. The noise from the monitor and my mother's caw deafens me.

My body lunges from the ocean floor onto the floor of the resident's room. As my hand grabs for the phone's receiver, one of my feet gets tangled in the chair. Before I have a chance to speak I have fallen onto the cold floor and the phone has fallen next to me.

"Hello?" I sit up.

"José, what's wrong?" my mother asks in Spanish.

When I hear her voice the tension in my face relaxes for a moment. Then my face gets hot and feels red. Without thinking I stand up, turn on the light, and plop back down on the floor.

"Mom," I say in Spanish. "It's…it's happened. Jack. I'm afraid that…" I begin to choke.

"Slow down," she says. "Take a deep breath and tell me what happened."

Tears trickle down my face. I look around the room for a Kleenex or some toilet paper, but I can't find anything. I sniff a couple of times.

"It's Jack," I say. "A car hit him when he was crossing the street this afternoon. Hit and run."

"Oh," she says. "It sounds serious."

"Yeah, he's in a coma and his back is broken. They have to do surgery when he's stable enough."

"How did it happen?"

"I'm not sure. I wasn't there," I say. "But one of the witnesses said that the driver yelled something as he left the scene."

"He yelled something?"

"Yeah, he said, 'Faggot, get AIDS and die.'" More tears stream down my face.

"Terrible, just terrible."

"He did it on purpose mom, on purpose," I choke on my sobs. "I must have just missed the accident on my way home. If I hadn't stopped at the bakery maybe...maybe..."

"José, you've wanted to heal the world ever since you were a little boy, but you aren't responsible for what other people do."

"Yeah, but it could be my fault, or maybe if Jack didn't look so gay."

"I know it might feel better if you could blame yourself or Jack," she says. "Because you think it would give you control over these kind of people."

"Yeah," I pull the sheet down from the bed and wipe my face.

"That's just something that people think because they don't want to face how vulnerable they are."

"I don't know." I blow my nose.

"You are not responsible for their hatred, but you and Jack, and others like you have to pay for it."

63

"Maybe."

"You're just tired and stressed."

"I know." My fingers twist and untwist the telephone cord.

"Did you call his family?"

"Yeah."

"Is everything okay?"

"No, I don't think they've changed at all in the last ten years. They called me Juan Valdez."

"Juan Valdez? I don't understand."

"It's a character on TV who sells coffee. It's like saying everyone like us is the same, so our names are interchangeable."

"How awful."

64

"That's not the worst of it. Joy's husband said that they're entitled to everything that Jack owns…if he…if he dies." I start to cry again.

"What hateful people."

"God Mom, what a mess."

"Would you like me to come for a visit?"

"Could you? It would really help."

"I'll take the first plane I can."

"I…I can wire you some money." I wipe my face with the sheet again.

"Don't worry about me. Just take care of you and Jack."

"Thanks, Mom."

"Are you going to be able to stay with him?"

"I don't know. I'm supposed to start work at 3AM."

"Try to take care of yourself."

"They'd give me time off if we were legally married." I sniff again.

"We'll work something out."

"I love you Mom."

"I love you too. Goodbye."

"Bye."

My mom was right. I have tried to feel in control by pretending that this was my fault or Jack's fault. The weight that I've felt on my shoulders since late in the afternoon has lifted.

I check my watch. Jack's been alone for a little over an hour so I need to get back to him. I throw on my clothes and shoes and put everything back together and race out of the room.

When my coworkers see me as I come through the ER doors they call Nan's name. This makes me nervous, so I decide to find Jack on my own. I walk back to his bed, but it's empty.

"How're you doing, José?" Nan asks, coming up from behind and putting her arm around my shoulder.

"Where's Jack?" I ask.

"We've moved him into an ICU bed in the trauma wing."

"Why didn't you call me?"

"One just became available and I wanted to make sure that he got it before anyone else."

"Oh," I say. "Thanks."

"Did you get a hold of your families?"

"My mom's going to try to fly out."

"That's good. What about Jack's?"

I look down at my feet. My head shakes back and forth. I start to sniff again but stop myself from crying.

"Well, I can't say I'm surprised."

"Yeah."

"I need to go home and see Rebecca and the kids, at least for a few minutes. We'll both come if we can find someone to watch them. Otherwise, it'll be just me. Okay?"

"Okay. Thanks," I say, and Nan gives me a hug before she leaves.

65

I feel apprehensive when I get to Jack's room. Once my hand touches the door handle though, my strength returns. I slip into the chair next to his bed. He's still unconscious, on a respirator and heart monitor. The machines beep and wheeze to his rhythms, the only sign that he is still alive.

I take Jack's hand in mine and hold it. My fingers brush the hair from his closed eyes. I whisper in his ear that his family loves him and that we care and want him to get better. I stroke his arm and tell him that my mom, and Nan, and our other friends, will bring us flowers and food and other little things.

I will think of this day many times to come. Our relationship that had begun so long ago has had many summers, and now, an autumn follows. I am still here next to Jack. I will be in his room all night and I'll be here just in case he wakes up in the morning.

Baby, Beautiful

C. Adán Cabrera

Truth was Ramón almost didn't get on that plane. He almost made that cabbie turn around and drive back to his tiny Bronx studio where he would lie on his mattress and listen to the 5 train get swallowed up by the subway tunnel one rusted car at a time. Even as he buckled himself into the seat he had visions of hauling his luggage back up the three flights of rickety stairs, and then trudging through the storm of snow to that bodega on Barnes and buying some bacalaitos or some empanadas—or hell—even some of that bomb-ass bread pudding and eat all of it, every crumb, without wanting or wishing to stop. The last thing he needed was more weight. All six feet of him were already stuffed with three-hundred and two pounds of Salvadoran stoutness, but with no one around to scold or scorn or even notice—what did he care about a few extra pounds, or a dozen?

In the end Ramón flew back home to Los Angeles, wedged between two teenage girls who rolled their eyes at him whenever they tried to claim an armrest, bumping into Ramón's chubby elbows that were already there, as if they had always been there all ashy and wrinkled and immovable as an elephant's knees. One sighed and slumped into her seat and he thought he heard the other whisper a not-so-whispered *fat ass* as she flipped onto her side to watch the black sky roll by her window one threaded cloud at a time. Ramón, for his part, had gotten used to the taunts of gordo and porker and even called himself *Ramón el Jamón* around the other cooks at the pie shop, because even though he hated his sweat and his mound of gut he could always laugh at himself, *ja ja ja ja ja ja ja ja ja ja ja ja ja ja ja ja ja ja ja ja ja ja ja ja ja ja ja ja ja ja ja ja ja ja ja ja ja ja ja ja ja ja ja ja ja ja ja ja ja ja ja ja ja ja ja ja ja ja ja ja ja ja ja ja.*

As the plane tilted, turned, and tipped toward the house he hadn't seen in a year, three months, and two days, Ramón wondered what he had to lose, better yet what he would gain after he told his family the truth. He knew it was a gamble, a risk, like the games of naipe he'd watched his uncles play as a boy. But instead of cards and cash he was playing the unknown for his future, gambling for love, and if he lost well then ni modo—at least he'd tried, and hell, anything was better than the solitary confinement to which he'd become inured like frozen pipes in winter, or like the shadows that crawled toward him every evening, every day, taunting him with memories and stealing all of, yes, all of his breaths.

Ramón was glad he'd laid down his pride like a fork after a meal you'd regretted eating and agreed to come to his parents' Christmas party because it was a special occasion, as it had been years since the last one. Ramón decided he would tell them everything: that he'd dropped out of school again, that he worked part-time in the pie shop, full-time as a clown, and about the overpriced box that he lived in with a view of the tunnel's black throat, and yes, he would even tell them about Marc and how they had been friends, but more than friends, yeah in that way, and how that puto had lied and cheated on him with that fat Haitian kid soft as pudding across the hall, and that he was sorry he had left. I'm sorry mamá y papá, and you too, Xiomara. Perdónenme.

And now, as the plane pulled into the terminal, and as the teenagers rolled their eyes at each other across his bulge of belly, Ramón could barely hold back the burn of salt in his eyes when he thought about embracing his family. He pictured them waiting for him tired and tearful at the terminal, waiting for the son and brother that had flown to the other side of this huge *Gringolandia*. The pilot thanked the passengers, the crew ushered them out, and Ramón sauntered toward the waiting area where he expected his mom to cry and his father to cheer the second they saw him approaching.

Instead, he saw only Xiomara, whistling in the arrivals lounge, wrapping and unwrapping her scarf around her forearm as she thumbed through a magazine. When she ran over to him, he bent over to hug his sister and felt ashamed that her arms couldn't wrap all the way around him. He felt her palms warm and separate across his back, each hand like the tip of a continent stretching toward the tip of another, waiting to collide.

The next day, on the morning of the party, the family shared a late breakfast of fried plátanos and salty black beans. After they had greeted each other (*We missed you!* his mother confessed; *My New Yorker returns!* his father chuckled), Don Ramón had a million questions for his son about the food, the sights, the people, the city.

"How can you last in that cold, m'ijo?" his father asked. He continued in Spanish: "I've never even seen snow. I don't think I'd last a day!"

Ramón finished chewing his plátano before answering, "I'm still getting used to it." He reached for another tortilla.

"People in El Salvador would go nuts with that kind of cold," Doña Maritza, his mother, interjected. Her words were heavy and measured, like always, as if they were ice cubes balancing precariously on her tongue. "We're used to a warm, sticky Christmas. Christmas here is so dull. Back home all the kids are well behaved and thankful for every little thing the Christ child brings them. Some coconut candy, a few marbles—if they're lucky maybe a teddy bear. Here parents buy their little gringuitos their Barbies, que Transformers, que Spiderman, que X-Bots ..."

"Mom, it's X-*Box*, not X-*Bots*," Xiomara said in English. She continued in awkward Spanish: "And anymore, we're not in El Salvador."

Doña Maritza corrected her daughter. "We're not in El Salvador *anymore*." She stirred her coffee vigorously.

Don Ramón leaned a little toward his son and muttered under his breath, "I hear your mom's making pupusas for tonight's party. Just don't tell her that."

"I heard you, cabrón." Doña Maritza reached across Ramón and pulled some of Don Ramón's arm hair. Her hand felt cold and rough as it brushed against his arm. "Pupusas are hard work to make, you know."

Don Ramón pulled his arm away and laughed. "Ay, vieja, relax. It's a special occasion. Besides, Xiomara will help you. She needs to start learning how to cook now that she's getting older. Her husband will want a wife who knows how to make him some carne guisada, some caldo, pupusas."

"Dad!" Xiomara cried out.

"It's not her fault she's the only girl," Doña Maritza said. "If I had another daughter or maybe a *daughter-in-law—*"

She nudged her son.

"Leave the boy alone, Maritza," Don Ramón set his mug of coffee down on the table. His fork trembled on his plate.

"Achis, it's for his own good," Doña Maritza insisted. "We haven't seen him in more than a year—and before he knows it his whole chingada life will have passed him by." She dabbed her eyes with the corner of the tablecloth.

"You and all your pressure, making the boy feel bad because he hasn't found the right woman," Don Ramón said. "Not all of us marry because there's no other choice."

"Well no one's forcing you to stay here, pendejo," Maritza crossed her arms.

Don Ramón sighed, shook his head. "And we wonder why you haven't gotten married yet."

The ceiling fan whirred overhead.

"I just don't want him to die alone, so far from us, surrounded by all those Puerto Ricans," Doña Maritza's voice cracked as she put an icy hand on Ramón's arm. Her gaze was fixed on the cold bowl of beans in front of her.

"He won't," Don Ramón said, softer. "Once he's done with school, he'll find a woman to love and take care of him. Isn't that right, Ramón?"

Up until this point, Ramón had enjoyed his breakfast. Now he felt he had to earn it.

"Right," he whispered.

Later that afternoon, while his family had gone out shopping for some last minute party favors, Ramón went into his old room to unpack. He had brought only two sweaters and a pair of faded jeans, along with a few gifts for his family: a shaver for his father, a bottle of perfume for his mother, a pair of earrings for Xiomara.

He'd also brought the bracelet that Marc had given him last Christmas, a bracelet made of solid silver with his name engraved on it in long, curly letters. He sat on the corner of his bed and traced the raised surface with his thumb.

Ramón would never have imagined falling in love with Marc, or that two weeks after meeting him at some party in Hollywood, he would agree to move into his flat in New York City, when he had never even been out of California (other than Las Vegas and that one trip to Tijuana).

Ramón had never made any "big decisions" and never amounted to much after high school. He had no real friends and lost count of how many times he dropped out of City College. He had no steady job and was embarrassed to be in his late twenties, having only unquenchable desires to beat off and eat pizza. So when love finally found him and made him happy—why not move in with Marc, the boy that loved *every inch* of him? He was cute and called Ramón a "beautiful baby" even though he had only seen him in the black mouth of a hotel room and really only said that when he was inside of him, that first night, saying *oh baby oh baby oh baby, you are so beautiful.*

Ramón didn't tell Marc to stop when it started to hurt because it was his first time and didn't want to ruin the moment, because making love is beautiful and he loved Marc's hot breath on his ear, his big tongue in his mouth, and the sound of their flesh slapping together. Hadn't it been his mother who said that God worked miracles? So he grunted along with Marc and when Marc finished Ramón put a sock back there and tried and tried and tried to pretend that he didn't feel the trickle running down his legs.

Ramón had known better, but he had made "the decision" one year and three months and two days ago, because it felt right even if it didn't seem right to Xiomara or his mamá, who begged him to stay, or to his father who sat quietly in

the corner. He wouldn't allow Marc to come into his goddamn house because that hijo'e puta could wait in the car
while the family talked about "the decision" goddamn it, and
if that hijo'e puta didn't like it he could suck on the tip of the
.45 Magnum he hid in the drawer underneath his calzoncil-
los.

Ramón started to reconsider, but in the end listened to the
chatter of his heart that called him east—and to his hard-
on that pulled him like a tuning fork to New York City. He
didn't listen to his mother who cried in the doorway as the
truck pulled away, her eyes all puffy and swollen, her face all
scrunched up with sadness.

So he moved and spent his first Christmas away from his
family. Instead of watching mamá and papá dance silently
in each other's arms to a soft cumbia, he instead watched
Marc prancing around the fireplace in his green Christmas
sweater, drunk on eggnog and yelling for Ramón to turn up
the music. Instead of atole and tamales, Ramón sipped on
cognac and nibbled on pretzels, half of which were sodden
with soda that Marc had spilled earlier. Marc vomited in a
corner. An exchange of wet, sour-breathed kisses. Tulip pet-
als littered the floor. Cocaine.

In the end Marc had produced only one present: a silver
bracelet engraved with Ramón's name. Marc was too drunk
to fasten it around Ramón's chubby wrist but tried to anyway. He held still, trying not to wince while Marc pinched
his skin and pulled his arm hair.

"I'm glad you're here," Marc had stammered, after finally
fastening the bracelet. "You're so baby, beautiful." His breath
smelled of whiskey. There was powder on his nose. He started to lean forward to kiss Ramón, but instead toppled head-
first into his lap and fell asleep. Ramón smoothed his hair
softly and thought how unexpected and fragile and noisy a
thing love could be.

He learned to look past Marc's late nights, past the hushed phone conversations in the hallway, past the hickies he found on Marc's ass, because he didn't pay any rent or bills here; he just worked at that pie shop on 35th and Broadway. Wasn't it his dad who'd said that unless you pay your way you have no say in what goes on under my roof, goddamn it? *New York is fun, Xiomara,* he'd said over the phone and *Dad, tell Mom to stop worrying* and *I told you, Mom, classes are hard right now and that's why I don't call so often anymore, but yeah things here are cool, real cool chivo, 'ama really don't worry.*

And then he'd found Marc with the chubby Haitian kid soft as a vat of pudding. He'd come home from the pie shop to see Marc grinding in and out and in and out and in and out and in and out and in and out and in and out and in and out and in and out between the fat kid's hips. Ramón remembered that they continued to grunt even after Marc (that *bastard*!) had turned around and seen him standing there, winter coat half off, a look of pain frozen on his face, but he smiled (that *bastard*!) and kept going as if Ramón was a customer a dollar short knocking on the restaurant door one minute after closing time.

Ramón ran out of Marc's apartment, ran and ran and ran and ran and ran and ran and ran past the deli, the bodega, the old Chinese woman selling newspapers, the crazy homeless man on 67th, the pervy man who always called him m'ijo and asked for fifty cents as he walked to work. He even ran past the garden of sunflowers looking silently for the sun that he marvelled at every morning, every day. Ramón ran and ran and ran until he couldn't run anymore, until he sat down on a bench in Central Park and tried to figure out what he would do now that he was homeless and so far from home. He wanted to call mami y papi, admit that he'd fucked up, that he should have listened to Xiomara—who warned him that he'd be back, but he hadn't called in weeks

74

and last time he'd lied and said he was happy, when in reality, he could barely sleep and spent most nights counting Marc's snores until he lost count and then consciousness. In the end he had inherited his mother's stubbornness and his father's pride, so he'd have to get through this on his own. He cried and cried and cried and cried to his coworker (that kind Nicaraguan lady) about Marc (that *bastard*!) and she let him stay with her in her tiny Bushwick apartment until he had saved up enough money to rent his little shoebox in the Bronx.

But he kept up the front with his folks, and with Xiomara, and told them that everything was cool, because one day everything would be cool and soon life became a beating heart, a deflated lung, a crusty eye, and a year and six months had been spent like a paycheck on the lotería.

75

Damn.

He was snapped out of his thoughts by Xiomara's laughter echoing down the hall as she approached his room. He stuffed the bracelet back into his suitcase and wiped his brow with the sleeve of his sweater.

The Lozanos were the first to arrive, as usual. Ramón watched Niña Magdalena, a matronly woman with jet black hair, turtle toward the front door, hugging a tub of what looked to be macaroni salad. Don Felix, her husband, trailed a little behind, supporting himself on a metal cane that caught glimmers of street light as they approached.

Ramón opened the door to let them in. A squeal of delight went up.

"Look, Felix, it's Ramón!" Niña Magdalena pulled him toward her and smacked a kiss on his cheek. Her lipstick left a greasy stain on his cheek.

"Mira, how healthy you look!" Don Felix stepped into the foyer, reaching for Ramón's belly.

Ramón stopped it midway and shook his hand instead. "Great to see you, Don Felix, Niña Magdalena. Feliz navidad."

He was relieved when his mother came out of her room, after nearly two hours primping and pressing to get ready on time. Her hair was still in curlers and she smelled strongly of perfume.

"Magdalena! Felix!" She kissed both of them on the cheek. As they exchanged pleasantries Ramón recognized his mother's other persona, the cheerful, social one where even her voice seemed a little bit fuller. Don Ramón then came out wearing the shirt he only wore to church and a pair of sad, faded shoes. Xiomara followed in a tight-fitting turquoise dress.

Ramón hated his dirty jeans and light green sweater with the small hole in the back, and maybe he looked like a lime but no one would notice, or at least not say, anything he hoped—at least not to his face. Ramón watched them chat and hug some more until he knew, just knew, they were talking about him because he heard Niña Magdalena suddenly say that maybe God (the only uninvited attendee) would answer their prayers.

They sat chatting in the living room on his parents' old, cracked, but very sturdy, leather couches until more people—the Escobares, the Garcías, the Sotos and their snotty lawyer son—arrived. Doña Maritza asked Ramón to lead everyone down into the garage where the party was going to be held.

Ramón and his sister had spent the afternoon clearing out boxes filled with their father's old vinyl (Metallica, Barnabas), carried out the food the dead family dog had left behind, and stuffed the dirty car cover that Ramón had used for his first car into the trash can, leaving its mouth ajar and filled with cotton. They cleaned and scrubbed and set up lawn chairs around the perimeter of the modest two-car garage and hung green and red streamers from the rafters to hide all the dust. Xiomara then stacked all the cups and beer and soda on top of the washing machine even though their mother would scold them when all the guests had left. Ni modo.

He'd tried to tell Xiomara then, just as she was sweeping out the last few cobwebs. It was the perfect opportunity, dusty with silence. But then maybe she'd freak out or maybe she'd just hug him, but in the end too many maybes got caught in his throat and he said nothing when she caught him staring at her. *I'm just thinking*, he told her.

Ramón helped all the ladies down the two small steps. As they stepped into the garage they admired the décor and the pile of tamales his mother had made the day before, and the tower of pupusas next to the boom-box, and even the little Christmas tree in the corner.

Soon they were all here, crowded into his parents' garage. Emiliano Nubes guzzled a beer with Don Antonio while the latter's young wife, Estella, nibbled away at a tamale. Nancy del Rio, his mother's friend from elementary school, shouted her bits of conversation to Leticia Porfirez, Juana Martínez, and Estephanie Rodríguez, over the loud cumbia that rattled the garage's one window. A bunch of couples he'd never met before stood against the walls, sat in the chairs, chewed, spit, smoked. Little kids wearing stiff new clothes fluttered about and between the dancing legs of adults.

As for the men, Don Ramón was talking with a group of them—Alvaro Porfirez, Beto Martínez, Salvador Rodríguez, Mario Guerrida—all of whom held a beer or a cigarette or both. Don Beto pointed at Ramón with the tip of his bottle, playfully asking if he wanted another one.

Ramón took another one, though he was already drunk, the result of one too many questions by his father's friends. About the women in Nueva York, whether he stared at their televisores as they walked away, if he liked black girls or Chinese girls or those freaky Puerto Rican girls or maybe he'd score him a güera like they had all fantasized. They wanted to hear all about Ramón's escapades, about his sexual trysts, about the morenas in Harlem, and if he even saw any Salvadoreñas at school, or at the lab, or at all in Nueva York.

So Ramón lied, of course, using the memory of the kind Nicaraguan lady and recast her as sexy waitress with the sweetest culito he'd ever seen. The beers that the men kept passing him helped. Between sips he'd look up to see his father looking on shyly, before leaning over to switch the CD.

After eight beers Ramón had to piss and was grateful to have an excuse to leave. So he went and pissed and then sat down heavily on the sturdiest lawn chair he could find next to Cristobal. He was drunk, so drunk that he even sang along with the music. No one could hear him singing over the blaring music, but that was okay with him. His hands kept time with the music and though he never ever danced in public, he felt his hips strain to ride the beat. He was sad, but didn't want to think about it, and so he thought about Cristobal, sexy Cristobal, the uncomfortably handsome son of the Guerridas.

Cristobal had been a last minute arrival, and as soon as he walked in, Ramón was already mentally undressing him, boxers or briefs, or maybe neither. When he lusted, he felt most like a man, and seeing Cristobal's shaved head and muscles—and that thick neck—made his manhood shift hungrily and alert in his pants. To make matters worse, Cristobal seemed like a really nice guy, uninterested in talking about women or booze, but instead asking Ramón about his work in the lab and about the books he was reading in college. Ramón imagined Cristobal, oh so sexy Cristobal, on top, inside, just near him, while he named books he'd never read and kicked himself for forgetting he worked in a medical lab and instead mentioned the pie shop, but Cristobal didn't seem to notice because he glanced every now and then at a woman but didn't make it apparent—and so what if he did—what could he do?

They talked and drank and talked.

Cristobal stood up. "Let's go have a smoke," he said. "Outside."

He smiled and Ramón smiled back and Cristobal smiled back, and when Ramón didn't move he tugged at Ramón's arm with his hand, and when Ramón felt his wrists wrap around him for that moment he smiled back again and followed him because maybe God did have another miracle up his sleeve and put Cristobal in his path—and maybe he wouldn't have to go back to the Bronx after all and would instead stay here and keep his secret a little longer.

Ramón stepped out into the December night. The clink of glasses and the machine gun laughter of the neighbors floated over to them. A cold, brisk wind rustled in the trees. The air smelled of firewood. The sky above them was black velvet stitched with tiny pinpoints of light. The city's lights competed with midnight. Christmas had come to Los Angeles.

Cristobal offered him a cigarette. Ramón plucked one out, more nimbly than he would have liked. Cristobal lit his, and when he held out the lighter, Ramón watched the flame bowing and bending; he felt his heart do the same and thought that maybe he would act instead of thinking so goddamn much.

He grabbed Cristobal's hand and kissed it. The lighter bounced with a metallic clang onto the concrete and disappeared under the bushes. As Ramón tumbled onto the cold concrete he wondered how he would explain what felt like a cracked jaw and a tooth knocked loose.

Maybe he could sneak away before they would see it and he could fly back to New York and pretend this never happened, like a bad dream, a bad movie, or that Haitian kid all naked and soft like a vat of pudding, or maybe he would never see Xiomara or mami or papi again, or maybe he'd finally enroll in school and make something of himself goddamn it, and then maybe he wouldn't be so embarrassed to walk into a department store instead of wearing the same shit day in, day out, day in, day out, looking like a goddamn photograph, or maybe if he woke up then maybe, just maybe, he would tell them the truth no matter how bitter or sour or awful it tasted.

Fairy Tale

JUSTIN TORRES

Father, I'm writing to tell you that Uncle Ramón has grown wings. It happened a couple of years ago, when I was still, in many ways, a child. They grew out of the side of his head, behind his ears. They aren't feathered wings, they're skin wings, like on a bat. He can't make them flap, but he can curl them in on themselves, roll them up like a sleeping bag, and then pop them out again. I remember when they first appeared—I used to follow him around, pulling on his pant legs, begging him to let me see and feel and smell them.

They smelled like cat piss.

"Come on man," I'd say, "give me some wings!"

He'd pretend like he didn't hear me, like he didn't notice me trying to jump up on his back and get a hold of them. He'd just whistle or hum softly to himself, ignoring me, then, all of a sudden he'd stop what he was doing, whip his neck around, bring his face down close to mine, and BAM! Out would come the wings, so fast they'd make a noise like someone had been smacked in the face.

He hides them now. He's grown his hair, not a far-out seventies deal, but just enough to cover the wings when they're curled down. He wears hats with earflaps. He's fallen in love with some woman named Carissa, or Carmen, or Carmencita—I can't remember which.

"She don't want to be thinking about them when we're out at a restaurant, or on the street, or what have you," he told me the other day, "but when the door's closed, them wings get her juices flowing, if you know what I mean."

I wasn't quite sure then, but now I think I know what he meant.

Turns out, Uncle Miguel grew wings too, tiny ones, like a moth. He tapes them down with bandages because they flutter constantly and the noise of the fluttering so close to his ears gives him headaches and makes him feel crazy. He says it's like a dozen helicopters landing on his head. Thing is, the taped down wings give him headaches too. "All that pent up longing," he says, "all that desire to flail and flap around."

"Them wings have needs," he says.

And just yesterday we discovered that Uncle Gabriel's growing wings, too. His are even smaller than Uncle Miguel's, they don't curl or flutter yet, and everyone's saying they hope, for Gabi's sake, that they'll stay small and hidden. But to tell the truth Father, I'm hoping for some big, badass wings, hawk wings, or eagle wings, big enough for Uncle Gabriel to cover his eyes with when he's afraid.

This might disappoint you, but after the whole affair with Uncle Gabriel, I went straight to see Uncle Tito at his place. I didn't tell anyone where I was going, because everybody acts like Tito's some kind of an untouchable, a creep, a black smear of disgrace on the family. But I knew that if all of my other uncles had wings, then he must have them too, and I was just dying to get my hands on them. I'm hot for wings, Father; I can't get enough.

Uncle Tito's wings were wilder than I hoped for. He couldn't even roll them up they were so huge, and they hung down the sides of his face like a bloodhound. He sat me on his lap and spread them for me with his hands. They were enormous, the size of pillowcases. The skin was thin and pink and translucent. Tiny, red and blue veins crisscrossed underneath the surface.

"Fuck," I thought, "them wings got my juices flowing."

"Watch this," he said, and wrapped them around my face, smothering me. It was warm and sweat-sticky and the stench of cat piss was overwhelming. I tried to pull the wings off me but they were elastic, the skin stretched and pulled like pizza dough. I couldn't breathe, and I couldn't scream, and Uncle Tito just kept pressing down harder and harder, until I had to slam my knee down into his crotch and get the fuck out of there before he killed me. But I'll tell you, Father, all day I've been smelling that funky, ammonia smell, dreaming about them wings.

The way I see it, your wings should appear anytime now, probably within the next year or so, and I thought I'd give you a heads up. Don't be scared Father, they're beautiful really, and nothing to be ashamed of. When they do arrive, I hope they're strong enough to fly you home, so you can come and see us, after all these years.

Picture it Father, I'll scrub them clean for you, I'll rub them with oils until they shine, and I'll massage them wings, when they're sore. Maybe you'll take me for rides, up and up until we're both dizzy and tired. Maybe I'll grow wings of my own someday and when we walk down the street to-

83

gether, all the old grandfathers will stop to shake our hands and clap us on the shoulders. They'll tell us they see the resemblance, they'll point their chins at me, they'll say, "This one must be yours."

pregnant boy

CHUY SÁNCHEZ

I let him cum inside me. I'm not sure why since I don't want to get AIDS, but I let him. It made me feel like I was giving myself all the way, you know? Like it didn't matter what kind of danger there was.

Last night was our first night fucking, real fucking. I'd sucked his dick plenty of times, but this was different. He came to my mom's house and was all like "¿Qué estás haciendo?" with a twinkle in his eye, acting all innocent—knowing full well his dick was hard for me. I was all coquettish, because that's how I do. I knew he wanted this. My mom was about to get home so I grabbed his hand and we went to one of the empty apartments in the building—the super always left them open.

Victor was three years older than me, seventeen. He was tall, super dark like an indio and had Chinese-looking eyes. He was cute and had big muscles. The first time I went down on him I thought, "Damn, how am I going to get that thing in my mouth?" But I worked it out.

Wasn't the first time I'd sucked someone off, but it was his first time feeling someone's luscious lips all around his Mexican stick. I remember the look of pleasure on his face; I'd never seen that before—not like that.

Victor was sweet, too. He opened doors for me, whispered in my ear, and bought me little things. He was jealous though, didn't want me doing anyone else but him. I was good, but sometimes it's hard to keep things on the monogamous tip. Bet you never thought I'd be on this one-on-one business!

He kissed me, last night I mean. My first kiss ever. I've done a lot of stuff with boys before, but never had I kissed and never had I actually fucked. I was like Adela Noriega in *Quinceañera*. (In case you didn't know, *Quinceañera* was the best Mexican soap opera ever made. It's my life except I'm not yet fifteen, don't live in Mexico, don't have a dad, and I'm not a girl. Everything else though—that's me.)

For a split second I didn't know how to respond to his tongue inside my mouth. It felt strange. I'm not sure why, since I've had a bunch of other things up in there. His tongue was sweet. That's what threw me off guard, that it wasn't rough. Usually boys are rough when you're with them. They just want to get off and be on their way—you remember. His tongue searched for mine and he wanted me to kiss him back. He touched me, felt me. I got scared. He licked my neck and—Lord have mercy!—it made me instantly wet. I knew I wanted him inside me. I wanted him to be the first one.

He was.

That shit hurt so good. I can't even tell you how good that was unless you felt it yourself. I'd had my finger up there before, but it just wasn't the same. Girl, he made love to me! He loved me. I loved him. I cried a little bit, not because of the pain, but because I had never felt anyone so close before. Well, you and me are close, but not in the same way!

"Estás sabroso," Victor said—that I tasted good. Heaven, pure heaven. He worried about me coming, too. Not once have I been touched down there and nobody ever worried whether I came or not. It was nice to cum with someone else holding you. Who knew that all the mushy-mushy shit you see in soaps could happen for real? When Adela got her first kiss, she made such a big-ass moment about it. Well, this was my big-ass moment—for real. I should start writing my own novela so I don't forget anything.

Victor walked me to my door afterwards. He made me feel like it didn't matter that I was a fag, you know? All the other ones, no matter how many times they came to get some of this, always made me feel dirty—like I was their secret whore.

87

Today at school I didn't mind that Leroy was being an asshole (again) and that Takwanda's fat ass punched me in science class—just because she's a bitch like that and she's huge and able to crush me if she wants to.

Chicago Public Schools ain't cute. Now that you're not here anymore, I don't have no one to get my back. Now they pound on me like never before. I'm an outsider now. I don't have a crew. You were my crew girl, and now you're gone.

I didn't see Victor today. We didn't make any plans. He just shows up whenever he's feeling it. I want him to feel it now. I want him inside of me again and again and again. I want to have his baby. I'm going to have his baby—a little baby girl that looks just like her daddy. I'm going to take real good care of her, so you're going to be an auntie.

I've got to go do homework now. This real life shit ain't so hot. School is a pain in the ass, but I have to keep up a front so everybody thinks I'm a good Mexican boy who's not gay, though everybody pretty much thinks it or wants it that way. To top it all off, I'm feeling like a whale. Later.

I got something to say and I wish I could say it to your face. I'm mad as hell that you're not here no more! The first time I saw your snot-nosed five-year-old self, I knew we would be girlfriends forever. I noticed you because that nasty big girl smacked your head and all you did was sit there with tears coming down your face. You had these cute braids with rainbow-colored clips. I smiled at you 'cause I felt sorry. You smiled back even though you were still crying. We became friends.

Fast forward nine years and you're dead. Just like that, you're dead. I don't get it. I don't even really believe it. I still walk over to your mom's house, though it's out of my way, 'cause that's what we used to do after school. Yesterday, I saw your mom. "Hi, Miss Maggie," I said. She opened her gate and hugged me so tight I thought all the air inside of me was going to disappear. Her eyes were so sad. She let me go and I walked away.

I'm falling in love for the first time and you are nowhere to be found, so you can tell me how silly I'm being or how stupid I look when I think about him. You were lonely. I saw you every day and you never said nothing. You could have told me something. I can't hug you. I need to.

I went to your wake. All these people from school were there. Kids that you didn't even like were there with their faces all turned upside-down. I walked in with my mom. I felt like a little child 'cause I had to hold her hand tight. Your dead body was in front of the church. I could see the tip of your nose from way back. I saw your mom and sister. They sat all the way in the front. I don't know how they did that, looking straight at you, straight at your lifeless face.

My mom tried to tell me that it was okay to cry, to feel what I was feeling. She told me to go up and say my last goodbye. She forced me. I walked up. There was no one else there but me. My mom said it was something I had to do by myself. Crazy. I listened to my mother.

Girl, your face was so quiet. Your hands lying across your chest. The color of your skin was different, lighter, weird. It was you, but not. Empty. I broke down. My mom took me in her arms and I didn't care that everyone was watching me. I'm glad my mom is around even though she's working all the time. She took that night off just to go with me. She liked you, too. She called you "negrita." You know, our mothers had never met before. They did that night. I think my mom met her first black friend and it's your mom, Miss Maggie.

I just ate four deep dish slices of sausage pizza, five glasses of pop, a box of cookies and two glasses of milk. I haven't seen Victor and I'm wondering why. Maybe I dreamed everything that happened. Maybe he's like all the others and just wanted to get inside me, to conquer me. I'm nervous girl, and there is nothing I can do to feel better except eat all this crappy food that tastes so damn good.

My mom just got home and yelled at me for eating like a pig. I didn't get a chance to clean up before she got here. "¡¿Qué te pasa?!" she yelled at me. I didn't say anything. She's got too much going on for me to tell her what's going on in my head. I'm scared.

Is this what you felt like? That you couldn't share parts of your soul with anyone? Your heart must've been hurting bad for you to do what you did. What kind of friend was I that I didn't even know you were hurting? All my insides are drowning in fat. My brain is high with sugar.

I'm going to tell him I'm pregnant. I'm gaining weight like nobody's business. He'll believe it's his. No one else has been inside me.

Girl, fuck you! Fuck you for not being here! Fuck you for killing yourself! Fuck you for making me feel like shit! Fuck you because I hurt without you! I still love you though, always. Smile with me.

Victor came over last night. We didn't fuck. He just held me in his arms. We talked. For real! All we did was lie with each other. I was cracking up 'cause in the middle of everything I felt like some white girl in a romantic comedy swooning for her man.

We were in my room. My mom was working the night shift so there was no problem there. I listened. Aha, my selfish ass was listening to someone else for hours without interrupting. Well, I did interrupt a little. It couldn't all be about him and nothing about me, right? You know how I do.

Victor is a dreamer. He wants to make it big here. His parents are in Mexico. He's living with his uncle and a bunch of other guys. He works and doesn't go to school. He has to send money to his parents every month. He misses them. He misses home.

Lucky. Am I? Victor thinks so. I never thought about it one way or the other. He kissed me and all I could think about was his tongue inside my mouth. Girl, that boy is for real. My fat ass has got a man. He said he was going to take care of me. I believe him.

I've seen my mom's boyfriends come and go. Not one has ever stayed long enough for me to care one way or the other about him. She does. I've seen her get bent out of shape over Ricardo, Arnulfo, José, Fernando, Ignacio and Elias. My mom is no fool, though. As soon as she sees something's not right she lets them go, even if it pains her. She cries.

She's taught me to not depend on no one. Not even her. All the work she puts in just to keep me safe and sound ain't easy. She doesn't complain. I do. She can't afford everything I want. I need more. Ever since Victor has come into my life things have been a little easier between me and my mom. I don't pay her much mind. She thinks I'm calming down. She doesn't ask. I don't tell.

They tried to rape Adela in *Quinceañera*. I can't remember if they actually did or if they didn't. Her best friend, Thalia, is pregnant. Teen pregnancy apparently is a big deal in their world. I haven't been keeping up with them as much. Been too busy living my own soap.

Victor scares me. He asks me things that no one has asked before. What do I want to do with my life? Do I miss my father? Do I love myself? Girl, I don't know that shit. That's the only thing that gets on my nerves about him, his damn questions. I try to answer, truthful and all, but I start to get the giggles and can't. He's so serious about stuff. I don't have no one to josh with. You were the Queen of Bullshit. That's one of the things I loved the most about you. Nothing was sacred. Not even your own life.

Victor made me remember about my dad. I don't think we ever talked about our pops. We just assumed they weren't there like so many other deadbeats. My daddy didn't leave me and my mom like that, though. He died like you did.

Not exactly. I don't really know. My mom doesn't want to talk about it. I used to ask. She would tell me bits and pieces. How their first date was to go see *The Exorcist*. I saw it, too. The movie is freaky. That little girl is no joke. Devil in her. I think they made me on their first date right after watching that possessed thing vomit all over Jesus.

I don't even know if I miss him. How can I miss someone I don't have any memory of? I was just a baby when he died. All I have are pictures. Everyone says I look like him. I guess I do. I suppose things would be different if he was still alive. He's a stranger. I have one parent and that's my mom. She's been everything to me even if she gets on my nerves, but that's what moms do. All I know is my mom and I are good. We do right by each other. Our little family is fine. I don't miss him.

A white girl joined our class yesterday. Aha, a white girl! I knew white kids existed but not around here. Little skinny bitch is pretty. All the black boys are up on her ass. All the black girls want to beat her ass. She smiles a lot. We got one thing in common. We're the only two students in the class that ain't black. I haven't talked to her. Maybe she'll be my new you.

Ooooh, I just felt a kick! I'm pregnant, girl. I'm for real this time. My belly been growing like nobody's business. I get morning sickness every day. I'm eating all kinds of shit that I didn't eat before, artichokes. With child like Thalia in *Quinceañera*. I'm gonna have to get back on it so I can see what happens with her. She's a rich girl, though. It's not gonna be the same. I wish Adela had gotten pregnant instead. Then I would know how to handle my own.

I haven't told Victor yet. I wanted to make sure. He's going to be happy. He's going to take care of both of us. I love him. He loves me. We're going to love our baby. I sing to her at night, real low so my mom don't hear. Cindy, that's what I'm going to call her. Like you.

"Victor is my baby daddy, so you best get your hands off my man! Faggot!" That's all I remember the bitch saying and then she started swinging like a dude. Yes girl, I got a black eye and that bitch is gonna need a wig 'cause I pulled off half of her hair. It has a name, Rocio.

I'd just gotten out of school. I was minding my business and all of a sudden I see this high school girl with a big ass belly walking my way. I keep on walking 'cause I don't think she got any business with me. She stares me down, calls me all kinds of names. At first I think she's talking to somebody else, but then I realize the heifer is looking me dead in the eye. Victor's name comes up and then all hell broke loose.

Girl, I didn't even have time to blink. Next thing I know we are rumbling on the street. All the crowd was around us cheering for her 'cause she's a female and pregnant. What about my baby, Cindy? I wonder what she's going to call hers.

My face hurts. I just got yelled at by my mom for fighting. She doesn't know it was with a girl; otherwise, she would kick my ass too. I don't know how to fight. Girl, we were never fighters. We knew how to get out of shit using our tongues, never our nails. I got my ass kicked good and by a pregnant bitch.

Victor. He's all I can think about. I want to hear it from his mouth. I want him to tell me that he put his seed in her. I want him to tell me that he willingly tasted that pussy. I want him. I'm eating a chocolate cake your mom sent us. The sweetness makes me forget. Each bite is heaven. So sad, this teenage eating disorder drama. Rocio is an evil cockroach!

He lied to me. That's his baby. I'm hurt. I'm sad. I'm an idiot. My baby is kicking right now. That shit is painful as fuck. Girl, you'll never know what it's like to be pregnant and you should be thankful 'cause it isn't easy. Every day I feel sick. My baby is never gonna get her ass kicked. I want her to be strong.

At night, I talk to her. I tell her all about her daddy and how we're all going to live together. She smiles. I can't see her but I feel her being happy, especially when I tell her about Victor. I tell her about how she needs to watch out for fools on the street. She's smart. I tell her about her grandma and how she needs to learn from her mistakes. I don't tell her about me. I figure she'll learn soon enough.

Last night my mom was telling me about the times when I was little. We would go to Kmart and I would come out wearing dresses. Anything for fashion, girl! You know me. I was a happy kid. No matter what was going on around me my dolls had my back. They used to crack me up. I had this blonde, blue eyed, chubby toddler doll named Lola. She was my favorite 'cause she looked exactly how I wanted to look. She was the most glamorous doll I had. When mom went off to work at night, it was just me and Lola chillin', watching TV and eating Twinkies. I don't know what happened to her. She's gone. Like you.

I'm going to have my baby in Mexico City. My mom is sending me away 'cause I've been acting up. Victor is gone. Rocio won. She got him and I didn't. I'm gonna be a single parent. I'm afraid of what that means. I haven't told my mom I'm pregnant, but she's noticing the weight I'm gaining. I'm a fat cow and I don't care 'cause my baby is coming. She's growing. I can hear her breathing.

Adela Noriega found love at the end of *Quinceañera*. I don't know what happened to her pregnant friend Thalia. She probably found love, too. I want that.

Tomorrow is the first day of summer. I turn fifteen in a week. Apparently, it's also Gay Day in the US. Gay Day. I'm going to march my pregnant ass on that pavement and scream with pride with all my queers. You're going to be by my side. I know it.

Javier

EDWIN SÁNCHEZ

I was never beaten up as a kid, which is odd, since I was both a sissy and a coward. I thought that being one meant I had to be the other and how could have I thought otherwise? I lived with my family in a six-story walk-up in the Bronx and would avoid going downstairs at all costs. I had to, of course, as I was the boy of the house. I had to run all the errands. Run being the operative word. I could amuse myself and make up games—that wasn't a problem. It was being amongst my peers that I hated.

I was the chubby boy who avoided eye contact and always tried to disappear in crowds. I was thirteen back when thirteen was still innocent. The tough kids in the neighborhood came up with a name for me, not Tomboy, but Tomgirl. To the Hispanic kids I was "Javier la loca." But things changed when I was allowed to ride the subway by myself—as there was a whole other universe besides the Bronx, a world I could get lost in.

It was the summer of 1969 and I was in midtown Manhattan. I had discovered that if you hung out where there were mostly adults you would be least likely to get harassed, because these were people leading important lives, going to important places, and I so wanted to be one of them.

A business man smiled at me one day and I smiled back as big as I could. *Maybe he thinks I belong here—that I'm one of them.*

He came up to me and asked if I could help him—if I could go with him to the roof of a building.

"Wow! Me? Sure!!!"

He had to take a piss and I could help him so much by holding his briefcase. I, being so idiotic (since there's no other word for it), was more surprised that a businessman would use the word *piss. Don't they have a high class word for that?*

"So can you help me out?" he asked again.

I, in all my innocence, suggested he go to one of the many hotels nearby. "The Sheraton might let you use their bathroom, maybe," I suggested, since he was dressed nice.

His smile faded, tightened. "But I really need to go now. Won't you please come with me to the roof of this building and hold my briefcase? It'll only take a minute."

I continued raving about the luxury of the Sheraton's men's room until he cut me off, staring me in the eye. Turning on his smile again, he said, "If your father had to take a piss you'd want a nice boy to help him, now wouldn't you?"

I guess.

I followed him into the building. We headed to the stairs. He wanted me to walk in front of him. I did, unconsciously swinging my hips left and right as we walked up. He asked me what I was doing. "Nothing," I told him.

I stopped, embarrassed. It seemed stupid to explain to him that when I had to take out the trash at home I amused myself by carrying the trashcan by the handle and swung my hips out far enough so that I could hit it.

"How old are you?"

"Thirteen."

That was it for conversation.

The building was filled with the sounds of televisions filtering through doors and the smell of burning meat. Someone cursed loudly and an oven door slammed shut.

"Why do you move your hips like that?" he asked with a stern look on his face.

I became very nervous. (You know how you get the sudden feeling you shouldn't be where you are—that's how I felt just then.) I told him I had to go home.

He said we were almost there.

I heard the faint sound of telenovelas as we passed apartments. I recognized one of them—it was *Simplemente María*.

"No. I'm sorry," I told him and tried to run down the stairs.

He grabbed my hair.

I hit him like a girl.

He punched me hard in the jaw and I hit the wall. His face changed and he took my head and slammed it against the wall again. I could taste blood. I slid down to the floor, thinking *I should've been in more fights, I should've learned how to take a punch.*

And I'm out.

When I woke up I was on the roof. Alone. It was still light out and my head throbbed. I opened my mouth and screamed and covered it to stifle the sound. I was sitting on the roof with no pants on. They were gone. So was my underwear. I was naked from the waist down, just sneakers and socks,

97

but, hello? Naked! I didn't care what Mister-I-Gotta-Piss
did to me, so long as he had the milk of human kindness to
leave my pants, but there was nothing.

*How will I get home? I'm trapped here. I can't call for help like
this. I can't run home, I'm naked! I'll have to die here. They'll find
my half-naked body months from now and guess what—they'll
still make fun of me, but at least I won't be around to hear it.*

I thought of my parents. The shame they would feel. They
would have to move, maybe get divorced—maybe even com-
mit suicide so we could all be dead. They would tell me for
all eternity what a disappointment I had been. I began to cry
with useless anger. I made promises to God.

*Drop me a pair of pants from heaven, please, and I'll do any-
thing. I'll give up playing with dolls and swaying my hips and
playing with my mother's jewelry.*

98

God was unmerciful.

My sobbing meant nothing to Him as surely as it would
mean nothing to the people who would find and make fun of
me, until I disappeared from this lifetime. I wished with all
my heart that I could be dead. Bent over, sobbing, I banged
my fists on the roof, knowing that my life would soon be
over.

Shortly thereafter I heard, "Hello? What's with all the
racket?"

It was a man's voice, but it wasn't Mr. Piss's.

"Little boy?"

I looked up but stayed crouched over, so as not to expose
myself.

"Where are your pants?"

I answered in a voice so choked with tears that even I didn't
recognize it. "He! Stole! Them!"

I was nowhere near running out of tears, they were eternal.

He threw me his shirt. "It's long, put it on."

I did, still not looking up.

"Come on, I'll get you some pants."

I followed him downstairs, beet red and staring at my feet the entire way. We entered his apartment. He put his hand on my shoulder. He was old. Old like my grandfather old. Another old man entered. He was introduced to me as Tony.

"That's quite a bruise you've got there..." Tony let his comment hang, waiting for me to say my name.

I don't want anybody to know my name!

My Savior then said, "This is Floyd."

"Hello, Floyd."

"He's a hero," My Savior added.

"Oh?"

"A gang of young thugs was trying to rob an old lady."

"Mrs. Santori?" Tony asked.

"Okay, that'll work. And young Floyd here took them all on. He was positively heroic."

"And his trousers?"

"Lost in a brutal man to man, mano a mano."

I began to cry less.

Tony seemed impressed and left to get me clothes and ice for my chin. I was led to a chair and told to sit.

"Did that hurt?" My Savior asked kindly.

"No."

"Then he didn't do anything to you. Really Master Floyd, you must be a little more selective in your encounters."

"Why did he do this to me?"

"To punish you for reminding him of what he secretly wants."

Tony appeared with underwear and pants. My Savior thanked him and Tony disappeared into the kitchen. I turned away and put on the underwear and trousers. I took off his shirt and held it out to him, as he turned his head to give me privacy.

"Keep the shirt. It completes the ensemble."

I didn't even know what "ensemble" meant at that age!

Tony brought me an ice-pack and put it to my chin, until I held it myself. And then, he left again. I'll always remember him as being in constant motion. I even wished I could've moved like him.

My Savior, whose real name I never knew, knelt by me. He looked into my eyes and didn't seem so old anymore. I leaned over and kissed him. I still don't know why, I swear to God.

He smiled and said, "Now, Floyd."

"It's Javier."

"Of course it is. You have a beautiful life ahead of you."

I shook my head, expressing no.

"Why not?"

I was too ashamed to admit that I didn't deserve it, so I remained silent.

Tony came back with ice cream and we sat and listened to old music. The girl from the *Wizard of Oz* was singing, and for the first time that day, I forgot all about my life and listened to her. I noticed Tony was crying. My Savior put his hand on Tony's and told me that they had just come back from Judy's memorial.

"She's dead?" I asked, shocked.

"Yes," they said regrettably, in unison.

"Oh."

We listened in silence for a while. Then, My Savior turned to me and asked, "Now, what would've happened had I not found you?"

"I would've died."

"No, you're a lot stronger than you think."

I shook my head and looked down at my feet.

100

My Savior assured me, "You get up every day, face your fears, and put one foot in front of the other and go on—even as people try to knock you down. That's an act of bravery right there. You think you're a coward, don't you? A coward? Young Master Javier, you may be the bravest boy I've ever met."

I felt like a desert that had finally found rain.

So we sat there as the girl they called Judy sang about the boy next door and the man that got away, Tony and my savior held hands and looking at them I believed that one could indeed fly over the rainbow.

The Team

JOHNATHAN CEDANO

I had anticipated this moment since I'd left Santo Domingo. Dreaming. Studying. Seeking. Watching. Planning. Building. I had played out how the encounter would be in my head a million times since I was a kid, but I never thought it would happen by chance on a rainy October afternoon on the A train as I made my way home to Washington Heights. I looked up and saw him, and to think that the train doors almost closed and didn't let him in—but true to form, he forced them open and slid right in, strong and confident, just how a good-looking Latino macho should.

My hands shook as he sat across from me and it seemed like an eternity before I got the courage to raise my eyes and take a good look at him.

At first I wasn't sure if it was him; his full head of hair had white interwoven where it used to be all dark brown.

He wore glasses now and his body, although still strong and muscular, couldn't hide the fact that he would soon be sixty. I had to admit that he had aged very well. My head felt heavy, I thought I was dreaming and wondered if the rest of the passengers could hear the pounding beat of my heart, now completely lodged in my throat.

I tried not to look too shocked when he got on the train; the one thing I always told myself is that no matter when or where I saw him, I wasn't going to let my true feelings show. The last thing I wanted him to do was notice me, and I'm happy to say that all those days of practicing in front of the mirror paid off. He had no idea who I was and that was exactly what I wanted.

The man whom I had sought for twenty years was sitting right in front of me—just a few feet away. Tears welled up in my eyes, but I held them back—nothing brings more attention in a crowded subway than a grown man crying—even in New York City. All I could think was, "Thank you, God."

My legs almost gave way when I got off at the 168th Street station to follow him. I could barely feel them as I walked up the stairs. At that moment, a rush of memories reserved for sleepless nights came rushing back. The smell of the ocean when we used to drive past El Malecón, the taste of chocolate ice cream from Manressa, our favorite ice cream parlor, and the taste of him in my mouth. I caught a whiff of his Grey Flannel cologne and a sharp pain stabbed my stomach, followed by a crippling desire to vomit. I had to slow my pace. That particular Geoffrey Beene creation had taken me back to 1970s Santo Domingo de Guzmán like an invisible vessel for time travel. The fact that he wore the same cologne as back then assured me he was the one.

He never once looked back; he didn't believe that he'd done anything bad to anyone in his life. It's not like he owed anybody anything, so why should he look behind himself? El que no las debe, no las teme. If you owe nothing, you have nothing to fear—as they say.

I stood outside of the building he entered for hours, waiting to see which window would light up, but none did. *He must live on the back side of the building*, I concluded. Perfect! *Be patient*, I told myself, I think it's him. I knew it was him. It had to be him. It was him.

Now, as I watch him peacefully sleeping without a care in the world. I can't believe he was actually there—in my house! The house that I had bought and remodeled waiting for this day, and in which I'd invested so much money, hoping that this moment would come and it finally had. It had been twenty years since I saw him last. Twenty years since he…

What would I say to him when he woke up? What would I ask him first? Was I going to lose my nerve? Was I going to panic? No! This is the moment I've been waiting for to have him here with me. Sleeping. Defenseless. Vulnerable.

The first one I told was Antonio. I told him to meet me at my house and didn't give him any indication of what I wanted to tell him, of who I wanted to show him. Antonio had been a policeman for close to twelve years, climbing the ranks at a record pace to become a detective. And bringing people to justice has been a secret motivation for Antonio to become the man he had become.

"I found him," I said, as he sipped the gin and tonic I had prepared for him moments earlier. When I uttered those words, the tough, rugged, wall-of-a-man that is Detective Antonio Báez crumbled into a crying, whimpering little boy. He held me as close and tight as I was holding him because he knew I had crumbled as well. As a kid he was the kind of boy you'd find climbing up a tree to shake down the fruit. He would be the one to throw the first stone at the kids we didn't like, the first to come to our defense when somebody was picking on us. He had an obsessive love for baseball and anything that involved physical activity and taught me how to swim one summer, when we all went to his uncle's "campo." He pushed me into the waters of a nearby river so I would "lose the fear," only to dive in right after me and carry me out like the superheroes we watched on Saturday morning cartoons. From that moment on, he was my Superman.

"Let's go get him," he said.

"We will, but first we have to wait for the others."

Pedro, the computer expert, had just finished a long, hard day at the brokerage firm where he worked and joined us shortly after Antonio arrived. "Where's the fire?" he said in that tone that only came with him thinking he had all the answers.

"I found him." I searched his eyes for a response.

He was cool and even. "Are you sure?" he asked.

"I'm pretty sure," I said. "He's sleeping in the next room. I slipped him a little something."

Pedro was always the brains in our little gang. He was the one we would go to for anything dealing with numbers or questions about how things worked. Pedro was the kind of boy who would pull his toys apart after growing tired of playing with them, just to see how things ticked, tocked, moved, and operated.

One of my most priceless possessions is a clockwork car he made with the motor of his sister's old music box when we were only seven years old. Once, after watching an episode of *I Love Lucy* where Lucy pulls the TV apart to put herself inside—and finally convinces Ricky to put her in show business with disastrous results—he attempted the same task, only to be stopped by a swift hit across his head by his mother, who caught him screwdriver in hand, hard at work behind the television set.

I often thought he would be the first Dominican to walk on the moon, or the inventor of a miracle device that would allow mobility for the handicapped.

I was about to tell them the A train story when the doorbell rang. It was Enrique, the last piece of our puzzle. As a child Enriquito was unequivocally beautiful. His mop of black, curly hair made him look like the most extraordinary chrysanthemum. His big, hazel eyes, surrounded by the longest most luscious eyelashes this side of Elizabeth Taylor, made me think I was looking into the most beautiful Venus flytrap. And as a Venus flytrap he would utilize those bewitching eyes to ensnare poor souls that lost themselves in their beauty.

Enrique had big dreams of becoming a famous architect. He would build intricate and very modern neighborhoods out of Lego pieces and old toys and populate them with those green plastic army soldiers every Dominican kid of our generation got on Three Kings Day.

Once he gave us the surprise of our lives. When Antonio, Pedro and I came back from school one afternoon we found that he hadn't been sick that day (like he'd told his mother), but had been busy in his backyard building our very first clubhouse out of old cardboard boxes, pieces of plastic, and tin planks he had been secretly collecting. We couldn't believe our eyes; he had thought out every little detail.

There were nooks with our names to put our things, working windows and doors, and a place for our baseball bats for after little league practice. Stints in various court-appointed rehab centers and a long history of domestic violence got in the way of Enriquito ever realizing his dream of being the next Calatrava. Of course, this hadn't stopped him from becoming the best contractor in New York City, and the fact that he'd help design and remodel my dream home was proof of that. Over the years, being in this line of work had built up his muscles and shaped his body to the point of making him completely irresistible to anyone he set out to seduce, conquer and sometimes con. In other words, a true ET— Emotional Terrorist—as I like to call him whenever I feel like teasing him.

"I found him," I said, as he put his umbrella in the holder he'd bought on his recent trip to London. He said nothing, just looked at me, then at Antonio, and then at Pedro, before collapsing to his knees. We rushed to him and held each other in the biggest and warmest and hardest embrace ever.

We hugged in silence for what seemed like centuries, looking at one another, four members of a dark fraternity we didn't choose to be in. United by childhood memories, schools we attended, single mothers who cried on each other's shoulders about what "those men" put them through, and him—he who sparked our collective nightmare of a dark figure chasing us.

We were also connected—not just for our preference for men in bed—but also by our especial predilection for older ones.

As I stood with my childhood friends, I also thought of myself, Ramón, the eternal rescuer and healer. I couldn't remember a time during my childhood when I didn't have a pet I'd found wandering the streets, or a creature given to me by a fed up owner who didn't feel like feeding another mouth in the family.

I remember being about two years old and crying my eyes out after seeing a man driving a horse-drawn carreta relentlessly whipping the poor and noble creature unfortunate enough to be given the task. This probably explained the repulsion I felt whenever the circus was in town. At one time in my life, I was the proud caretaker of two dogs, three cats, two cotorras as we call parrots, one rabbit, and a tank of fish. As I grew older, I mistakenly replaced the need to res-

cue animals for the need to rescue men—the difference being that most animals want to be rescued and nurtured back
to health.

Time and time again I found myself chasing after deeply
troubled, emotionally unavailable men who broke my heart
and sometimes some bones. But with all my inclinations for
healing and protecting, this man raised feelings opposite my
nature.

He was a beautiful man, with one of those bodies shaped
by years of playing sports. That's how he lured us. He was a
good looking, understanding, cool replacement for the men
that weren't in our lives. He caught me looking at his fully
developed body once when we were changing after playing
all day under the scorching Caribbean sun. His hairy chest
damp with sweat, his flat stomach giving way to his fully
developed manhood and the aroma of feet, sweat and "man"
you can only find in neglected locker rooms made me stop
dead in my tracks and stare. He must've sensed I was a bud-
ding queen when he grabbed his beautiful, semi-erect, uncut
dick and winked devilishly at me. God he was gorgeous! He
knew I was easy prey, I guess he knew we all were, he could
see it in all of us, and he took full advantage of that.

He asked me to come over to his house one afternoon, and
at first I didn't think anything of the fact that I was the only
one there. He opened the door wearing just a pair of gym
shorts. He hugged me tightly from behind as he said in an
almost whisper "you're so special and beautiful." His hard
cock pressed against my back. He turned me around and
kissed my lips. At that moment an electric feeling I'd never
felt shook my very core. He took my clothes off and kissed
me everywhere, including my little boy erection. He said the
fact that I was hard meant that we loved each other—that
we were connected. He took my hand and ran it down his

muscular hairy chest until I was holding his stiff dick. I remember how big it seemed at the time. "Suck it," he said.

After a few visits with all this softness and gentleness and once I had placed complete trust in him—he did it. He had me on my stomach. He was rubbing his large penis in between my butt cheeks, on my small hole like he'd done before which felt really slick and good. Then he did something different. He cupped his hand over my mouth and shoved himself inside. I screamed, sobbed and jerked to get him off me, but he had me pinned down. It was like he'd shoved a sword up my ass and kept stabbing over and over and over again. I tried to bite him, but my teeth couldn't make contact. He knew what he was doing. My tears wouldn't stop and neither did he. He continued to stab me until he shuddered and collapsed and I felt a thick warm liquid inside me. I squirmed and he warned, "Quédate quieto o te mato." (Stay still or I'll kill you.) I pressed my face into the pillow, letting it absorb my tears and felt his weight on me and the fire pulsing in my ass.

He gave me a rolled up piece of cotton to put in my butt to stop the bleeding. For Antonio it was a sock. For Pedro it was balled up toilet paper. Enrique got cotton, too.

As he cleaned me up he told me that what we did was normal and that the first time there was always blood. When a man and woman did it for the first time on their wedding night, the woman always bled. And that making love like that meant they would be together forever.

I was never with him again. After he fucked me, he moved on to Antonio, then to Pedro, then to Enrique, and to the other boys on the little league team.

We searched each other not knowing what to say, but we all knew that the moment we'd talked about for so long, for so many nights had come. Antonio finally said, "Are we still doing this?"

"Yes," we said in unison.

"Okay, then," Antonio said.

And that was that. The plan was in motion. We could've slit his throat or injected him with Drano as he slept. Instead, we watched him breathe deeply, curled in a fetal position.

I learned his routines and Antonio's police work helped with my surveillance. Meanwhile, Enrique built a sound-proofed, impenetrable room in the basement.

Pedro took to the internet, where he was king, and uncovered all of our guest's secrets.

Antonio coached me on what to say, what not to say, how to act and where to be, so that our man really thought he had found a kindred spirit in me. We could not afford to let him get away, not again, not like he did back home, like people with a lot of money often do there.

All those months of watching, following, and plotting, finally paid off because the all-night chats and the meeting in person made him feel sure I was "safe,"—and then he shared the pictures and videos he'd collected over the years. I felt like vomiting at the sight of all those boys "having fun," as he put it. I let the rage build up inside me, but never let my true feelings show. Especially when he showed me pictures of the boy I used to be.

But enough about that. It's game time. The team is here and ready to play. All that sacrifice, saving, building, waiting was not in vain, and the proof was chained to a chair, sleeping like a baby, not knowing that when he woke up, he would wish he never had.

Dark Side of the Flame

DANNY GONZÁLES

It smelled like burning plastic. I stared at the flame only inches from my face and sucked the glass dick for the first time. I didn't know what to expect but I held my breath, just as I was told to, before letting go a white cloud that hovered above me like a halo. As I exhaled, a sense of euphoria washed over my body. It was a tingling, numbing sensation. My eyelids were slightly shut, yet I was excited.

Shit was in slow motion. There was a slight ringing in my ears, but everything else was muffled. Like the laughter and screams of children when you dive underwater at Brighton Beach. I forgot where I was. I'd become a stranger in my own home. Everything had an ethereal quality to it. But all was fine with the world, because at that moment, this was all I knew of it. I forgot the problems I hid all day behind fake smiles and forced laughter. I forgot the sadness, the loneliness. I forgot reality. I forgot myself.

This was to be the stamp of entry into this sinister and seductive world. I was allowed access without a visa. I strolled in like a naïve tourist about to be roped in by a local guide who, for a small fee, would show you the sights. I took pictures in my mind because cameras weren't always allowed. My souvenir was my pipe, akin to those "shaky, shaky" things with glistening snow all over an urban skyline.

I didn't have a printed t-shirt. I probably sold it for a bundle. I declared everlasting friendship, with great effusion, to people I would never see again. I hurt long gone strangers that would haunt me forever. By the time my journey was over I was a native. I knew the game. I knew the hustle. I was one of them, selling my own crafts and schooling the newbies.

I grinned at my get-high partner Izzy. He reassuringly caressed my back. We spoke in a covert fashion. Maybe we felt guilty for our pleasures.

"You okay, bro? Do you like it?" he would ask. I didn't respond. Yet he knew I did and nodded in agreement. I wasn't afraid. I fucking loved it. I was hooked. Crack was my newest friend. Blow was shit. Fuck blow. I gave Izzy, my teacher, the pipe and watched as he carefully placed more rock in it, then placed it against his lips and smoked it.

He placed it on my lips and told me to suck.

In the beginning I felt in control. I experienced this intense high. But I knew I could stop anytime I wanted to. I was capable of using restraint. I was smarter than Izzy, who obviously had a crutch. Although I felt an immense connection and the high was beyond any high I'd known before, I knew that it and Izzy were only here for tonight. I had a full and important life. I was certain of this.

I watched as he skillfully removed the screen to clean it. He used the end of a wire hanger that he broke and bent.

This homemade utensil was used to scrape all the charred reserve in the stem out so we wouldn't waste any. On this night I was under his tutelage. I was a novice at this art, later a masterful pro.

We smoked for a few hours, I think. I didn't know for sure. I lost all sense of time. The clock—it had no face. We watched as the last ember of pleasure faded. *What next?* I thought.

Then it started hitting me. I felt blood rushing through my veins. It was cooler this time. I didn't like this shit. All of a sudden I was riddled with anxiety. My jaw was clenched tight and my mind raced. I could hear my heartbeat over my confused thoughts. I paced the apartment I was beginning to recognize—I was crashing.

Having been a coke addict for years, I had crashed before. But this was different. It was harder than any crash I'd ever experienced. It was a major collision with my real world. I needed more and quickly. Izzy was talking to me and in my slight panic I wasn't cognizant of his ramblings. I was busy playing it cool. I didn't want him to know I was starting to bug the fuck out.

"You got money? If you got money we could go get more."

"How much?" I asked stuttering, knowing it didn't matter. He suggested we would get better weight if we got bundles from a different spot and he would take me there.

We went to a bank machine and I pulled out a hundred dollars. Izzy politely kept his distance, trying not to see my PIN number. I didn't give a fuck where he stood because he would've had to take the card away from me and that shit wasn't going to happen. I was ready for anything. I always thought of these things; even for shit that already passed, my mind would be dancing with *coulda, shoulda, wouldas.* My upbringing wouldn't let me trust anyone. I anticipated the worst and knew well how I'd handle myself in a world of created scenarios. Well, that and the fact that Izzy was a hustler.

I had met Izzy on Eighth Avenue and somewhere around 48th Street. He positioned himself in the doorway of a tenement building with a broken door. He knew the minimal street lighting and neon would enhance his good looks and light eyes. He stood at my height, proudly, bordering on cocky, a bit cari fresco. I'm certain this was part of the appeal. He gave a slight nod of his head and pointed with his lips to gain my attention, the way only a Puerto Rican thug could.

He was dressed with a slight punk twist. He represented all that was unattainable to me unless I paid for it. He wasn't my first hustler but he was my most memorable. I don't know when I had my first, but I was always attracted to them. I was tired of all the queens and "homo-thugs" in the clubs.

My faithful companion and I got in a cab and headed back to Times Square. I was anxious as we headed to 9th Avenue and 50th Street. My stomach was tight, my chest was tight. I squeezed the door handle till the germs wore off. I screamed in my head at the cab driver—*hurry the fuck up, I'm in a rush motherfucker*—and turned to Izzy in our silent cab. He clenched his teeth as we passed New York's fabulous nightlife.

All these years later I still wonder how many cabs pass me by with a newborn fiend in the backseat, rushing to cop that first bundle, creating a façade of experience while looking green in a black world. I wonder. We copped three bundles and some munchies that we never ate. We then took a hit behind a dumpster before hopping in a slightly less stressful cab back to my crib.

Izzy wanted to get comfortable so he stripped down to his boxers. I did the same. We dimmed the lights and lit some candles. I shut off the phone and put on some music. The music didn't stay on long, as no song was right while we got high. We smoked much and spoke little, sometimes placing the pipe aside in a feeble attempt at rationing our shit, only to pick it up shortly thereafter. Izzy and I were comfortable with one another.

"You do you, I do me." You can't have somebody blowing your head.

He took off his shorts without saying a word. I stared at him for a second, but thought it was okay. He had tats all over his body. Some were from inexperienced artists you might meet in prison. Then he removed my shorts. Again, I didn't say anything. We both sat on pillows we placed on the floor.

Izzy placed rock in the stem and handed it to me and gave me a light. While I smoked he kneeled down before me. I leaned my head back as the high took over, as Izzy went down on me. I was near orgasm but couldn't explode. The more I smoked, the more he sucked—the more I moaned. I leaned my head against my shelves filled with art, classic literature, and self-help books.

I could barely see the frayed spine of *Your Erroneous Zones* as his hands moved all over my body. I pulled on his hair with one hand and held the pipe with the other. It was Izzy's turn. I placed rock in the stem and gave it to him. He lit it and inhaled. He pushed my head down.

He placed it on my lips and told me to suck.

I was reluctant at first. Then I closed my eyes and let go of any inhibitions I possessed. I knew I was doing shit right because of the way he ran his fingers through my hair and curled his toes (one was painted black by his girl). He put the pipe down and used both his hands to hold my head. We dealt in crack and foreplay till daylight.

I was dealing in a world of sex and drugs. I relished being high and getting my dick sucked. This was the closest thing to romance in my world. I would sit on the floor and spread my legs, so that whatever faceless, nameless, soulless get-high partner was there could have an all-access pass to my cock. Sex and drugs.

This lethal blend brought me somewhere I hadn't been to before and would never travel to again. This became a form of combinative therapy in my life. I didn't know I was desperate or lonely. I thought I had the "friends and family plan." But I needed the affections of a hustler on crack to make me feel good. He would touch me the way I needed to be touched, even if it was just for a moment.

Then the crash came back.

It was midday. We both fidgeted, not knowing what to do. I knew I didn't want to go outside in the daylight. After a while he left because—although he had nowhere to be—he needed to go. I was done with him and he didn't want to stay. No hard feelings. This is what I paid for; this is how he earned his living. I needed to be alone and he needed to be back in Jersey with his girl and kid. He showed me the picture and left with the vacant promise to return soon.

I curled into a fetal position under my Perry Ellis sheets and promised my tolerant God that I would never do this again if He helped me get over this crash. I apologized for not speaking to Him more often. Even though I felt neglected I told Him that I knew my actions were less than pious. I was full of obligatory remorse.

I told Him, "I needed to try that so that I would learn." I knew I was a good sheep who'd lost my way. But, not for nothing, you haven't carried me in the sand, damn it. I oftentimes blamed Him for my state of affairs. I also decided, fuck this religious experience. I can do this. I'm strong. I'm an achiever. I'm the golden boy. I can do anything. I've been the prodigy of the ghetto. Up until now, in spite of myself, I'd led a laudable life. I must strategize; it's how I do things.

118

I thought of how I would correct all the wrongs in my life. I thought of the dos and don'ts I did and didn't do. I decided to be more generous in my ways. I thought of how I would connect where I felt disconnected. I thought of the people I was letting down. I thought to be a better brother, a better son, and a better friend.

I thought of making pasta dishes, selecting paint chips, and buying shoes. I thought of past episodes of "The Odd Couple," doing laundry, and dusting furniture. It was an irrational stream-of-consciousness that required my immediate attention. I thought of all the shit I would do. I thought I would do it all tomorrow. Just let me get past today.

Baby, I'm Scared of You

(from *Mixtape*)

RICARDO BRACHO

Before Twilo. Before Sound Factory Sound Factory Bar Factoria (where I vogued with Girlina and saw La India sing pre-salsa). Before Sugarbabies at CBGB with Monster and the aforementioned Girlina. Before Jackie 60. Before Mother. Before Grey Gardens. (Bow down and honor Mr. Johnny Dynell.) Before the Tunnel and Save the Robots where Vin Diesel and Craig Ferguson worked the respective doors. Before Shelter and Body and Soul and Summerstage and the Warehouse (in the Bronx, por fa).

Before Stella's the Savoy Cats and La Bamba's cocaine hustler tranny banjee boy and Wall Street trader after parties. Before the Cock or the Hole and way before the Cock moved to the Hole. Before trips home to hear Tony Largo at Does Your Mama Know? Before I left home but would run away nightly to hear Doc or look at boys at Circus Robbie's Chico Woody's le bar y le barcito.

The Catch the Study Boy Trade. Before Cee Farrow's Apartment Plastic Passions Black Market Fresh Flesh. Egg Salad Alcohol Salad Alcohol Salad, no eggs. Funky Reggae, King King (the first one in the Chinese restaurant on 6th and La Brea next to the Pik Me Up). Before the Pik Me Up, Gorky's, Onyx Café, the Living Room. Before the Surprising Taste of No-Wax Formica. Before 321 and the Odyssey.

Before all that.

There was this song.

This album. Two smiling people whose easy beauty belied the title Love Wars (this was also before I knew or would use words like belie). My mom had it on heavy rotation; it always made her smile, a secret smile that exposed us all.

All of us being me, her, and Frederico. Her being Angela, me being Angel Junior (named after her), him being named after Frederich Engels. All of us Sanchezes, though only one of us, me, had the blood and birthright to the name.

But it was the song she said that made us a family.

Come, if you got real love for me.

Mommy loved this story even if she told it sparingly (another SAT word). How she made the mixtape and invited him over. Him being Frederico's dad, a Puerto Rican independentista who was underground and passing through L.A. with guns or dynamite or some such in the trunk of a sky blue Oldsmobile. Frederico's dad was the most unserious revolutionary I had ever met. He always had jokes and candy and liked to spend more time around the kids and their moms than the men and their guns.

He was the only one I didn't mind calling "uncle."

Mom says there's no way I could remember him so well, he only passed through a handful of times, often in a range of disguises, dye jobs and bigote/barba combinations, but I've known him since I was two, and I was ten when she had Frederico with him, and his smile and big paws nunca cambiaron. Plus, I was the only one who refused to learn his new name. José Manuel, Tío Manny to me, just wasn't no Ralph, just like his son, Frederico, could never get Fred to stick.

But Mommy had to make sure the zygote stuck. So this song had to come at the end of Side A. And so she had to figure out the minutes backwards to make sure not a second of this nearly six-minute (well five minutes, thirty-six seconds to be precise) track cut off. She had been enough of a Catholic at one point in her life to have practiced the rhythm method so she knew she was in prime ovulation mode.

She also knew José Manuel would be cool with knowing he had a child in the world, one belonging to two colonized, now revolutionary peoples who he wouldn't have to see for more than a few weeks each year. But with one more baby, one more boy, Mommy diverted the tragedy that would be family reunification Sanchez stilo.

See, the two people who loved me most in the world hated each other more than anything. My Yaya and my mom. And my Yaya didn't trust my Mom with caring for the absolute *bijou du monde, moi.* So Yaya was making a big play to lure me to live with her.

Mommy figured the only way to keep me from leaving her for the serenity of El Sereno and freshly made tortillas and a room of my own was to make a baby sister or brother so that Yaya couldn't turn my overnights with her and my dad and the whole Sánchez-Montoya clan into forever. Daddy was no longer a reproductive option as he had removed that brown beret and replaced it with a grad school graduation cap and married a woman he liked rather than one he just liked to fuck.

That's an exact quote. From my mother. About my father. *Stay away if you got games and tricks for me.*

By the time she got around to plotting Frederico's birth most plots to overthrow the system, the man, seize the state,

123

set up alterna-utopias new afrikas aztlan wimmin's land and the like had died. Sure they never caught them brinx job boricuas and we got Assata to Cuba without bloodshed, but the early 80s was all the gay dudes on the beach and in Boy's Town dying and women of various colors going on at meetings about white women and black and brown men and she just couldn't stand the noise and then she found the sound of L.A. punk so Mommy chopped off her honey brown trenza, dyed what was left bee yellow with carpet dye, and moved me and her from Venice Beach to a Hollywood bungalow. Our first two-bedroom.

I had a room of my own for one year of my niñez.

Then there was Frederico or Ping Pong. I gave him that name cuz he was so round-headed, but with that dimpled soft spot. Mommy taught me how to hold him, how to feed him, change him. How to be a little her. Of use. I had never felt more loved or in love, I'd race home from school and watch the end of *General Hospital* and make the baby's lunch. While Mommy or Tía Tere or any range of women with and without kids, all without men (but whatever), would put hand to hip and hmmph at how obviously gay I was gonna be.

That's what you get Ang, naming him after yourself.

I want a man that means everything he say.

And not a boy full of play.

No one ever calls me Junior though. Nor AJ, which I hate. But Jujube, given to me by my Yaya on one of our bus trips to the Highland Park Movie Theater, stuck to me the way that candy stick to a tooth and pulls out a filling. And ever since Alberto El Mocoso found out that my lil bro (who towered over me by the time he was fifteen) was half Puerto Rican he named him Congo. Frederico, who was Freddie or Rico on trips to see that side of the fam in New York and San Juan, Deric (with a c) when dating black girls, José Frederico when introduced to various Latin American left indignitaries, and Ping Pong to me, became Congo forthwith in our little mojado Mexican and Central American neighborhood.

Ping Pong ran and made such a lloriqueo all the way home, Mommy thought he was really hurt and was about to wail on my ass for letting something happen to him when I explained that he had put a push pin in the map on the world's longest standing colony when in his class they were all showing where they came from (besides L.A.) and the whole class laughed. Then, when relating the story to me and my friends on the way home Alberto El Mocoso called him Congo and everyone laughed at him again.

Mommy laughed and laughed and laughed so much she forgot to hit me.

So did the newly christened Congüito.

125

Pulling rabbits out of his hat everyday

Oh, Baby I'm scared of you

But there was no fear. Just three people who looked nothing alike: Mami all golden Venice Beach sunlight with a hint of Arizona desert sand olive, like her whole lithe body (Mommy liked to say we might have ruined her life, but hell if she was gonna let having babies ruin her body) was set up to match her angry hazel eyes, Ping Pong on the trigueño/jabao cusp with a trompa that was really a bemba and a knotty cloud of dark brown hair that girls loved to touch and lay into straight and simple or increasingly labyrinthine rows, and me an Indian stump, like a worry doll come to life, inscrutable slits for eyes and a solidly brown body, como el chocolate antes de echar el agua. A family, like the sandinistas say, living in solidarity under one roof.

Mommy's plan worked. Once baby and then boy and always 'lil brother even when he got bigger than me, was born there was no whining to go live with Yaya even when Yaya upped the ante with promises of weekly Toys R Us trips and since Mommy insisted that both my dads and Fredericos treat us like family, they're a package deal, they might have two fathers, she'd say through her sucked teeth, making us in her eyes and ours full brothers. Ping Pong came with me everywhere and I got my first trips to NYC and the island via him.

I always knew New York would be mine, until Mommy called me back with the news of her cancer. She couldn't let Frederico take care of her; he wasn't strong enough, we both agreed and Tere was long gone by then. And I wasn't much stronger than my brother but at least had spent the 90s changing my friend's diapers and watching thirty-year olds become ancianos in front of my eyes and in my hands. Come home, m'ijo, a word she had never called me.

So here I am and here she isn't. She left me with this apartment, added my name to the lease and everything, an unpaid phone bill, photo albums that have more flyers from demos and Whiskey gigs and Polaroids of drunk love than they do Sears portraits of me and Ping. The funeral costs and the hospital bills she cleared before dying.

My mother died and left me a shoebox of mixtapes.

Este Dulce Frío

MIGUEL ÁNGEL ÁNGELES

127

We are skirting along the desolate outskirts of Lindsay cuando he touches me for the first time. We drive with the top down on the white Bonneville, the frigid December breeze nos enreda as the sun's rays begin stretching closer and closer toward us, chilling my soul. Es el día que temo más para mí. Us. Al ratón, he'll tell me that it was because he was so carried away by the music or because he was in a hurry to fill up the gas tank o porque la chota nos andaba siguiendo or because he was speaking with his 'Ama on the phone o lo que sea.

I know fully well that that it is for fear, por la idea de que sólo podemos estar juntos cuando estamos solos, and even the smell, the sound, the very soul of the small town stalks him. Us. No importa. I, for my part, could wait hours, days, and even years knowing that at last I'll feel his hand upon my thigh. I, for him, would slip through an infinite universe to simply know that he loves me.

Finally, he begins edging the convertible off of the road to turn into the orchard. Nuestra huerta. He parks the car and we remain seated in silence. I remember years ago, helping him restore the Pontiac, the hours spent driving de yonke a yonke searching for a grill, stolen, broken, and shattered mirrors, a dashboard to replace the one I broke the day I found out about 'Mando. The day we graduated and he held me as I wept for my eldest brother.

For myself. Por las promesas que nunca serán cumplidas, que sólo serán palabras tiradas al aire. Por siempre. That day he held me, told me he loved me in a way that escaped him and only I could understand. A love that he had denied me until he saw how broken I was and knew that he was finally ready to give it. For me. That day that seemed so far away that created a new promise for me. For us. That day created (for) us.

128

We are surrounded by the incessant hum of the immense fans that blow away the nightly frost to keep the harvest from spoiling. Gigantes nocturninos. Just like us. He turns to look at me and I at him. Finally, he leans in and takes me by the hand...he kisses me and I kiss him. Un besito peligroso robado en la oscuridad. We get out of the car and walk hand-in-hand through the orchard, twigs and branches and tree bark and dirt crunching under the white Nikes he keeps a meticulously sparkling ivory.

The oranges that surround us fresh and sweet and juicy and ready to be picked. He, with his sack large and open, begins filling it with those fruits just as our hearts with moments bitter and sweet and abundant. I walk ahead and lose us, so thick is the infamous valley fog. *Esto es CalifAztlán*, I tell myself, and my mind drifts to the so many lost in the fog, lost by the fog, lost to the fog.

I call out to him as an ever-present reminder that he is with me in this sweet chill. Frozen are the both of us in this moment and content. Happy. The oranges we pick for our families, para su 'Ama y la mía. They are our gifts for them, large and sweet. Just as they have given us so much and continue giving. My fingernails tear into the skin and the acidic spray spurts out and the bittersweet aroma relaxes me.

Me regresa a mi niñez, long walks through the orchards at night, losing myself in the labyrinthine paths etched out for me. Escapándome. My hands dripping, oily and sticky, I bring them to my lips y lamo. Chupo. I tear a wedge of fruit and take a bite, the chilled nectar me regresa a mi presente y lo veo. He takes my hands and runs his fingers over my fingers and stops me among the trees.

129

"I love you here y por todo el mundo, ese," he murmurs, and I believe him.

"And I you, in my heart y por siempre, güey."

The Fermi Paradox

BEN FRANCISCO

Sometimes I like to go to the bars in Gay City to bring a little joy into the hearts of all the lonely men there. I see one now, a lonely guy, sitting across from me on the other side of the bar. He's young and has glasses and he's tearing away the final remnants of the label on his Heineken, staring intensely at it as if this were extremely important. Shy people do things like that, immerse themselves in objects to pretend they're not bored or lonely, and I am intensely attracted to shy people because to me their shyness is like being challenged to a duel. *En garde!*

I sip away the last of my cosmo and set the empty glass down on the bar with a decisive plunk. I've already given the bartender a tip but he's a friend and I'm a big believer in over-tipping so I leave another two dollars anyway. The song playing has a great bass line that gets under my skin and into my joints, so I shuffle my way across the room, doing a little basic jazz two-step. Some of the men are staring at me thinking that I'm weird and others are staring at me thinking that there's something strangely attractive about my exuberance but who cares so long as they're looking.

I sit on the stool next to the cute shy boy with glasses, and my timing is perfect. He has just finished his project with the Heineken label and his hands are looking for something to do.

Hey, I say.

He looks around, wondering who is saying hey to whom, but I'm the only one there, looking right at him, and finally he says, Hey, a cautious mirror image of my hey. His jeans are faded in all the right places and even though he's sitting on a stool I can tell he has a gorgeous ass.

Can I ask you a question, I say, very serious.

I guess so, he says.

Are those Jupiter pants that you're wearing?

He looks at me confused, and of course he is confused because he has never heard of Jupiter pants.

I don't think so, he says.

Oh, I say, nodding. I just thought they might be Jupiter pants, since your ass is out of this world.

He looks at me like I'm crazy, and then I let myself fall onto the bar laughing, and only then does a smile work its way across his face, slowly turning into a chuckle.

I'm Manny, I tell him. His name is Jeff, which makes me think of Josh, how could it not make me think of Josh when both names start with J and have exactly one syllable. For a moment I feel a tidal wave of sadness in my stomach. I order another cosmo and sip the waves away.

I ask Jeff whether he believes in God, because I hate small talk because you'll never get to know someone by talking about the weather, so you might as well cut to the chase. But Jeff does not like my question, I can tell, because he says that he's agnostic. If he were atheist, we could have an intense ontological debate, which would be an exciting form of foreplay, but since he's agnostic all he thinks is that he doesn't know, which is another way of saying he doesn't care.

Well do you believe in life on other planets? I ask.

I can't believe you asked me that, he says, and explains that he is a Ph.D. student in physics, which is hot, much hotter than chemistry because physics is all about things that are in motion.

Then he asks me a question in response to my question. Have you ever heard of the Fermi Paradox?

No, I say, but I'm a big fan of paradoxes.

We've been looking for life on planets for a while now, he says, and for the first time he seems comfortable speaking, giving me a lecturette on something he knows he knows something about. If there's advanced extraterrestrial life they'd be looking for us too, he says. But there's been no radio waves, no signals, nothing. So the Fermi Paradox basically says that if there were intelligent life beyond Earth we would have seen some sign of them by now.

So you don't think there's life on other planets, I say, thinking that the Fermi Paradox is not really a paradox at all, which is disappointing. But aren't there like millions of planets and millions of stars and millions of galaxies?

That's true, he says. So there probably is life somewhere else in the universe. But it's probably really far away, maybe not even in this galaxy.

But it's out there, I say, somewhere.

But it's physically impossible, he says, to go faster than the speed of light. So it's unlikely that we'll ever meet them. Best case scenario there might be something within a few hundred light years, and we could trade messages with them with a lag time of hundreds of years between responses.

133

Well that doesn't sound very fulfilling, I say, and he shrugs.

Utterly unsatisfied by our discussions of God and the Fermi Paradox, I change the subject to exotic matter, because for a while now I've been hoping someone would explain it to me. At first Jeff is shocked that someone at a bar is asking him about exotic matter, but he also seems grateful, as if it were a quiz and I were lobbing a string of easy questions at him. The words roll out of his mouth and he's gesticulating wildly with his hands, like a still-life portrait that's suddenly become an animated movie, and this is it, the thing that I love the most, the moment when you stumble across someone's passion and they can't help but share it with you.

I listen and enjoy imagining something that goes in the opposite direction from the one you push it in, which falls up instead of down. Unlike the Fermi Paradox, exotic matter lives up to its name.

I ask him about black holes and quarks and other physics things, and he tells me all the juicy details, as if he were the neighborhood gossip and subatomic particles were the people next door all having affairs with each other. Then he realizes he's been talking for a long time and a moment of self-consciousness stops him in his tracks.

So, um, where are you from? he says to me. A standard small-talk question. I attempt to steer us back to big-talk.

The conversation goes on like that for a while, until the call of the word suavemente cuts through every conversation in the bar, and the room is filled with the gently irresistible percussion of a merengue beat. Without thinking about it, I'm standing up, shaking my hips, closing in on Jeff's stool with a smile. He gives me this look of utter embarrassment, like I'm his mother and I just announced to all his friends that he wets the bed, and then he turns back to the bar and starts peeling off the label of the new Heineken I just bought him.

No more label peeling, I say, taking his hand in mine. You've already met your daily quota. Elvis Crespo demands that we dance.

Trust me, he says, you don't want to see me dance.

There's nothing I want more, I say, and then wish I could whip myself for such a stupid line. Anyway, merengue is easy, I tell him. I can show you the steps.

He lets me drag him to the dance floor. It's still early but there's already a few other guys out there. I show him the basics, how to bend at the knee to throw your other hip out, to keep your upper body tight as your legs and hips do all the work. But instead he bends his right knee at the same time as he throws his right hip out, which I never even knew was anatomically possible, and every time he shakes his hips his whole body follows. He's one of those white people who lack the ability to isolate the different parts of their body with any precision.

Is this it? he asks. Am I doing it right?

You're doing fabulous, I say. I follow his lead, dancing a foot or two apart from him, letting my whole body bop to the beat with a casual North American patternlessness.

The song ends, and I can't tell if he's disappointed or relieved, but whichever it is we come to a silent covenant to retreat to the deck out back with the smokers and the flirters. We sit down on the wooden bench that lines the deck, and I lean back to look at the nighttime sky. Ever since I was a little kid, any time I'm outdoors at night I feel an instant compulsion to look up and take in the stars.

I look over at Jeff and see that he's leaning back too, looking up at the stars and taking them in the same way as I do. It's one of those moments, one of those times when you're looking at someone and even though you saw them a while

135

ago you only really see them now. Recognition. And for the first time in weeks I think that maybe I really can get over Josh, maybe it really is possible to fall in love with someone else, and maybe that someone else is Jeff or maybe not but either way he's given me the gift of possibility.

Not that many stars, I say, casual. Even though it's not that cloudy.

Light pollution, Jeff says, still looking up.

Of course, I say. Light pollution. And I find that my lean is leaning closer to his. I turn my head and there they are, his lips, right there on his face. He doesn't pull away so I pull in, my mouth making a gentle landing on his. Our kiss is dry until it's wet, oh so wet, I could lose my entire body in the wonderful wetness of his mouth.

136

But then the wetness disappears and my tongue tastes the dry emptiness of air.

I can't do this, he says. And he's leaning forward now, away from me, his head between his knees like he might throw up but still has high hopes that he might be able to hold it in.

What's wrong, I say, and I'm so pissed at myself because I must have gone too fast, I always go too fast.

Look, he says, I'm sure you're really a nice guy and every-thing. It's just, it was humiliating enough to walk through the door of this place, but now to come in here, to a place like this, and to be talking with a guy like you, and dancing with a guy like you, and kissing a guy like you. It's just.

What do you mean a guy like me, I say. What exactly is a guy like me like?

He looks at me and shakes his head, and he gives me that embarrassed look again, that bedwetting-embarrassed look, but now I realize I was wrong, it's not embarrassment, it's humiliation, and I'm not his mother, I'm the piss.

You're just so, he says, but doesn't finish. I'm sorry. I gotta go. And then he's off the deck and out the door.

I'm sitting there on the deck alone, just me and a bunch of guys in one corner smoking and two guys in the other corner making out and a handful of stars you can barely see because of the light pollution and all I can think about is *so*. I'm *so* what? A rain of so's fall through my mind like confetti on a lonely New Year's Eve. So silly so gay so femme so foolish so brown so ugly so unlovable. Josh said I was *so*, too. I am always *so*.

Joshua, I whisper to the night. His name is a ritual prayer I can't resist, a futile rain dance that I enact with a single word. Joshua, I say again, despite myself, and hope that no one hears.

Now I'm not sure what to do, so I do what I always do when I feel like this, I follow my body, which takes me into the bar and onto the dance floor. The small dance floor is packed now, dozens of bodies pulsing to the techno beat. I jump into the crowd and let myself get lost in it, finding comfort that there are so many men crowded so tight together you can't be sure who is dancing with whom. The man nearest me has his shirt off; his t-shirt tucked into the back pocket of his jeans, and so does the man next to him and the man who is two men away. It's an epidemic of t-shirts tucked into the back pockets of jeans. Two men near me are dancing pelvis to pelvis, the music irrelevant to their grinding hips and their nearly touching lips. Two young guys are dancing with a woman, the three of them pressing together for a few moments before letting go in a fit of laughter. A man in a wifebeater, all muscles and skin, is dancing by the mirror, and a bunch of guys are looking at him as he looks at himself.

After a few songs, three strippers come out, wearing nothing but one purple thong each. They stand on top of the little black boxes in the middle of the dance floor, and they dance, their bodies slow and their faces serious. All the heads of all the men tilt upward toward the strippers. The gravity of the room shifts. The shining bodies of those naked men are the sun, drawing all the eyes of all the men into their orbit.

Except for me. I am Pluto, with my own eccentric orbit, resisting their gravitational pull. I've never been a fan of strippers, not because I'm a prude but because I'm a populist. I look at the men around me one by one and each one is unique, each is beautiful, each deserves a moment of glory atop the little black boxes with a room of gazes on their skin. I fantasize of leading a revolution against the stripper oligarchy but I know in my heart that I'm too far ahead of my time, so I just leave the dance floor and go sit down at the bar by my friend Sandy Shore.

Ready for your show, I say to Sandy, as I flag down the bartender for another cosmo.

You know me, sugar. I'm always ready. How you doing tonight?

Bad, I say. I think I met Josh's doppelganger. Just so he could reject me one more time.

Oh, sweetie, been there, she says, puckering her lips. There's nothing worse than running into an ex-lover's doppelganger.

This is why I adore Sandy. She always understands.

So what do you do? I say. When you run into a doppelganger?

You know the funny thing, sweetness? The more I get over a guy the less doppelgangers I seem to find.

I sip at my cosmo and nod. One of the strippers walks past us, his thong stuffed with dollars all around his waist.

What is it, I say, about guys like that? What have they got that demands so much of our attention?

Don't ask me, sugar. I have to put on a sequin skirt to get any attention from this crowd.

Part of me wants to jump up onto one of those black boxes and start ripping off my clothes, I say, surprising myself as the words come out of my mouth.

Mmm, Sandy says. That's a show I'd pay to see.

I don't know, I say. I'm not feeling very performative tonight. Also these clothes are too hard to take off. Not conducive to a sexy strip tease.

Just get up there, she says. They'll eat you up.

I picture myself on top of the box and imagine people looking at me with disgust or not looking at all, and the thought of it terrifies me, and I know that means it's something I have to do. Sandy gives me a good luck kiss on the cheek and I work my way across the dance floor, squeezing my way past sweaty torsos.

139

The black boxes are empty now. The official strippers are in between their sets. I climb onto one of the boxes. A few people glance at me and decide I'm not important and look away. My head is only a few feet above everyone else's but I can see all of them from here, every person in the entire bar.

I dance. Not the way the strippers dance, with movements that are serious and slow and small. I dance *my* way, my joy in the music showing on my face, my movements too big for the little box beneath my feet. A couple of guys look up at me and smile, and it's a species of smile that I recognize, a smile of appreciation. My confidence is boosted by the smiles and the music's shift to Lady Gaga.

I pull up my shirt, twisting to the music with my shirt around my head, as if I were caught in it. Then I pull it off the rest of the way and let it drop to the floor beneath me and I bounce up and down like a jack in the box celebrating its release.

There are catcalls and whistles, and it's only then that I look down and realize that a whole bunch of guys have gathered around the box and they're looking up at me. I feel a dozen pairs of eyes on me, their desire dancing across my torso, their longing pressing into my skin. I've never felt so beautiful.

Take off the pants, someone shouts, and I oblige by un-buckling my belt and letting my jeans fall around my ankles. It's harder to maneuver so I just shift my weight from side to side and let my upper body do the dancing. One man holds out a dollar and looks up at me expectantly. I sink down to my knees so that I'm within his reach. He gazes at me, tak-ing in every inch of me, and slides the dollar into my boxer briefs. I return his gaze, but his eyes don't meet mine. His eyes are looking everywhere on me but my eyes.

That's when I realize it's all the same. They're orbiting me instead of the men in purple thongs but it's still just one body revolving around another, the vacuum of space an un-breakable wall between us.

I pull up my pants and climb down from my box, pick my shirt up off the floor and slip it back on. I feel like someone should be giving me a high five or something because that was a brave thing that I just did, but the men who were around me just turn away from the box and go back to their dancing.

I have another cosmo and watch Sandy's show. Then I dance a little more, but the music isn't carrying my feet across the floor the way it usually does. I can't stop myself from whispering Joshua's name when the songs slow down.

Then the music is off and the lights are on and all of a sud-den it's not a party anymore. Everyone is walking out and everyone is in pairs or clusters or superclusters and everyone is holding hands or smiling or talking about going to a diner for omelets. And some of these eyes are the same eyes that were all over my skin only a few minutes before, but now my skin is uninhabited by anyone's eyes. I look around for somebody, anybody, even Sandy Shore, but there's no one, so I walk out alone.

Outside people are hanging out and smoking cigarettes and lining up for the pizza joint across the street. The rainstorm earlier today turned out to be only a drizzle, not even enough rain to leave puddles, but there are bits of water in the cracks of the sidewalk, and the concrete is shimmery with a thin layer of damp.

Joshua, I whisper to the night air. Joshua. Joshua. Joshua.

A guy in a windbreaker brushes past me and gives me a look, like, are you just talking on your cell phone or are you actually crazy? His eyes dart away from me, and I think crazy is his verdict.

There's a line of yellow cabs out front, cabbies waiting for the 2 AM rush. I could go to one of the after-hours clubs, more dancing and more cosmos, but no. Sooner or later I have to go home and face the inevitability of my empty bed. I flop into one of the cabs and tell the driver my address.

141

We drive north, away from the bars and clubs of Gay City, and after only three blocks the streets are empty. The city feels like an old widow at night, sitting by the window in a lonely, creaking chair. This is not New York. This is a city that goes to bed promptly at 11 PM.

So you always work late? I ask the cabbie. It's a small-talk question but even I know it's easier to start with small talk if you don't have anywhere else to start.

Yes, he says. The fares are good at this hour. His accent is Indian or Pakistani or somewhere South Asian.

Have you lived in Port Haven long? I ask.

Three years, he says. I came here from Sri Lanka.

The way he says Sri Lanka I can tell that he thinks that I think it's far away, that the world he comes from is some unimaginable and insurmountable distance from the world I know, and all I want to do is reach through the little plastic wall between us and shout, *no*, we are only as far away as we allow ourselves to be.

I was born in Puerto Rico, I say, putting my hand on the seat in front of me, just inside the opening in the plastic wall between me and the driver. I'm an islander too.

That makes him smile and he asks, Do you have a boyfriend? For a second I wonder how he knows that I'm gay but then I remember where he picked me up.

No, I say, looking down. Not anymore.

We stop at a red light and he turns to look at me, reaches back to touch my hand. I touch him back.

You are so beautiful, he says, caressing my fingers. How can someone so beautiful not have a boyfriend?

That's a sweet thing to say, I say. Now he pulls my index finger into his mouth and starts sucking on it. This is unexpected. It's nice the way this person who happens to be in a car with me has decided he wants to taste me.

The light turns green, but he doesn't notice till I tell him so. He drives on, still caressing my hand. We cross the Desmond Street Bridge. Along the river below, the houses on boathouse row are all lit up. They always look like Christmas lights to me, as if this handful of houses was determined to hold onto Christmas all year round.

We hit another red light after the bridge, and he kisses my hand again, but more gentlemanly, no tongue this time.

Come sit up front with me, he says.

He says it like a question, like a humble request, which is sweet, and I never liked the way passengers are supposed to sit in the back of taxis, as if the cabbie were nothing but a chauffeur, so I get out of the car and get in the front seat. He holds the wheel with his left hand and with his right he touches my hand, my arm, my chest, my thigh. I wonder whether he's a righty or lefty or possibly ambidextrous.

142

We pull onto my street and I say, This is it, up here on the right, which feels strange, because it's the standard thing you say to a cab driver except that this cab driver is rubbing his hand against my crotch.

He pulls the cab to the side of the road, right in front of my building, reaches over and wraps his arms around me and kisses me. It's a wet, sloppy kiss, lots of tongue and very little subtlety. It makes me think of the first time Josh kissed me, because it's the polar opposite. When Josh kisses he uses barely any tongue, he does it all with his lips and what he does with his lips is amazing.

I try to kiss the cabbie back because it's only polite but his tongue is so aggressive that it's colonized the entire interior of my mouth and there's no room for me to do much of anything. Out of the corner of my eye I see that the meter is still running and while I believe in being a generous person, it feels wrong to pay forty cents a minute to make out with a guy.

I pull apart and say, It's late. I should get inside.

Stay, he says, reaching for my hand.

I give his hand a squeeze and say, I really have to go. But thank you. And I give him the fare plus a too-big tip and then he reaches in for one more kiss and after thirty seconds or so I pull away and pat him on the shoulder and get out of the car.

He waits and watches until I unlock the door and get inside, like a concerned parent dropping off a child. From the window I see him drive away.

I walk up the stairs. They're steep and it's tricky with I'm-not-sure-how-many cosmos in my system. I fumble with the keys and open the door. The apartment is dark and my housemates must be sleeping so I try not to make too much noise as I work my way through the living room and into my bedroom. It's still only 2:15 AM, which means it's only 11:15

143

in San Francisco and I feel like I need to talk to someone so I call Josh.

Dude, Josh says. It's like 2 AM. your time. Why are you calling me so late?

I love that I can call you at this hour, I say. That's the best part about having a friend in San Francisco. I almost say ex instead of friend but I stop myself because Josh hates when I call him my ex because according to him we were never even boyfriends only best friends who hung out all the time and had sex whenever Josh wanted us to have sex.

Is something wrong, he says, and now I'm starting to feel like I have to argue the case for calling him.

No, I say. I just had sort of a weird night. I went to Seventh Heaven and I met this guy Jeff who seemed cool at first but then he turned out to be an asshole. Then I did an amateur strip show which was cool because everyone cheered for half-naked Manny and then I took a cab home and ended up making out with the cab driver, but I decided I couldn't afford to make out with him for very long because the meter was running, and then I came inside and called you.

You made out with your cab driver? he says, chuckling. That is such a Manny thing to do.

Yes, I agree. It was a very Manny night.

The phone is quiet and I wonder if one of us has lost the signal. We live in the era of lost signals. Are you there?

Yeah, he says, I'm here. Listen, let's talk later, ok? I have work tomorrow morning, and so do you, even if you don't mind waltzing in at 11 AM.

I would never waltz in, I say. I might mambo in, though. Or cha-cha.

He doesn't laugh, he sighs. I can picture the eye-roll that goes with the sigh. You're drunk, he says. Go to sleep and we'll talk later.

Okay, I say. Just one question. Did you move away from me because you wanted the Google job? Or did you find the Google job because you wanted to get away from me?

I thought we agreed you were going to stop asking me questions like that.

I think I have a right to know, I say.

You're drunk, Josh says. And we're not having this conversation now. Good night, Manny. Make sure you drink some water.

Good night, I say, but he's already hung up.

Josh is right, I should drink some water, but the kitchen is very far away. I let my body collapse onto my futon. As soon as I'm horizontal I realize I must be drunker than I thought because the room is not staying still.

I lie there, letting the room spin around me as I think about the Fermi Paradox. I wonder if Jeff is right that there's no other life in the universe, and even if there is, it's too far away for us to find them. I hope he's wrong. I have to keep believing that there's something out there, that there's something more on the other side of the emptiness.

Antología

ANTHONY HARO

It all started with a bad haircut.

I took the 266 MTA bus and made it to Freddy's house a little after 8PM. I don't know what I was doing at my ex's house, but I know what it looked like on the outside. I was trying to be that cool guy that could be friends with his former boyfriends: *Let's keep in touch—let's remain friends—let's hang out soon.* These were the flags that were waving above my head ready to be plucked and used if anyone were to ask why I was out with him so soon after our breakup. On the inside I missed him and was still attracted to him. I wanted to see if there were any sparks left.

I knocked on Freddy's door and some guy I didn't know opened it—mistake number one. I thought it would be just us going to Circus that evening. He asked who I was. I explained. As I walked into the living room, I could hear Freddy getting ready in the hallway bathroom. The house still looked and smelled the same. *What the hell am I doing here?*

Words and fake smiles attached to even faker handshakes were exchanged. We had a drink, maybe two and left soon after. We climbed into the guy's car and took Interstate 10 west to the 101 Highway. I was in the backseat hating myself for being such a fool, but I was planning an escape route— you should always have an escape route.

We got to Circus just before ten. If you don't know what Circus is, let me explain it to you this way: Every Friday night it becomes the center of the universe if you're gay, Latino, and live in Los Angeles. As soon as we got into the club, I made some excuses and took off from Freddy and his friend. I knew for a fact my friends Arnold and Oscar were going to be there. I planned it that way just in case something went wrong.

I made my way into the main room, and as usual, it was packed from wall to wall. The music was bumping bass so loud you could feel it on your skin. Hot guys everywhere the eye could see. Flashing, multi-colored lights, smoke machines, and go-go boys in every corner. Everything was in its right place. I walked toward the back of the main dance-floor where my friends always held a spot.

As I squeezed between the dancing crowd and the guys posted on the sidelines, I caught a glimpse of a cute guy staring at me. I walked deeper into the club, figuring I could catch a better look of him; he was dancing with friends in the middle of the dance-floor. In between flashes of light and dancing bodies, I could see that his eyes were following me. He was about five-seven, thin, tanned—and damn he knew how to dance!

I ran into my friends sooner than I had hoped. After being showered with hugs and kisses I got made fun of, because of my new haircut. It was shaved too close and way higher than

I usually had it. I tried to play it off as a new look, but no one bought it. It was good to be around my friends Byron, Oscar and Arnold—even my old roommate Shawna made it out that night. I turned around to look for the guy who had been following me with his eyes, but he was gone.

Our regular bartender Juan hooked us up with strong drinks and we were good to go. We walked around the main dance-floor checking out the guys, as we headed to the outside patio area so that Oscar could smoke a cigarette. I told the gang about the little fiasco that occurred earlier that night with Freddy and I got the expected chorus of *I told you so* mixed with a lot of rolling eyes.

We laughed and drank and were soon back inside dancing the night away. Song after song, the DJ knew exactly what to play to keep the crowd dancing. While dancing with Oscar I noticed that cute guy again. I got nervous and excited and smiled at him when I noticed that he was smiling at me. It was hard to get a really good look at him; there must've been about fifteen or twenty guys between us. All I knew was that he was staring at me.

The guys wanted to go to upstairs to dance to hip-hop, so we took off. I waved goodbye to the cute guy and up the stairs we went. After more dancing and another round of drinks I took off to the restroom, but didn't return to my gang. I instead went to the smaller room by the front of the club, which was the Latin music dance-floor. I ran into my friends Saul and Gustavo there and hung out for a while. At midnight they started the drag shows, which were a lot of fun. The hostess spit out insults and dirty jokes to the drunken crowd, while drag queens mimed popular songs.

Saul and Gustavo took off to the main dance-floor and I found myself alone, watching this one particular performer singing the pop songs of a recent female singer that had just come out of Colombia. The room was dark and filled with

149

smoke and I was enjoying the show. I turned to my right and standing right next to me was the cute guy I had seen earlier that night. I was so happy to see him I didn't have time to be nervous.

I tapped him on the shoulder. When he turned around, he broke out a beautiful smile. I introduced myself and he shook my hand with his soft and delicate palm and fingers. His name was Fernando. I asked him if he was enjoying the show and he said yes. He kept smiling throughout our first few exchanges. He leaned in and told me how much he loved this new singer and I told him I was into her, too.

The performer started her third song of the evening, which was strange since most only got to do two. Fernando got closer and asked a funny thing. He asked for a small favor. He asked if I would mind pretending to be his boyfriend. *Am I dreaming? Have I had one too many drinks? Am I imagining this?* I laughed and asked him to repeat himself.

He explained that he had run into a coworker that night that kept bothering him to go out with him. He asked if it would be okay if he introduced me as his boyfriend—if the guy came around again. And strangely enough as soon as he was done telling me his story the dude showed up.

Fernando laced his fingers into mine and introduced me as his boyfriend. The guy gave Fernando a beer that he had bought him and said hello to me. I gave the guy attitude. He left after he saw Fernando get close to me. We turned and faced the stage and both laughed hard while the dude disappeared.

The crowd began shouting for an encore and the hostess was going crazy trying to calm them. I teased Fernando by daring him to go on stage and tip the drag queen when she performed her next song. He laughed and dared me to go instead of him.

I said, "Okay, I'll do it if she performs the song 'Antología'."

"No, I'll go up and tip her if she sings that song."

"It's a deal!" I told him. In the back of my mind I knew I was safe. That song was a ballad and the drag queens there never performed ballads. Never say never in this world. Fernando and I giggled when we heard the opening chords of "Antología" being played over the speakers.

I took out two one-dollar bills from my wallet and started to walk to the stage. Fernando held my hand tightly. When we got to the steps of the stage, I turned around to look at him. We both cracked up. As I climbed the first step, I stared into his brown eyes and pulled him up with me. We tipped the singer and climbed back down into the crowd.

The song was soon over and the hostess thanked everyone for coming out—it was two in the morning. The regular lights came on and the crowd started pushing toward the exits. Fernando and I made it out to the parking lot and talked for a while about small stuff. I asked him to come with me to the spot where my friends met after the club, our usual rendezvous, and he agreed.

We chatted and waited for my friends to arrive. The night was cold and the moon was almost full. I asked him what it was that made him notice me at the club and he said it was my haircut—that it was different, that he liked it. I told him it was a bad haircut and how I had missed my appointment with my regular stylist.

He insisted he liked it.

I told him that it was his beautiful smile that made me notice him. I wanted to lean in and kiss him so bad at that moment. A homeless man passing by asked us for change, interrupting us. I gave him a couple of dollars and he thanked me. He turned back and yelled, "You guys make a cute couple."

We laughed and said we were just friends.

151

"Are you sure?" he asked. "You look like a couple to me."

I looked at Fernando and thanked him for letting me be his boyfriend for the night. He smiled and said, "You're welcome."

I offered him a ride home, but he said he didn't need one. I could see my friends coming. I wanted to introduce him to them, but Fernando got shy and started to say good night and walked away. I didn't know what to do. I asked him for his number. He asked me what I was doing the following night. I said I had no plans and he asked me to meet him at Arena. That he would be there.

He said, "If you really want it, meet me tomorrow night and I'll give it to you."

152 I grinned as he waved goodbye and watched him walk toward the Seven-Eleven on Santa Monica Boulevard.

My friends asked about him and I told them it was the cute guy from earlier that night, the one that had been following me with his eyes. I told Oscar that we had to go to Arena the following night because I really needed to see him again. Arnold, Byron, and Shawna said goodnight and left. Oscar and I stood a while longer, as I told him what had happened, while he finished one more cigarette.

I met up with Fernando on the following evening and we danced the whole night long. I got his number and we kissed for the first time. It was a kiss I'll never forget. That first kiss led to many nights in downtown Los Angeles, where Fernando worked, and in Silver Lake where he lived. He lived with his aunt, who loved me right away, and with his brother, who wondered what the hell we were doing.

Every weekday, at seven on the dot, I would meet him by the waterfall in Pershing Square. He demanded hugs when I wouldn't give them, telling me he didn't care who saw us. So many happy dinners on Olvera Street and passionate late night kisses by MOCA. We took buses, trains, and taxis everywhere. We held each other secretly and in plain sight.

Moments lasted far longer than I'm capable of describing with words. Voicemails filled with messages of love would suck the oxygen out of a room the moment I heard them. Days and weeks passed, so many happy days filled with love and adventure. Nights filled with made up stories, just so I could spend the night.

He dedicated songs to me I can no longer listen to. Songs that once brought so much joy now only bring nostalgia and lumps to my throat. Time passes and things change. I don't like to remember this part. I don't like to think about it because it raises too many questions. So many things unanswered.

153

Even now, thirteen years later, things are fuzzy and hard to explain: Your accident at work. My best friend James and when you saw us hug and go in separate directions. The two movie ticket stubs. All I can tell you is what I am sure about, what I know to be true—one hundred percent true. I didn't cheat on you, Fernando. I would never have destroyed something so perfect, something so pure.

I know I was letting work get in the way. I know things looked fishy. I know I was taking you (and us) for granted, blindly thinking those days would last forever. I was so stupid and weak. I should've fought harder. That's what haunts me the most to this day. I should've fought harder, you were worth it—love is worth it. I don't know how I let it slip away. And for that I'm so sorry. This is what all of this is: an apology to you.

My Hero Abel

JESUS SUAREZ

They would arrest me. I was a runaway, and if they decided to search me, I had a gun. I was fucked. I was sixteen and a guy. If I had been a girl the cops would've taken it easy on me (unless I was a whore, then they would've run me in for soliciting). But being a Latino guy—and gay on top of it—I was in deep shit trouble. Even if that group of guys had jumped me with or without the sex, the cops wouldn't have given a shit because I was just a little spic faggot who had it coming to him.

Maybe if I had been a good little faggot, and pretty after all, and I wasn't too beat up, they would've let me suck their dicks and called it a night so they wouldn't have to fill out paperwork. They weren't worried about complaints or accusations from someone like me. Everybody knows that fags lie anyway. I almost started to cry. I was scared. I swallowed it down real hard and started thinking up excuses, but couldn't figure out what would be convincing.

Maybe if I pay some guy ten bucks to walk me to my car...

"Abel? Like Cain and Abel in the Bible?"

"Yeah," he answered, a slight smile on his lips, his hand gently massaging my wrist.

"Where are you from?" I asked.

"Texas," he answered proudly, jutting his chest out. "West Texas, San *Antone*," he said with a twang.

"That's San Antonio, right?" I asked for clarity. Texas is a big state. Who knew—maybe it harbored some small town called San Antone for all I knew. I had driven through Texas a few months before and it had gone on and on and on—I couldn't wait to get the hell out of it.

"Yeah," he finally answered, looking at me as if I were an idiot. And with all the troubles I had brewed up for myself in recent days I definitely felt that I was. But I wasn't caring all that much about that—I had bigger fish to fry.

My wrist began feeling better (he had healing hands, who would've known?), so I thanked him and pulled my hand back and set it on my lap to keep from hurting it again.

"And where are you from?" he asked.

I told him I was from Miami, that I had a job in Hollywood and lived there too. We kept drinking and talking about our families, which we had left behind.

Abel told me he was married but was in the process of getting a divorce, that he had a three-year old son that he was very proud of. He pulled a picture from his wallet to show me. His name was Abel too, and he was adorably cute. He was dressed like a little cowboy, or so it seemed; he looked a lot like his father.

When I told him that, he said, "I hope he doesn't because I'm not good looking, I'm ugly."

"You are *not*," I protested, "I think you look very handsome, in a rugged sort of way."

He laughed and asked, "What do you mean rugged?"

"If you trimmed your moustache it would make you look younger."

"What do you mean younger, how old do you think I am?" Abel asked.

Since he had been gentle toward me I figured he was older. "I don't know, twenty-nine or thirty. Right?"

He exhaled and his shoulders dropped down. "I look that old and beat, huh?" he asked, dejected.

"No, don't think that. What do I know about guessing peoples ages? I don't know anything," I added, realizing I'd put my foot in my mouth.

"I've had a really tough year with the divorce and not being able to be with my son."

There, I did it. I depressed this really nice man. I felt like such a jerk. The way his eyes grew sad pulled at my heart. "Now come on, that's not fair, go ahead and ask me how old I am," I implored him, sitting up straight, nodding my head up and down. I hoped he would guess twenty or so.

He looked at me and answered, "I don't know, about twenty-two or twenty-three?"

"That much, really? Thank you!" I responded, patting him on the arm. I hadn't expected that and felt it said a lot about how well I was handling myself.

Taken aback by my excitement Abel asked, "You got so happy…so how old are you güerito?"

"Güerito, who the hell is güerito? My name is Jesus," I said, confused.

He laughed and said "Güerito is not your name, it's what you are. You're a white boy."

A white *boy? What the hell is he talking about? How am I a white boy?* "I'm Latino and proud of it," I corrected him.

157

He laughed even harder. "You're proud of being Latino?" he asked, amazed.

"Yes, I am. I'm very proud. Yo soy muy orgulloso de ser Latino y particularmente de ser cubano. Okay?"

He cackled and slapped his knee; he liked pissing me off.

"Are you laughing at me? Don't laugh at me!" My blood began to boil. This was not my night, or so I thought at that moment.

"Güerito, your eyes get so beautiful when you're angry. Let me see them. Yes, they're beautiful—I want to be with you."

He wants to be with me? What does that mean? I asked him what he meant.

He told me, "I want to spend time with you. I want to get to know you. I've never felt this way about a guy before, but I'm feeling it for you."

What the fuck? Is this guy crazy? I didn't know what to say. Confused, I asked, "But how can you know that if we just met?"

"Because I know," he shot back.

"What if you're not who you say you are? I haven't seen any ID. What if you're somebody else?" I asked him.

He smirked and pulled his wallet from his jacket pocket. I pulled mine out of my pants. He gave me his ID and I handed him mine. I prayed he wouldn't notice my age. I looked at his picture and saw his name. It was the name he had given me. He too saw that it was the name I had given him and that I was indeed from Miami.

As soon as he acknowledged where I was from I took my card and gave his back, before he could discover my birth date. His ID stated that he had been born in 1956. I started doing the math and realized what a mistake I had made. He was only twenty-four!

Abel nudged me, asking, "Okay, so now you've seen my ID and I've seen yours. Can I spend some time with you?"

"We haven't even kissed!" I protested, "What if you don't like the way I kiss? What if I don't like the way you kiss? A kiss is very important to me."

He cut me off and asked, "What do you want me to do? Kiss you right here in front of everybody?"

I thought to myself *now I've got the upper hand and maybe Pancho Villa…err…Abel will chicken out and leave me alone to figure out how to deal with my dilemma and get back to my room at the hotel in one piece.*

Thinking I was going to scare him away, I said "Yeah, kiss me right here in front of everybody. Prove to me that you want to get to know me. You're a man and so am I. We're adults, prove it to me," I dared him.

159

Abel grabbed my head and kissed me deeply; it made me forget what I was thinking. Then he sat down and studied me with a sly grin on his face. I stared right back. Overwhelmed, I opened my mouth to say something but he kissed me again, this time embracing me and playing with my tongue using his. Some chicks walked by and one of them yelled, "Get a room!"

That was amazing, I thought to myself. I put my hand on his face and kissed him back as tenderly as I could. He tasted like alcohol, cigarettes—like a man. The cologne he was wearing smelled perfect on him. I closed my eyes and got dizzy, as if I were getting drunk. His pheromones must've been raging because I had never smelled nor tasted anything so amazing in my life.

I had a hard-on and noticed the magnificent bulge in his pants. Squeezing me in his arms he said, "I need some cigarettes. Why don't we get out of here?"

"Sure, where do you want to go?"

"Anywhere, I don't care. I just want to be alone with you."

Could this even be possible? I thought.

"I have to go to the bathroom. Why don't you come with me?" Abel asked.

"No thanks, I'm all right. Don't need to go."

"Well then walk with me and wait for me there." He pulled me by my good hand and led me to the bathroom.

We got to the men's room and I stopped. "I'll wait for you here, okay?" I said to him.

"Don't you go anywhere—you hear me?" he warned, looking me in the eye.

"I won't, I promise," I said with a grin.

He grabbed my head again and planted another kiss on my lips to mark his territory; he made sure I got the point.

I did.

160

As soon as he went in, Gabriel, the guy I had been avoiding all night, stepped up to me, out of nowhere. The fucker spotted me. He grabbed me by the arm and pressed it hard. His dark-haired friend was at his side. "Hey, time's up and we want to go home. So how about you come with us?"

From the way he said it I knew he wasn't asking. "Sorry," I told him, wondering what the hell I was going to do. "How about tomorrow night? I ran into a friend from work that wants to take me somewhere else."

I could sense that Gabriel was getting angry. "I got a little party together for you. I know how much you like sucking cock—stop being such a little prick-teaser and come back with us." Gabriel began pulling me away with him. I pulled my arm out of his strong grip; it hurt.

Abel stepped out of the men's room just as I freed myself and noticed I was upset. "What's up?" he asked, assessing the situation.

Abel and Gabriel sized each other up. Abel looked so handsome, so masculine—so manly—that Gabriel and his friend looked like little boys next to him. They shot me a dirty look and walked back into the club.

"What was that about?" Abel asked, a little pissed off.

"Oh nothing—just this guy who lent me money last week and I forgot to bring it, but I told him I would get it to him tomorrow," I lied.

"You're coming back here tomorrow night?" he asked with suspicion.

"I have to pay him his money."

"Well how much do you owe him? I can give it to you and you can pay me back whenever you want to."

"Come on, you don't have to do that," I told him. "He just probably wants to use that as an excuse to hang out with me."

"Hang out to do what?" he asked sounding jealous.

161

"Why the twenty questions? It's nothing okay, weren't we going somewhere?" I smiled as seductively as I could. I was tired. My legs were weak and wobbling and my heart was beating a million beats a minute. I felt dizzy and overwhelmed. He never knew what he saved me from that night. And, I never told him.

I parked the car facing the ocean and made sure to engage the emergency brake, since one never knows when some idiot might hit your car and send you careening over the cliff onto the rocks below. Abel pulled out a couple of beers and opened them. He began talking about how he missed his son and how he regretted not being able to help raise him. He said it broke his heart.

I asked him why he and the boy's mother were getting divorced, but he changed the subject. That the whole thing was just too complicated to explain. It was too painful for him. I was able to feel it coming from his heart and heard it in his voice. He drank his beer with one hand and held my hand with his other.

I put his hand to my mouth and kissed it, hoping to minimize his pain, even if just a little. I discovered that it didn't take much to please him. He reached over and began kissing me even deeper than he had the first time; Abel was strong and passionate. One kiss at a time, he was stealing my heart away.

I took his hand and placed it on my crotch, showing him how I liked getting it rubbed. I also put a hand on his and could not believe what I felt there. Abel's kissing became more passionate when I did. I undid his large belt buckle and lowered his zipper. The needy pole in his pants was too long and too hard to manipulate out, even when I had the zipper all the way down and his pants completely undone. He had to raise his ass off the seat and pull his pants down past his upper thighs to free it.

When I saw it, I almost ran out of the car. *What the hell is that thing?*

Abel could tell that I was freaked out. "Don't worry I'm not going to hurt you," he said tenderly.

How is he going to keep this promise?

I had never seen a cock so big. Not that I had that much experience; the only cock I had seen comparable to Abel's was Bill's, my benefactor, but that was it. It left me breathless. The one-eyed monster stared me in the face, expecting something. Abel's testicles were the largest I had ever seen as well.

"Don't be afraid," he assured me, and took my hand. He wrapped it around his shaft and guided it up and down. He was so gentle and patient that I decided to give it a go. I bent over and kissed it. I stuck my tongue out and began to lick and suck as much of the immense head as I could. I massaged my tongue and lips up and down his shaft, giving as much pleasure as I could, while pumping up and down with my hand.

The windows in my car fogged up and I could feel the heaviness of Abel's breath on the back of my neck. He let out a low moan. I needed a kiss from him if I was going to continue; I could tell he was approaching orgasm.

I sat up while giving him a hand job. "How do you like it? Am I doing okay?"

He looked at me with disbelief. "Okay? No one has ever done that to me before."

I didn't know what to make of his confession. "Come on, quit playing around. Do you like it or not?"

"I'm serious. None of the girls I've been with would even kiss it. I was lucky if I got a hand job from them and real lucky if they had sex with me. Even whores told me no. How do you do what you're doing?"

The answer to that was easy. It was that I didn't know any fucking better, that's why! I didn't know that I could've said no in those days. I thought that once a man exposed his need to you, you had to pleasure him—that was what my first boyfriend Andrés had forcibly taught me.

I began to feel like a whore and blushed. "Do you think I'm a slut?"

"A slut? No babe, you're not a slut. You're just making me very happy. Why don't you drive us to a motel so we can get comfortable?"

"I live in a dumpy hotel, so if you don't mind we can go there. That way we don't have to spend more money"

"Babe, if you told me you were going to the moon, I would be there next to you. Let's stop wasting time and go. My balls hurt because of you, cabrón!"

I wrapped my arms around his neck and shoulders and kissed his cheeks and face. He kept trying to kiss me back, but I was too fast—I giggled as I did it.

"You really like me that much, babe?" he asked with disbelief.

"You know, I was going to ask you the same thing."

"I think I'm falling in love with you."

I turned to him and said, "Ditto."

He flashed his most charming smile.

Gathering my senses, I asked, "Aren't you going to put that cock away? You can poke somebody's eye out with that thing."

Abel let out a deep belly laugh and said, "I can't fit it into my pants until it goes down a bit. Stop making me so horny. Cut it out!" he teased.

I hightailed it back to the Saint Francis Hotel in record time—forty-five minutes—the happiest I'd been in a long time.

Thunderclap

DAVID CALEB ACEVEDO

"Are you telling me that you want to be gang-banged by a bunch of strangers?"

"Yes. Does that bother you?"

"I told you already. No. Let's go then. Tonight."

"Do you think it'll be safe? I mean—to drive all the way to the warm springs at night?"

"We won't know if we don't do it."

They rode in silence the entire hour-and-a-half drive to Coamo. The breeze that came in from the friction of the car's velocity plugged their ears. Marcos thought that perhaps the silence of words was the product of having gone too far with his petition.

One thing was Charlie's outrageous sexual history; another entirely would be to imitate some of his boyfriend's greatest deeds. He tried to touch Charlie's hand while the other drove, but there was an absence of sound and he knew that sometimes a wall can come from it. He pulled his hand back and into the pocket of his gray hoodie.

As they climbed down the freeway away from the mist-clad mountains of Cayey, Marcos started to think about the time when his boyfriend told him he had been fucked in the warm springs by nineteen guys, one after the other. He thought about the things that had been left unsaid, the probable facials, the piss circle, the incredible sexual stamina of his boyfriend's sphincter.

And then he turned on his iPod. "Thunderclap," by Eskimo Joe.

"Nah—too depressing, papa," Charlie said, turning it off.

So it was silence again.

Great.

They passed the Salinas toll station and Marcos shifted in his seat. His ass-ring twitched in anticipation. He imagined walking to the huge lone Ficus tree close to the latrines, finding a horde of males in heat—as in his boyfriend's tall tales—and satisfying them with his cute, little hole.

He twisted uneasily at the pain that he would feel.

"The more pain you feel, the greater pleasure it will turn into," his boyfriend had once told him. He imagined the feeling of being hosed up with sperm and his groin protested against his stonewashed jeans. He really wanted it. His chest grew heavy with the rush of blood as they turned at the school to the left. The wait gave him pain. In a way, he wanted it to be over already. The way his knees jumped gave him away.

Charlie warned, "You know, you should take it easy, papa. This here is a lottery. There may very well be nobody in there."

"Okay."

"Okay? So everything is just okay?"

"What do you mean?" Marcos asked.

"Whatever…"

Marcos knew very well. Charlie was probably under the impression that he wanted to follow in his steps. The HIV had not been enough to scare him away when they had met in the stalls at the park. He had gone right down on his knees and sucked hard on Charlie's 9x6 until he put a condom on, took him by the arm to the handicap stall, and fucked him hard.

That kind of liberalism wasn't an issue with him either, but Charlie wanted it to be that way. It's one thing to be a whore and another to turn a young boy into one. Charlie frowned hard at this, as he continued to drive in silence.

When they arrived, there were plenty of the daylight's residues permeating the clouds. The moon was hidden, but it would not be excessively dark.

"All right, here we are," Charlie announced with a groan.

"Okay," Marcos replied.

"So this is what we're going to do. There are many cars here. Some of these people may be straight and we don't want trouble with them. They usually keep to themselves in the pools. But then again, there is action in the pools too, so you may want to trot back and forth between the pools and the Ficus tree. Do you follow?"

"Okay, yes."

Charlie tried not to look frustrated. "Well, you go do your thing and I will go and do mine. And papa, please be careful."

"Okay," Marcos answered, silently cursing himself for being so nervous as to be unable to say anything else.

"Are you nervous?"

"Very."

"Don't be. I'm going to be around to protect you."

"Thanks, papa. I love you. Tons."

"Me too."

They got out of the car. Charlie opened the trunk, took off his shorts, and stayed in his underwear. He beckoned Marcos to do the same. They took off their shirts and grabbed a pair of black towels. Charlie changed into flip-flops and Marcos followed suit.

As they ventured down the half-night road, completely lacking safe illumination, Marcos grew restless. He grabbed his lover's hand. The gesture was well received, as Charlie closed his much bigger hand around his puny one. There was lightning far above the town's center, but Marcos could not hear thunder louder than his heart.

"Damn, I really hope it doesn't rain."

"It seldom does in this town."

As they approached the latrines, Charlie registered movement in the shadows. His experience told him that in such darkness, it is always best to look at things from the corners of his eyes. Marcos's experience told him to leave, that no good thing could happen in such a dark place.

"Let's go to the pools first," Charlie said quietly.

When they climbed the ramp, they heard male giggles and grunts. A cloud of moaning, laughter and virgin's gasps of pain and shock mixed with water vapor from the springs. When they turned at the corner end of the ramp, they saw several men in the middle pool going at it relentlessly, splashing water everywhere. Two bears were sitting on top of the hill, observing with lit cigarettes and baseball caps, if nothing else on.

"Ha. They didn't bring their leather. I guess chaps and warm water don't mix," Charlie said with a grin. "Okay pa, you go into the pool and have some fun. I'll go with the bears."

Marcos watched as Charlie left with the hairy men; they headed into the bushes, further up the hill. Suddenly alone, he jumped into the middle pool. The sixteen or so men who were there quickly turned to look at the innocent virgin who had stepped into their dark realm.

"Sup, papi?" asked a black man who was seated at the edge of the pool with his hand on his hard-on.

"Nothing much."

"Want to taste this? Come here."

Another thunderclap erupted with light in the distance, not far from the springs. *Better decide already, papi. It sure looks like the storm's coming this way.*

Marcos got closer and kissed the man's curved ten inches. The latter shoved Marcos's head down, gripping his hair tightly. Marcos protested gutturally but could do nothing to disengage. The black guy forced him up and down until he erupted in Marcos's mouth.

"Swallow it, you lil' bitch."

Marcos obliged, while tears flowed. When he was able to pull off, almost sick, he went to the edge of the pool and threw up. His mouth felt slimy in certain parts, metallic in others. He coughed deeply.

The black man laughed and called to some of his friends in the other pools. He grabbed Marcos from behind and covered his mouth while the others played with him. A white man with a mustache played with his nipples, gently at first, then out for blood. Two guys played at sticking their fingers in Marcos's ass.

They twitched here and there, making sure that Marcos could feel the difference between fingers by their movements. Another guy kissed him hard, brushing each tooth with his tongue. The other four watched as the black man kept forcing Marcos's mouth onto another man's dick.

Part of him wanted to cry out to his boyfriend, another wanted to let them rip his ring, to give in to the submission, notwithstanding the hemorrhoids that would surely follow the next day, not caring about the precious blood that was already leaking into the pool. But he could do nothing, even if he were able to choose. They pinned him to a corner and penetrated him, one by one, sometimes doubling into him. He was gagged the whole time, either by a dick or a sadistic hand.

Tears continued to flow.

The pain never ended and pleasure never came.

"What the fuck are you doing? Leave him alone, immediately!" Charlie rushed at them brandishing a knife over his head.

"Sorry, man. We thought this was what he wanted," the black man replied, abandoning his South Bronx accent for a more Southampton flavor.

"Let him go. Now!"

The men dispersed and Marcos got out of the pool. He vomited once more and cried.

"What's wrong, papa? Tell me, what's wrong?" Charlie asked him.

"They raped me!"

"Hey, we didn't do that shit! He wanted it," said one of the men.

"Let me get you out of here, papa. Let's go," Charlie assured him.

He took Marcos's arm and placed it around his shoulder. Another thunderclap made itself heard clearly, this time over their heads. Within seconds, it started to rain full fledge. Charlie carried him all the way back to the car. In the distance they could hear the other men approaching, although consciously trying to keep their distance.

They drove away under the deluge, stopped at McDonald's for coffee and burgers, and at the gas station in Santa Isabel for two packs of cigarettes and a lighter. They smoked in silence, as rain and thunder followed them all the way back to San Juan.

"Papa, I'm so sorry," Charlie said.

Marcos said nothing. He lowered his seat back, pulled down his wet briefs, inserted two fingers in his anus, and began masturbating.

"What the fuck are you doing?"

He paid no attention to Charlie and kept jerking off; he recreated every detail of the scene he had just survived with his own four fingers and came hard.

"They didn't rape you, did they? Answer me, damn it!" Charlie protested.

171

Marcos didn't reply.

He turned on his iPod.

Same song.

Then he cried.

Much more.

Empanadas

MIGUEL M. MORALES

Manuel fantasized about being a porn star. He wanted a hard body, lean torso—and most importantly—he wanted a bubble butt. However at thirty-nine, five-foot-seven, and 240 lbs, he realized he should probably fantasize about something else. Even his imagination knew it would never happen. It's not that he wanted to be stuffed like an empanada; he just wanted to be wanted, much like an empanada.

Manuel spent his days working in the library, trying not to stare at men's crotches or at least trying not to be obvious about it. For their sakes, Manuel pretended not to see the nervous young men walking past the gay section. On his hourly rounds he coughed as he entered the men's restroom and made sure the metal door hit the broken tile doorstop which usually brought a few young men scurrying from the stalls.

He volunteered to shelve books, to make sure they were in order according to the Library of Congress—screw Dewey. Everyone loved Manuel and they told him so. He brought cupcakes to the office birthday parties. He smiled but wondered if they would still love him if he didn't write the newsletter, cover shifts, or if he actually made porn.

On days like today, Manuel held on to the thought that he was lucky people loved him, even if not for the reason he wanted. After work he stopped by Ramos's panadería, as he did every Thursday, to pick up the last of the day's pan dulce—broken banderas and crushed conchas.

Omar, the owner's brother, would sometimes save him a few of the day's pumpkin empanadas. When he began working at the panadería last year, Omar immediately brought familiarity to the sparse and troubled Kansas bakery. He offered the women of Sacred Heart Church a place to sell their handmade rosaries and spent Saturday afternoons teaching neighborhood children how to make papel picados, which he displayed in the store window.

The most significant change came when he began using his mother's pan dulce recipes and his favorite, pumpkin empanadas. Omar drew in the community. He helped create a strong business for his family and their employees. The twenty-nine-year-old embodied everything Manuel wanted and wanted to be. Tall, handsome, kind, and Mexican. He always greeted Manuel with a smile and handshake made firm from years of working in construction and maintained by various projects at the panadería.

Manuel knew that Omar's brown eyes could tunnel effortlessly into his soul, unearthing secrets. Sometimes they did. Omar made Manuel feel young, attractive, and noticed. Being near Omar overwhelmed Manuel, causing him to stare down at the crumb-filled trays inside the empty display cases.

Crossing the icy parking lot, Manuel walked toward the windows heavy with condensation from the ovens. Through Ramos's decorated plate glass he saw Omar wiping his hands on his apron. Soon Omar stood holding the door open, which sent a shot of adrenaline to Manuel's heart.

"Oh! Omarcito—did you save me some pun-kin empanadas?" a voice from behind Manuel asked.

"Sí, señora," Omar answered, looking past Manuel.

"Señorita," she said correcting him, as she walked through the door, her heels clicking with every step.

She paused for a moment to brush against him.

"It's señorita," she repeated.

Manuel grabbed the weight of the door as Omar walked the woman, who was obviously a prostitute, to the counter.

Stop being so mean Manuel thought to himself. *She's not a prostitute. She's just being—did he just give that bitch my empanadas?*

Manuel watched her red fingernails carry the bag past him. Again, her heels clicked responding to her internal rhythm. Her hoop earrings danced and her necklace bounced off her tight and rather busty turtleneck.

Manuel watched her cross the parking lot and drive away.

"Ah, I owe you some empanadas," Omar put his hand on Manuel's shoulder.

Manuel breathed in the smell of fresh pumpkin and cloves emanating off of Omar. As Omar slid his warm hand off, Manuel felt the cold returning, the cold of winter, the cold of reality, the cold of loneliness.

"That's okay," he said facing Omar. "It was worth it."

Omar sighed and slid into the nearest booth.

"She wants to be my girlfriend," Omar said with a thick accent. "She wants to marry." Omar looked up at Manuel and tunneled into his soul, adding, "I know how you look at me, I'm not stupid."

Manuel felt air escape his lungs; his muscles tightened as he struggled to breathe. He leaned against the door—he wanted to fall through its glass.

Omar drew close, looking deeper into Manuel. "And I know you put money in the jar for rosaries but never take one. I know you go to the bank before coming to the panadería so that you can pay me in crisp dollar bills."

Trying to escape his shame, Manuel turned his face away. He shut his eyes, pushing tears down his cheeks. His eyes burned and his head pounded.

Omar stepped back. He looked around the bakery, and all his work, and went into the office.

Manuel wiped his eyes with his shirtsleeve, sniffed his mocos away, and pushed the door open. Hearing the jingle of the bell on the door Omar yelled to Manuel, "Wait!"

176

Omar emerged sorting through an old black notebook. "Un momento," he said placing the notebook on the table. He stopped on a page, looked at it carefully, and pulled it out of the rungs and folded it. "I owe you some empanadas," he said placing the recipe in Manuel's hand.

"No," Manuel whispered in disbelief. "No, amor—I mean *Omar*," he explained.

"I know," Omar said with a half-smile and a flash in his eye. "Look, I'm going home. I want you to keep that for me."

"You mean the . . ."

Omar leaned in, looking into Manuel's soul, "Just keep it for me."

Requiem
Sertanejo

RICK J. SANTOS

Stuck in traffic on the 59th Street Bridge on my way back to Queens, I listen to the first Portuguese music CD that Zeca made for me when he decided I had to learn the language to speak to his mother. "Baby, I'm all love, vamos *pra* Babylon. *Viver à pão-de-le Moët & Chandon*." As Fagner and Zeca Baleiro sing, I get lost in their words and my memories of my own Zeca. I look for the city behind me in the rear view mirror, but all I see is my own face frozen, streaked with tears that fall uncontrollably, unconsciously, acknowledging the presence of an absence.

Last August my ex-lover unexpectedly passed out on the A train platform and was admitted to St. Vincent's hospital. They had to close down the uptown A service at Fourteenth Street for two hours. Commuters were in a venal mood and there were speculations about possible terrorist activities. Drama, with a capital D! Of course, life with him was never casual or ordinary. Never a dull moment. So him becoming ill and passing out in the subway could not be any different.

Over a decade has passed since we separated as lovers, and my visits to him now are always spent wondering how much time we still have left. I wonder how much longer we will be able to hang on to summer dreams in the midst of a brutal winter.

As motorists honk and curse at each other, I weep. Oblivious and insulated from the world around me, I slide smoothly over the East River, in spite of all the bumps and potholes.

My great solo hero boyfriend who sang with gusto all the arias of his life never failed to surprise me. Even now, his melodies still resound in my mind as fragments of incomplete songs. He vibrated with sound: shrieks of joy, gasps of pleasure, bellows of rage, or impromptu musical performances in unconventional places.

During the time we lived together, a train ride to the city could easily become the occasion for a spectacle as, bored with my silent involvement with a book, he'd softly hum a few lines of some popular song that soon escalated into a powerful Ray Charles-like solo. On the seat next to him, I cringed.

"What?"

"Nothing."

"What you mean nothing?"

"I didn't say anything. You are the one who is singing."

"Not with your mouth, but I know you. Why are you curling up like a grotesque fetus in those pro-life ads?"

"Zeca, please"

And much as I tried to resist or be indifferent to him, I couldn't move away. I was his captive. Like a charmed snake I was drawn to his music.

On my commissioning day, as we sang the National Anthem his rich tenor soared above the instruments and resounded from the back of the auditorium. As I stood up on the stage next to my fellow officers who recognized his voice, I cringed.

I spent most of our affair cringing in embarrassed denial of the spectacles he made and, perhaps, in terror of the power and fury he exuded. I wished only for an ordinariness in him that would have made me feel less alien and less helpless.

After graduating, I opted for the Reserve Corps because I knew I could not live with him on base, and more importantly, I could not live on base without him. Together, we got a beach cottage at Point Lookout. The house was simple but very comfortable, three bedrooms, a glassier porch leading to a wooden deck backyard, and a working fireplace. All of this just one block from a private beach. In the summer, we would invite friends and his coworkers for barbecues or just for casual sunset happy-hour drinks. I preferred mojitos, which he'd make with fresh mint he planted in our yard. On these occasions, he would always insist on a toast and at least one glass of champagne.

179

"May our husbands never become widowers."

Veuve Clicquot was his favorite, but anything French with bubbles would quench his thirst for style and celebration.

"Drinking is an art. Americans just don't get it. In this country people drink to get smashed. They value quantity, not quality. No wonder Americans are huge."

At these gatherings there was always singing and dancing. After two or three glasses of whatever, someone would inevitably pick up a guitar, a tambourine, or any of the other musical instruments he kept around for decoration purposes. In no time beautiful music would rise, filling not just the backyard, but the whole house. Sitting not too far from him, I was always amazed to watch him dominate the singing with unselfconscious joy, overpowering our guests. And yet again, I would cringe.

He was extraordinary! Like Eliot's candle flame reflected on a scratched mirror in a 19th century novel, he could not help but draw to himself the unrelated, haphazardly scratched lines, making them converge and meet, creating the illusion that they either stemmed from or ended in him. This was not out of arrogance as I assumed for a long time. It was his nature. And his curse.

Standing six-two with broad shoulders, his proportions were large, his responses were large, and he surrounded our world with largesse. He'd spend thousands of dollars in clothes which packed every closet in the house, books, *objets d'art*—literally anything could and would set off an uncontrollable shopping spree in him. Even a supermarket with merchandise burgeoning from the shelves in endless varieties excited him so much that he had to daily, not from necessity, but for pleasure. I remember reluctantly spending weekends racing behind him as he moved with ferocious speed down the aisles, waving to vendors and bragging about some great deal he got on what seemed to be soft fruits and decaying vegetables that he purchased "on special."

"There is nothing wrong with a little brown. Real fool gets a little bruised. Only pesticide-preserved, colored with cancer-giving stuff stay pretty for months. In this country fruits and meat have more hormones than transvestites and teenagers together. The trick is buying organic and cooking it right away, while it's still fresh. You can't freeze life."

He had a grand vision capable of seeing beauty buried in the most plain things. He also had an unparalleled knack to bring it out to the surface where everyone else could see it as well. A simple school notebook cover had to be perfected with mythological figures, a modest jeans jacket decorated with colorful patches from exotic and distant places. He seemed to need a lavish external world to mirror the enormity of his expectations. I told him that with an accusatory tone during one of our first heated fights. To my surprise, in the midst of bellows he stopped and looked straight into my eyes with an inquisitively, placid look of a little boy and whispered softly as if he were in a trance: "Yeah, I know I expect too much. But look at whom I've got."

That was one of our most intense fucks.

He once told me that as a teenager, he took upon himself the daily chore of working in his mother's garden, pulling out weeds, selecting different kinds of flowers and arranging them in symmetrical designs. Appropriately, he majored in architecture and continued his mission and delight in adorning the ordinary after he left his mother's nest and ventured into the world.

Not surprisingly, our home, too, reflected his elaborate vision. Texture and color spilled beyond lavishness in a variety of rugs, paintings, and handmade crafts he collected from all over the world. And mirrors everywhere—reflecting back endlessly, all the mystic colors of our home and the daily routine of our domestic lives.

"My Aunt Leah says that mirrors are more important than photographs. Photos show us who we were; mirrors remind us of who we are. Besides, they ward off evil spirits and when we are lost, they help us find ourselves."

"If you get lost, you can always call me, silly."

He paused for a moment. "What if you are not around? Or, what if you just can't hear me calling?"

From the corner, at his piano, his figure dominated the room every time he played half-remembered melodies with his acrobatic fingers. Music was the only vessel that provided him with an ephemeral outlet for his feelings. Certainly, the spontaneous bursts of joyful music he emitted could easily become an explosion of unexplained rage. His untamed energy held me captive as I vacillated between terror and some other equally frightening feeling of orgasmic delight.

I cringed in our bed as his constant complaints rose from the bathroom in the morning, filling the house.

I cringed in the driveway when angry screams of sorrow accused me of lacking the courage to take him to business dinners at the army post.

I cringed at his joyful melodies and maniac cacophonies, bewildered in each case as to their sources—both hopeful and terrified that it might be me. It was only with the perspective acquired after a decade living apart from each other that I came to understand that like all epic heroes, he sang his happy songs in exquisite, quivering expectation of some cosmic fulfillment, and made his angry outpourings against some mythical betrayal. Betrayal of what? What had he hoped for that was never fulfilled?

Because our life was a constant roller-coaster ride, I grew to accept the unpredictable. A romantic Valentine's dinner in Montauk could unleash a nightmarish display of repressed anger and violence as, if by mistake for example, I were to pick the wrong type of wine. Later, as I would lay cold in the dark room, he would creep in and smother me with apologetic kisses. He knew better than to use words. No words, just touch. He knew instinctively how to make my own body betray me and as much as I hated to admit it, I loved it. On those occasions, he would fuck me like no other man had or ever would. By morning the incident was barricaded for us both. Although unable to make sense of him, in my naïve wisdom, I somehow intuited he was railing against something much larger that I.

Still, I kept seeking continuously the nature of my fault. As his hyperbolic praises and critiques enveloped me, I felt unworthy.

After nine years together, we finally broke up for good. At twenty-eight I had never really loved anybody else and did not know how to. For many years I struggled to separate myself from the power of his personality. Of one thing I was sure: Never again would I experience either sadness or happiness so intensely.

We did not see each other at all for another nine years. Then, three years ago, with the conviction that I was no longer in thrall of his sorcery, we reunited. But, it was a reunion of strangers.

It was not until he fell sick last April that I finally found in him what I had yearned for all those years when we were lovers: ordinariness. Time and the acknowledgement of death tamed his ferocious energy and modified his exotic beauty. For the past seven months I have made my weekly pilgrimage to New York City to see a mellow forty-year-old man whose hands shake and whose lungs need help breathing. We greet one another with affection, but restrained embraces. The emotionally-charged quarrels of the past have been replaced by casual chats about our cactus plants.

"Oh, Lilly seems to be having a hard time coping with this weather."

"She's like me. We are wild desert creatures from the badlands, not fit for the urban jungle."

"Don't be so sentimental. You always loved New York. I was the one who learned Portuguese and always dreamed of living in Ceará. Don't worry, I'll get you another damn plant when I come back next Saturday."

"I hope you don't mind, but I gave them your name and number."

"What do you mean?"

"It's just in case they need to call, but I told them you are very busy with your platoon and that they shouldn't bother you."

"Are you okay, ba—? What are you talking about? Who did you give my name to?"

"They asked me for a family member contact in case of emergency. I guess you are all that's left. You are the closest person I have ever had. I hope you don't mind."

"Don't be silly. You know that it's okay."

"Good. I'm glad. You know what? They asked me to specify how we are related, so I told them that you are my 'X-of-kin.'"

When the phone rang this morning, for one last time, I cringed.

Midnight Waters

JIMMY LAM

In my early years my mother would take me with her to visit Bonao. Our distant cousins had a little shop there, in the middle of town, and used to invite us over. It was horrible back then in the 60s. My little cousin Toni was a nerd and my aunt's cooking was terrible; her endless conversations with my mother bored us all—interminable monologues about bingo, lotto, soaps, and alien husbands.

Their talking made me go as far away as I could, to the front of the shop right on Bonao's main street, to watch people pass by—mostly poor peasants trying to sell their crops on the sidewalk, looking as if they barely made enough to survive their days. Shopping at my aunt's place was out of the question for them—they stared at the glass windows filled with plastic bottles and cheap underwear.

Years later I returned to that small city in Cibao Valley, when I was fifteen and traveling alone. Some friends from the Episcopal Church took me. They were opening a branch with a new chapel and asked me to take part in a popular theater piece about—who else?—Jesus himself. I would negotiate anything not to play the role of the son of God.

After the small presentation and benedictions took place, everybody went into town to hang out. As odd as it may sound, every town in my country is built around one of three main things: and old fortaleza, a church, or a central park.

Upon our arrival in the central plaza, the mayor's band was playing, as was usual on Thursday evenings. The tunes were old and they played inside a beautiful marble gazebo that was shocking in comparison to the town's poverty; it looked as if they were playing on top of a pink wedding cake—dropped right there in the middle of the park.

Dozens of guys, girls, children, parents and nannies (they could not be completely differentiated) walked around the park making small talk and giving each other "eyes" (the Dominican word for flirting or cruising). People even sent little notes and other silly things to each other.

I had to endure this and didn't enjoy a minute of it, for by then, 1970, I was already thinking about boys. Even more, I was enthusiastic about being by myself and enjoying those dirty little crushes, those thoughts boiling in my mind. In an unknown city with some money—and being a foreigner for the first time in my life—being around all those chicks was impossible. So I escaped and returned to the church building to find out that Marino was alone in the back bedroom—alone and naked on top of the bed where I was supposed to be sleeping, too.

Fifteen years later I returned to Bonao to see Marino who'd become a gynecologist. As a gay man, he had balls to establish his medical practice in his small hometown after schooling in the capital—one-million miles away from the not as advanced Bonaenses. Although Canadians had arrived in the town and established themselves over ten years prior, Bonao maintained almost all of its old mentality, sensibility.

The Canadians cleaned the streets, organized transit and provided more than electricity to turn on the lights. They brought other modern measures and an open-sky nickel mine that caused the sky at sunset—and for twenty miles around town—to turn flaming red and changed the color of nights in the valley. With all that technology the possibility of having a job also arrived in Bonao.

Marino became successful and guys flew around us like flies on cake every time I went to visit him. He rented a complete third-floor apartment with a long open terrace overlooking the blue mountains that separated the town from the nickel mine. Visitors to Marino's place arrived early in the morning and stayed until very late, all weekend long. They had little or no sense of time.

187

In the beginning I felt overwhelmed by so many handsome men and the attention given to me. They made themselves clearly available, at any time, and always seemed hungry and never in a hurry. The big thing back in those days was getting drunk and taking a plunge in the river around midnight.

When I discovered this paradise, my visits to Marino increased. I used any pretext I could to show up at his apartment for the weekend. He never made an issue of it. I'd had a fling with him myself when I was in college and he understood who I was. I guess that our past experience alone welcomed my constant weekend presence.

His lover at the time was married with two children (both of whom Marino had godfathered in the Catholic church in front of the plaza) and had a lovely wife who loved to cook for us. We all pretended to just be "friends," but one night Marino had to go away to tend to an emergency in a nearby village and his lover made a pass at me. I felt pretty bad for not rejecting him, but knew it would happen eventually (most of my friends' lovers tried to get me or vice versa—those were the 70s!), so I reasoned that I should have him before he started making life difficult with the other guys who were always around.

Besides, he was the one who introduced me to the river. On that hot full moon night, full of rum, we rode his motorcycle for two miles into the mountains, to a pond that he claimed only he knew about. I had him on top of a rock, from where later we'd plunge into the dark fresh water. He was young, with the hard body of a miner. He cried loudly when I fucked him; he knew we were alone and almost free. From that night on my heart would always cry water after midnight.

Returning to my routine in Santo Domingo became an agony; I felt desolated every time I had to take the bus back to the capital. I would miss the midnight waters. Urban Santo Domingo couldn't offer what the Canadian dollars had helped bring to a small town dying of poverty at the border of the most beautiful mountains on the island.

They arrived with their Caterpillars to expose nickel, the sensuality of the young miners and the independence that having a job means. What a difference from my first couple of visits to Bonao, back when nobody had the slightest idea of the presence of nickel in their lives, before I yearned for the midnight waters.

Centenario

(Novel Excerpt)

ALFONSO RAMÍREZ

New York City, mid-June, 1999

What's happening? What are you feeling?" The therapist leans forward in his chair.

"Strange." Max stares at the wall. "This is something I haven't thought of in years. I was so mad at my father for dying, as if he could have helped it or changed it. But, I was mad for selfish reasons, for what it would do to me, how it would affect the rest of my life."

"Are you still angry?"

"Yeah, but now I'm angry at myself for not being more sensitive."

"Don't pathologize. You said you were just—," he glances at his notes, "twelve years old when he passed. You should be more patient with yourself."

"That's another thing we had in common. My mother used to tell me that my dad had no patience. He hated standing in lines or waiting for people."

The therapist nods, as if that made sense to him. "Go on."

"I don't gamble or bet on anything. That's something he drilled into my head. He'd say, 'You take your money and you flush it down the toilet. Same result, but it'll save you lots of time.' Let's see…this is going to sound stupid—I always look at my stools after going to the bathroom just to make sure there's nothing unusual."

"Is that something you actually saw your father do?"

"No, but I knew he did that. I never saw him, you know, in the bathroom. He was careful not to expose himself to me, whether he was showering or urinating."

"So, you never saw him naked?"

"What you're asking is if I ever saw his penis?" Max chuckles out of nervousness. "No. I think he was afraid to give me a complex."

"Did he have, shall we say, a very large member?"

"Yes, and a big dick, too. But that wasn't the reason. According to my mom, he was uncircumcised, but I was. He kept that part under wraps, cloaked—incognito, you might say. Maybe he was afraid I would make comparisons."

"We all do. We can't help it. Do you think what you've been searching for all these years is not necessarily your father, but rather, your father's penis?"

"If you mean on an emotional level instead of physical, maybe." Max takes a couple of seconds to consider the concept, spinning it around in his head like a top.

"It could be figurative, it could be literal. That's a question for you to answer. It would certainly explain the sexual compulsiveness you claim."

"You know what's so interesting; all these years my memory of the events of the past has been so selective. I can never remember the faces of those men who were so instrumental in my sexual education. But I can easily summon up what their penises looked like. I remember every single cock. I guess you could say I've always had a pornographic memory."

The therapist glances at his wristwatch. "I think this would be a good place to stop."

As Max walks home in the twilight, he wonders how they got on the subject of his father. Where did that thread of conversation begin? He was talking about Alex and his fear of losing him, even though he's only known him for barely a month, and the next thing, they were on to the subject of Papá. *God, I hope I can manage to hold on to Alex without having to work through these paternal issues first,* he says to nobody in particular. He'd prefer to focus on the present with all its glimmering possibilities and not dwell on the immutable past with its dark secrets and repressed memories. *But, how do I keep from making the same mistakes?* he asks himself. *Maybe I do need to focus on papá before I can figure it all out. Cherchez le père.*

"Broadway and Fulton Street, please," he directs the driver.

As the cabbie peels rubber down Seventh Avenue, the radio plays an old Mexican tune he almost recognizes, if only he had the energy to focus on the lyrics. He leans back against the cold headrest of the seat and closes his eyes.

The song reminds him of the day three weeks earlier, when he and Alex had finally managed to communicate in person, rather than through their respective answering machines or e-mail, and had agreed to meet at the South Street Seaport for their first 'date.'

"Thanks for indulging me," Alex said as they embraced quickly at the Fulton Street subway exit. "I know this place

191

is a tourist trap, but I like being around old boats and piers. I like the salty smell of the water. I don't know why."

"Maybe you were a sailor in a former life," Max snorted out of nervousness.

"Or a grimy, old, syphilitic prostitute," Alex shot back, putting Max at ease as they both laughed.

Max led him toward the water's edge. From the bench where they sat they could see Governor's Island in the distance, the Statue of Liberty, and beyond that the twinkling lights of the Verrazano Narrows Bridge, which were like stars caught in a big net.

"Are you hungry—or did you just want to have a drink?" Max felt his stomach doing Nadia Comaneci somersaults. He was as nervous as a virgin at the sacrificial altar. He wanted to bite his fingernails, until he remembered that his fingers were still tinged with chemicals from his darkroom sink.

192

"Not just now," Alex responded. "Do you mind if we just sit here and talk a while?"

"Not at all. What shall we talk about? Sports? Politics? How about religion?"

Alex laughed and nudged him in the ribs gently. "You left out sex."

"Believe me, if I had my druthers, we'd be at my place right now playing Hide the Chorizo. I'm incredibly attracted to you—not just sexually, but in so many other ways. I can't explain it. To paraphrase Cole Porter, 'you do something to me.'"

"That's fine, don't try to explain it." He looked right into Max's eyes. "And by the way, what exactly is a 'druther?' My parents never explained that one to me when they talked about the birds and the bees."

"Stop! You're making me feel old," Max laughed. "I don't really know what it means. I used to have a teacher in college who used that expression. Isn't it odd how many words become parts of our vernacular and we have no inkling—that translates as 'no idea,' for the teenagers in our midst—of what those words mean."

"That word I've heard before," Alex paused.

There transpired a few minutes of silence, like a fat German tourist stepping between them and cutting off all conversation. As they sat there, Alex reached a hand out and placed it over Max's. Max felt like he'd stuck a finger into an electrical socket.

Max squeezed Alex's hand. "So should we have that drink now, or did you want to walk down and get a closer look at the tall ships?"

"I'm going to break one of my steadfast rules and go with my instincts, for once." Alex moved in and embraced Max. "Honestly, I'd much rather go to your place. This is too, I don't know, too exposed. I'd rather be someplace more private."

193

"Are you sure? I wouldn't want to be arrested for corrupting the morals of a minor."

Alex stood and held his arms out. "Please! Corrupt me all you want. Just promise me one thing: you won't kick me out in the middle of the night. I hate that feeling of trying to find a cab, especially after being corrupted for an hour."

"An hour?" Max stood up. "What twinks have you been dealing with? It takes me that long just to unpack my instruments of torture." He paused awkwardly. "I hope you know I was kidding."

Alex snapped his thumb and middle finger together. "Darn it! I was hoping you might have some kind of Marquis de Sade fixation. I need to cross that one off my list of Things to Try Before I Die."

Max laughed. "I promise not to torture you— too much. My apartment's just a few blocks from here."

They began to walk away from the water. Alex leaned into Max. "Do you have anything to eat at home—I mean, besides that proverbial chorizo you mentioned?"

"Sure, I have lots to eat. I'm a good cook. Do you prefer wine or beer with dinner?"

"Either. I'm partial to red wine, but, as Dorothy Parker once said, 'Wine's fine but liquor's quicker.'" Alex pretended to hiccup.

"That's funny! I've never heard that one. Wasn't it she who said, 'Men don't make passes at guys who wear glasses'?"

With that, Alex removed his eyeglasses and stuffed them into his shirt pocket. "Maybe."

Max smiled. "I can't wait to show you my photographs."

"Photographs, etchings, call them what you will. I know your intentions are less than honorable, Mr. Márquez."

"You're so funny. No wonder I like you so much."

Two hours and three bottles of wine later, they were on the bed, flanked by sweeping views of the Twin Towers through one window and the gothic arches of the Woolworth Building through another, exploring each others' bodies with the ferocity of teenagers in the backseat of a red convertible.

Alex noticed Max had tears in his eyes. "What's wrong? Am I hurting you?"

"Nothing's wrong, nothing at all. I just feel so high."

"Must be the wine. At your age, you should watch it. That ticker's got too many miles on it." He patted Max's chest. "Lucky we flight attendants know CPR."

"Well, it's been more than twenty years."

"Since you had sex?!"

"No, God no! Since I felt this way." Max kissed Alex's palm. "You make me feel so happy it hurts."

"Should I stop?" He started to pull out.

"Never!" Max pulled him back toward him, sliding the sheet around his shoulders. "It's just that I was suddenly seized by this terror of losing you. How crazy does that sound on our first date? But I'm so delirious with joy that you came into my life, I want to be careful, I want to hold back so that I don't frighten you away."

Alex eased out slowly, removed the condom, and lay down beside Max, taking his face in his hands. "Sweetheart, just relax. Let's not start choosing china patterns just yet or renting a U-Haul. Let's take this a day at a time. We're not in a hurry, are we?"

"So, I should cancel the mariachis?"

Alex chuckled. "Yes! Unless you plan to serenade me." Alex grabbed the nearby cum towel to wipe away Max's tears. He placed the towel over Max's nose. "Now, blow nice and hard for me. Good boy!"

This made Max cry more.

195

"Shit! Should I have used a Kleenex?" Alex frowned.

"No, it's just something my father used to do." He rolled over onto his stomach and blew his nose into the towel. "I'm feeling so vulnerable tonight. It's been so long since I let my guard down. It's also been many, many years since I was in that position."

"Should I be flattered or worried?"

"Definitely flattered. It felt great. I was hoping it might happen again. My father used to say, 'you can't rush fate. When the student is ready, the master will appear.'"

"Ah, so does that make me the master and you the disciple? I think it's the other way around. Some of your moves tonight I've only read about in magazines. Do you read the Kama Sutra in your spare time?" He knelt on the bed and prostrated himself before Max. "You're the master and I'm the disciple kneeling at your feet."

"Don't kneel at my feet, not ever." Max reached out and pulled Alex to him. "Just stay here and let me look at you and thank my lucky stars for whatever it was I did to deserve this moment with you. If I had my camera handy I'd snap an entire roll of you right now just to capture that look in your eyes."

Alex kissed him on the top of the head and sat cross-legged on the bed. "Tell me about your photography."

"Suffice to say that it's like being a lepidopterist. That's a—"

"I know what that is. My favorite writer, Nabokov, was a lepidopterist. Go ahead."

"It's kind of like in that one split second that the shutter snaps and you capture your subject's likeness, you're pinning a butterfly to a board. That expression, that image becomes frozen in time. It's a moment that will never be repeated again. It's very powerful. You feel as if you're stopping time, or like you're trying to catch your breath while driving a car super fast and sticking your head out the window at the same time. It's unbelievable and indescribable."

"Yet, you just managed to describe it for me."

"Nah, I don't do it justice. Some of it is boring, like photographing Hadassah fundraisers and birthday parties for cats, yes, I said cats. And then there's the occasional laundromat opening. Once a year I get to shoot beefcake photos of firemen for their annual calendar. Talk about prima donnas. They're worse than the cats."

"I like the way you talk, the facility with which you express yourself. You never cease to amaze me."

Max pulled Alex closer. "For one whole year when I was fifteen, I took pictures of everything I saw. I would pose my family, my friends at school, even perfect strangers, and I'd fuss and make them wait until the light was just right. When they'd ask me later to see prints, I'd make excuses that the photos weren't good or that they didn't turn out at all." (Laughs.) "Truth was, I couldn't afford to buy the film. I spent almost a whole year like that. But I was very serious about getting the aesthetics right in the meantime. When I applied to colleges, I had to get a portfolio together, so I bartered services for rolls of film with a photography studio in Hollywood."

"Did you have to take pictures of graduations and first communions?"

"No. Let's just put it this way; for every roll of film there was a roll in the hay."

"So you were a whore for your art?"

"Yep."

Alex yawned. "Sorry. It's been a long day. I should get dressed and go."

Max grabbed him around the waist and wrestled him back into bed.

As they were cuddled up next to each other and falling asleep, a neighbor, just coming in from work, cranked up his DVD speakers to fill the entire floor with the sound of Ricky Martin in concert singing, "Living La Vida Loca."

Riding in the cab, Max remembers the episode and can't wait to talk to Alex and find out how his week has gone. He can't wait to share the therapist's theory about his father and the issue of his penis. *Issue of his penis! Technically, that would be me.* Max laughs at the semantic coincidence.

The next day, Max and Alex strolled through Battery Park City together. "It's like trying to put together a big jigsaw puzzle, except I don't have the box cover to see what the end result should look like, and a bunch of small pieces are missing."

Alex squeezed his hand. "Well, you're searching for some-one who doesn't exist. How could you possibly find him?"

"You're no help."

"What am I supposed to say? Do you want me to lie or pretend I have the answers?"

"Yes. No." Max stops, regards Ellis Island in the distance. "I just don't know what to do anymore. Sometimes I wish I had a father not so much to tell me what to do, but what not to do." He hesitates. "You know, I never really said goodbye to him, to my father. I never mourned him properly, and I certainly didn't miss him. I mean, not like a father."

"You were just a boy, not even a teenager, right? How were you supposed to know how to act, how to react?"

Max stops to look at Alex. "I wish you'd been here last night to make me a cup of tea or rub my feet, whatever, just to calm me down. Sometimes I wish I did smoke pot."

"Nobody's stopping you. You're lucky you don't have to undergo drug testing like me."

198 "The last time I smoked, I woke up the next morning feeling like I needed to shampoo my brain."

Alex takes Max's hand in his. "I'm sorry. Maybe it is better that I wasn't here. You might not be able to process those feelings. It's good that you're confronting this issue head on."

"How is it you know so much?"

"Clean living and ten years of therapy."

The two of them sit on a bench in front of the Holocaust Museum. "All my life, I've accomplished so much, but I've had nobody to share that joy with. I wanted someone to be proud of me—like the time I was valedictorian of my senior class, for example. Buying my first apartment. Winning a Pulitzer Prize for my photographs of the Mexico City earthquake in '86. I was always alone. It's not the same."

"You won a Pulitzer? Wow, I'm proud of you. You can share those things with me, you know."

Max throws his arms up in defeat. "Ay, I don't like feeling so vulnerable. It seems the older I get the more sentimental I become. Why is that?"

"And you don't think that's a good thing? Sweetheart, to paraphrase Freud, 'that which doesn't kill us will make us stronger.'"

"Are you saying I'm weak? Anyway, I thought it was Anne Frank or maybe Joan of Arc who said that."

"No." Alex gives Max a playful slap on the arm.

Max stops dead in his tracks. "Holy Shit!"

"What?"

"I just got this sense of déjà vu."

"What was it?"

"One time, when we were in Mexico, it was my dad's birthday, Cinco de Mayo. He and I were in this park together. I think my mom was pregnant with Cirilo and María Elena was too young, so they didn't come along. Anyway, we're sitting on a bench in this park watching this incredible fireworks display and I asked him, 'Who is this party for?' and he answered, 'It's for my birthday. The whole city is celebrating.' I felt so important, that an entire city was celebrating my dad's birthday, and it gave me a chill. He took his coat and opened it up and hugged me inside of it until I warmed up." Max shivers. "Wow! I haven't thought about that in so long. It was the best feeling ever. To be so close to him that I could smell his underarms and his hot breath. It was—magical."

199

"See? I'll bet there are lots more good memories lodged up in that ancient brain of yours. You just have to get the wrinkles out and shake them loose like an old blanket." He smiled at the comparison. "Let's go. I'm still tired from all those quick turnaround flights last week. Remind me, I have to call my dad tonight and wish him a happy Father's Day."

As the two of them board an uptown train, they're joined by a trio of kids who start dancing in the middle of the subway car to the sounds of Madonna's "Ray of Light" blaring from a boom-box the size of a large suitcase.

Eden Lost

(novel excerpt)

W. BRANDON LACY CAMPOS

CHAPTER ONE

And now the angels of Thy heavens are guilty of trespass,
And upon the flesh of men abideth Thy wrath until the great
day of judgment.

Enoch 84:4

The empty bottles of wine stood on the counter like accusations. Festive labels with jolly
Australian marsupials and mosaic butterflies stood in tight
regiments. Bitter December sunlight cut through the for-
est green glass sending rigid emerald shadows skittering
around the living room.

Enoch sat on the floor, the thin apartment gone suddenly
quiet. The green tinged sunlight created a vivid frame for

the fresh bruise rising from his back, onto the lower part of his neck, jutting from his Scooby Doo pajamas.

The angry mark quivered across his young skin as if it wanted to open up and tell its own story. When Enoch stretched out on a dull orange polyester shag carpet, staring at a mute and dark television screen, more of the bruise was exposed. The edge changing from a grimace into the clear imprint of a spatula that went from a tool for creation into a weapon of acute destruction.

Enoch sighed. His short curly, black hair was half standing, half flattened, by a long night of dreams of rampaging stepfathers. His battle, in truth, was against the Smurf sheets that wrapped keenly and tightly around his young body as he struggled in his sleep. Every morning he woke up sweating, his chest heaving, and his body wrapped like the Egyptian dead in a tightly wound bed sheet with Papa Smurf's cheery grin stretched grotesquely across the shroud.

202

Slowly pushing to his feet, Enoch checked the large clock on the wall above the doorway to the apartment's small kitchen. The small hand was on the nine and the big hand sat squarely on the eight. Starting with thirty, he quickly counted by fives on his fingers. It was 9:40. He had to wait twenty minutes before he was allowed to turn on the television. Waking up his mother before 10AM on weekends was a sure way to reignite the Pinot Grigio-fueled wrath from the night before.

Since he was hungry he did the customary safety check. His eyes darted to his parent's bedroom door. It was closed and no sounds of early movement were detected. Next he checked the open doorway to his little brother's room. The crib was empty. He remembered that Big Mama had the toddler for the night.

His young heart pounded against his ribcage as he quietly tiptoed into the kitchen. The sink was piled high with empty wineglasses and dishes caked with the crispy skin from his mom's fried chicken and bits and pieces of homemade macaroni and cheese. Dots of Louisiana Hot Sauce flecked the plate like dried blood. Enoch's stomach growled.

Gently, he slid a small white plastic stool from the corner. Like a spider monkey, he swiftly mounted it to the counter, his small brown feet avoiding contact with the dishes and silverware that created lopsided sculptures on the countertop. Opening the center cabinet, its façade sporting large white polka dots where the powder blue paint had peeled, he grabbed a bag of puffed rice cereal and a bowl from the shelf beneath it and set them on the counter.

Turning to climb down from the counter, he miscalculated as he stepped onto the footstool, and his toes slipped. He landed hard on the kitchen floor, and the plastic stool shot from beneath his foot, clattering like an insane tap dancer across the linoleum and coming to a deafening halt against the far wall.

In an instant his heart went from hummingbird to full stop. The air around him thickened. A fight or flight panic shot from his stomach to his head and back again. Every muscle in his slim frame tensed, and he leaped to his feet in an instant, ready to bolt, even though there was no place to run. No safety inside these walls. No place to go outside the front door.

Like a caged animal, he rocked, ears straining against the screaming silence. After a moment, when no slamming doors announced his impending doom, he began to relax.

Someone giggled behind him.

His heart leaped back into motion with a dangerous ache. He jumped looking quickly over his shoulder. He saw a small face, all sharp angles, with a long crooked nose, and wicked curving eyes staring up at him from the whorls and swirls of the old cracked grey tile on the floor.

Enoch blinked and rubbed his eyes. When he looked again the face was gone. Slowly, Enoch reached up and grabbed his bowl and cereal. Without removing his eyes from the spot on the floor where the face had been, he reached into the nearest drawer and felt around for a spoon. Backing quickly away from the spot, he reached the refrigerator. For a moment, he pulled his eyes away from the floor to find the milk carton. Just as quickly his eyes jumped back, scanning the four square tiles where the face had been and just as rapidly checking the rest of the floor in the area, in case the face had taken up residence someplace else.

With the milk in his hand, the bag of cereal under one arm, and the bowl and spoon in his other hand, Enoch's careful caution gave away to a healthy childlike respect for the things that go bump in the night, or, in this case, early on a Saturday morning.

He bolted from the kitchen.

In less than a second he reached the relative safety of the cheap orange carpet. Without any discernable patterns, he'd experienced the carpet as safe from the unannounced appearance of laughing devilish faces.

With a last look tossed over his shoulder through the kitchen door, he moved to the small dining table that sat wedged into one corner of the living room. He checked the clock. Still ten minutes to go before he could blithely lose himself in the embrace of the Snorks. He climbed into the chair. At six, he was small for his age, given to slenderness. His feet dangled a half-foot above the pumpkin shag.

Pouring himself a bowl of cereal, his new fear of the kitchen floor gave way to his complaining stomach. He lost himself in the crunch of the puffed rice. His spoon lightly touched the bowl, sending soft chimes into the stale apartment air that smelled of old cigarettes, cheap wine, and cooking grease. The constant clinking of his spoon against the rim of the

204

bowl reminded him of the sound of ice cubes falling into an empty glass.

The night before came rushing into the morning.

His mother's favorite Keith Sweat song was playing loudly from the turntable in the living room. Her long blonde hair was teased up into a cloud of thin filaments supported by the magic of Aquanet. She moved slowly, a soft smile spread like butter across her face, her hips rocking back and forth to the R&B standard.

She was wearing her new outfit, a gift from Enoch's stepfather. She sported a leather aubergine top with shoulder pads that made her look like a Vikings linebacker. Matching the top was a short leather skirt, the same deep eggplant. On her feet she had stilettos with long supple straps that created spider webs up her calves. Her lips were a soft red; above her long eyelashes she wore purple mascara that brought the whole ensemble together.

205

Enoch thought his mother was the most beautiful creature in the world.

Enoch's stepfather lounged on the old green leather couch against the far wall. Its cushions cracked and creased from age and ill use. It had been crafted at the height of the Black Power movement, when Panther's roamed the streets, oiled afros and assault rifles held against shoulders pinned back by race pride. And like those days, only a memory of the couch's original glory remained. In 1983, the cracks were visible metaphors for the crack that euthanized the movement.

Enoch's stepfather was a tall man, over six feet. His hair was clipped short to the scalp, his ebony skin broken only by the occasional stoned smile. His teeth a brilliant white in contrast to his skin, but up close, Enoch knew, his teeth were yellow. Up close, the illusion was shattered.

"Teeny! Turn up that song. This is my jam," his stepfather shouted, carefully leaning over the glass coffee table in front of him, unrolling a sandwich bag filled with dried green herb.

Enoch's mother spun smoothly around in her heels and turned the volume dial up on the turntable. Briefly, Enoch wondered why his mom was called Teeny. He knew her real name was Lucia. She was thin, that was true, but he would hardly call her Teeny.

"That's it. That's it!" His stepfather, called Frank by his friends, shouted as the music blared from two speakers, taller than Enoch, sitting on either side of the stereo stand.

Enoch sat at the dining room table with crayons spread out in a rainbow stockade around a new oversized coloring book. When Big Mama had stopped by to pick up Baby J this evening, she had brought the new 64 crayon box of Crayolas for Enoch as well as a giant coloring book of fairies, goblins, elves, unicorns, and other fantastic creatures that he loved.

Enoch looked over to his mother, she smiled at him, and he smiled in return.

"Mama, you look beautiful," Enoch giggled.

"Thank you baby, come dance with me." Teeny grabbed his little hands.

She picked him up from the table and swung him up to her hip.

"Uff-dah," she said as his weight settled on her. "You are getting big!"

Enoch giggled again, his laughter loud and strong and ringing. It quickly turned to laughing shouts as his mother began to tickle him. There wasn't a part of his young body that wasn't ticklish to an almost torturous degree.

"Mama! Mama! Mama! Stttt—ooo—ppp." He gasped for breath between hysterical high-pitched squeals.

He began to squirm and wiggle, and his mother, finally relenting, let him slide to the floor.

"That boy is gettin' too damn big for all that foolishness." Frank frowned and shook his head.

"He's my baby." Teeny retorted her forehead creased.

Frank didn't respond. He just shook his head and cut a sidelong glance at Enoch. Enoch hid his face in his Mother's miniskirt.

Frank continued combing the marijuana seeds from the leaf as he rolled the contents of the now empty baggy around in the top of an old shoebox. Deftly, he pulled a cigarette paper from a small rectangular box, spread some of the dried leaf onto the paper, rolled it, and licked the edge of the paper, sealing the joint. "Pass me a lighter."

Teeny looked down at Enoch, rolled her eyes and shrugged her shoulders. Enoch covered his mouth to keep the laughter from spilling out again. Teeny snatched a lighter out of an ashtray on the dining room table, pulled out a cigarette from the pack on the coffee table, and lit it. As the thin, pungent smoke curled from the cigarette, she handed the lighter to Frank.

"Damn. My chicken." Teeny ran to the kitchen.

Enoch trailed after her as Frank lit his joint. When Frank was smoking marijuana he was okay. But sometimes Mary Jane made him want an even bigger high, and that's when he sniffed the powder. And when he sniffed the powder he got mean. Very mean. The combinations of cigarette and marijuana smoke and fear twisted Enoch's stomach.

As he entered the kitchen after his mother, the smell of chicken frying made his mouth water, and an earthquake rumbled from his midsection and released his tummy's uneasiness. With her cigarette in one hand and a spatula in the other, Teeny flipped the chicken like a pro. Wings, legs, thighs, and a large breast did gymnastic floor routines in the coal black cast iron skillet on the stove. The grease in the pan jumped and sizzled, scoring the acrobatics with an aroma that screamed 10! 10! 10!

Teeny removed a couple of crispy golden wings and legs, which emerged from the Crisco hissing with a delicious popping sound. She dropped the chicken on a paper towel-covered plate and removed three uncooked pieces from a large brown paper bag.

Enoch watched as his mother did her alchemy. Fascinated by the entire process, he memorized her spell as she grabbed flour and cornmeal, Lowry's, garlic, and, for heat, dashes of hot sauce. She mixed them all together in a large paper bag. Into the bag descended the raw chicken. She expertly rolled the top of the bag and shook the entire ensemble violently. From that magician's hat emerged raw chicken with a new, snow-white skin, which, when put under fire, became a rich powerful golden brown, full of flavor.

When his Mom was cooking, the too early wrinkles on her young forehead were smoothed away. She lost herself in the subtle rhythms and invisible clues that tell a good cook when and how to shake and move and season. With her Lee Press-On nails, she gingerly tore a piece of leg meat from the plate and popped it in her mouth.

"Now, that, little man, is some good chicken." She smiled at her little boy. He smiled back as she pulled a bright blue plastic plate from the cabinet. One of the wings was deposited on the plate, and from the fridge came a bottle of Louisiana hot sauce; she unscrewed the top, sprinkled some sauce onto the chicken and handed the plate to Enoch.

With her cigarette dangling from her lip she said, "Take this to the table and eat it. It should hold you 'til the rest of the chicken is done. The macaroni will be out in a minute and I have to put these beans on." His mother turned back to the stove and started snapping green beans from a bowl she grabbed from the refrigerator. She squinted as the cigarette smoke rose up to her eyes and began humming the new song blaring from the speakers.

"Thanks Mama," Enoch said.

"Hmmm. Mmmm." Her answer trailed after him as he moved back into the other room.

Stepping out of the kitchen his nose wrinkled at the clouds of marijuana smoke. He hated that smell almost as much as he hated the man blowing the clouds.

For someone who was halfway through his first year of kindergarten, Enoch knew a lot about hate. His smile was replaced by an earnestness that transformed his six-year-old face. For a moment, an old man stared out: milky eyes set in a worn walnut face peeking out of his pupils, into a time that the old man scarcely remembered.

Frank, who happened to glance at his stepson, jumped and let out a shout. He had seen the old man as clearly as he could see the fire bright tip of the joint smoldering in the roach-clip in the ashtray on the table. He looked at the boy, who stared at him with a hard look. A look he'd seen before on grown men's faces. He looked down again at the roach-clip and let out barked laughter.

"This some good shit!" he said, amused by what he interpreted as the hallucinatory power of quality weed.

"Sit down and eat that chicken, little nigga'." He waved Enoch towards the table.

"Yes, sir," Enoch said, his voice flat, on the edge between courtesy and rebellion. Climbing up to the table, he pulled apart the chicken wing and popped a piece into his mouth. He lost himself in the flavor. The skin was perfectly crisp. The grease was still hot but bearable, and it flooded his taste buds with a warm, soft embrace. The salty perfection of it curled up his tongue in juvenile erotic pleasure, lulled, for a moment, until the hot sauce that had soaked into the meat ignited his mouth. His skin flushed from the heat. His brain, unable to tell the difference between the spice in the pepper sauce and actual fire, sent chemical signals racing down synapses at nearly the speed of light alerting his mouth that it was burning. He began to sweat.

In less than a minute, the chicken wing was scalped. The fragile wing bones were split and cracked. The marrow surgically removed. The ends of the bones had been gnawed for their edible roasted cartilage. Enoch was comforted by the love his mother had dashed into her cooking, like a rare spice; it was addictive.

The doorbell rang. A sickly buzzer that sounded like a half-dead bee trapped in a plastic bottle.

"Teeny! The door!" Frank shouted from the couch, not bothering to move, as he started singing softly under his breath and rolling another joint.

His Mother shouted back from the kitchen. "I'm trying to get this chicken out of the pan. If you want to eat tonight, you better get up and get it yourself."

Frank rolled his eyes. "Damn, I got to do everything around here myself." He lifted himself off the couch.

Enoch stuck out his tongue at Frank's back. Frank didn't do a damn thing around the house. What Teeny didn't do, Enoch had to do himself. He was willing to put money on the fact that he was the only kindergartner in the entire city that knew how to wash and wax a kitchen floor.

Frank pushed a button set into an old yellowing box, random brown and red wires reached ominously from around its edges. They looked like insect antennae searching blindly from the wall.

"Who it is!"

"Yo, Frank, it's Sleepy Floyd. Open up now here." The familiar voice was hazy and slightly slurred, laid over the sound of teeth chattering. A woman's voice followed, "Yeah hurry up Frank. It's cold as a witch's titty in a brass bra out here tonight."

"About time your slow asses got up around here. Come on up, niggas."

Frank pushed another button and held it. Enoch could hear a door slam far away, several floors down, even over the pulsing music. The building they lived in was old, heavy, weighted down with memories, and hungry.

Whenever Enoch heard the door to the building slam shut, he imagined it was a mouth. He could hear the building chomp.

At one point the building had been a convent. The narrow hallways still boasted windows with the cold, abeyant forms of long dead saints and avenging angels frozen in colored glass.

A decade ago, the building was converted into apartments for people who couldn't afford to pay rent without help from the government. Once it had embraced the prayers of the faithful and now it held only the outcries of the desperate.

A rapid-fire knock at the door followed by a loud, "Open up bitches. Let's get this party started right."

Frank yanked open the door revealing his best friend Sleepy Floyd, dressed in a tan pantsuit and vest, butterfly collar shirt with wings wide spread, and an oiled short afro with a black power fisted pick sprouting from the top. His mouth spread wide in a minstrel show grin, and a thick mustache that looked like a dead caterpillar stretched above his upper lip.

Frank let out a laugh that sounded like a cross between a machine gun and a cock's crow, "What up Sleepy!" he said, their hands moving in a slick handshake ending in a snap.

"Damn, something sure smells good." Sleepy Floyd brushed into the room.

Behind him came Janet, a mocha-skinned black woman with long silky black hair fanned out in homage to Farrah Fawcett at the sides. Her full lips, slender waist, and wide hips had Frank licking his lips in appreciation.

"Damn girl, what you been eatin'?" He slapped her ass as she walked by.

"Hi Frank," she responded, her voice flat and her eyes narrowed to ice cold slits. She grabbed Frank's muscular forearm and dug her nails into it.

"Ouch, bitch, turn loose my arm."

"Slap my ass again and I will tear this arm off," she said, her voice sweet and dripping with venom and an undisguised distaste that she spat, boldly, into Frank's face.

Enoch winced. No one talked to Frank that way. He watched as Frank's face clouded up—a storm gathering in his head. Enoch stopped breathing. Janice continued to stare Frank dead in his face. Her eyes spitting sparks and her lips turned up into a 'fuck with me if you dare' smile.

And then a miracle occurred. The gathering storm blew away. Frank broke into a hangdog grin.

"Girl, you crazy," he said, laughing and waving a hand dismissively at her.

"Yeah, Frank. Real crazy. Real fucking crazy," she said.

Enoch caught her looking at him as he sat at the table. He was coloring without looking at the coloring book beneath his crayon. The plate with only a memory of the chicken wing had been pushed to the center of the table.

"Hey, baby. How you doing?" She walked over to Enoch as Sleepy Floyd and Frank, ignoring her and the boy, moved to the couch and lit up the waiting joint.

"Hey, Aunty Janice. I'm good." His shy smile broke into bloom.

"Let me look at you for a minute. Child, you jus' keep getting bigga and bigga," she said, her voice holding on still to the deep South after more than fifteen years up North.

She searched his face. He felt she could feel the heaviness he carried. He was young and he was beautiful. His skin was the perfect intersection between black and white. Golden brown with saffron and cinnamon highlights, she had once said, it was smooth and soft. His cheeks were round and dimpled, baby fat just beginning to give ground to the young man that he would someday become. His eyebrows were full and naturally arched, and long, thick eyelashes framed Asiatic eyes, almond shaped and slightly upturned.

His eyes gave her pause. They didn't fit his youthful body. They had seen too much, too soon, and in too short of a time. Janice had said it before and she saw it; she started to tear up.

213

Coughing and pretending to have something in her eye she said, "Ohhhh, baby. My mascara is getting all up in my eye!"

Enoch nodded solemnly as if he had a world of experience with the vagaries and shenanigans of mascara.

"Give me some sugah, baby!" Janice's eyes lit up when he gave his sweet smile. "You are beautiful. And you going to be a heart breaker." She watched his careful approach, the soft way he laid his hand on her arm. She was distracted from her thoughts as he placed his lips on her cheek and then blew outward as hard as he could. It made a loud farting sound.

"I flerbitzed you!" Enoch doubled over in laughter.

Janice's own laugh caught up with his and hugged it. She ran her manicured nails through his loopy curls and gave him a playful slap on the back. "Come on boy, grab that plate. Let's go see your Mama before I flerbitz your little narrow behind," she said, as Teeny's voice called out from the kitchen.

"Janice, girl, I am in here trying to dish up this food. Come give me a hand."

Enoch grabbed his plate and hopped down from the table. He trailed after Janice into the kitchen.

As Janice and Teeny kissed each other in greeting and exchanged pleasantries about hair, clothes, and eye shadow, Enoch slid his plate onto the counter and wove through the taught calves of his mother and her best friend and deposited himself on the white plastic stool on the far side of the stove.

"Girl, I had to let Frank have it a minute ago." Janice pulled a compact out of her clutch and checked her face.

"What did he do now?" Teeny sighed, grabbing an oven mitt and releasing a heat wave into the kitchen, as she pulled open the oven and removed a baking pan that hissed and bubbled underneath its tin foil blanket.

"Nothing more than usual, and nothing less than expected."

"Meaning what?"

"Nothing child. I just don't know why you put up with his shit."

Enoch watched the verbal ping-pong and shifted on his stool, which creaked sharply.

Janice smiled, covering her mouth, "Sorry baby. I mean stuff." She grinned at Enoch as she helped herself to a tall glass full of wine.

"Girl, don't worry about that, baby. He has heard worse in this house."

Janice's smile turned down at the edges. Then she whispered, "Is he still layin' his hands on you?"

"Naw. Girl. Naw." Teeny refused to meet Janice's eyes while she busied herself scooping mounds of molten macaroni and cheese, then topping each one with a piece of chicken.

"Uh. Huh," Janice said unconvinced. "Let's get this food out there before someone starts to holler."

"They can wait a minute."

Teeny still wouldn't meet Janice's eyes. She reached down and pinched Enoch's cheek and passed him a plate with a volcano of macaroni and cheese with a chicken leg erupting from its crater. "Take this one out to Frank, baby. I need to talk to Aunt Janice for a minute."

Enoch turned to leave when his mother's voice stopped him, "Wait a minute baby. Come back in here and grab this plate for Sleepy Floyd when you are done, and then do Mama a big favor and take this trash down to the bin."

"But Mama! It's dark outside."

"Ain't nothing out there going to hurt you."

"Please, Mama."

Teeny arched an eyebrow at Enoch and pressed her lips together in a thin, sharp line that meant any further protest would result in swift repercussions.

"Yes, ma'am."

"That's what I thought. Now get that food on out there to Frank," she said flatly.

"Teeny, let the boy be," Janice said. She'd watched him. When his Mother asked him to take out the trash, he tensed, his body ready for danger. He was terrified. She didn't know why. But she knew his fear was real even if the danger wasn't.

"Go on now," Teeny said waving at Enoch. Her voice had softened slightly.

As Enoch left the kitchen he caught his mother's lowered voice. "That boy could work a saint's nerve, but I love him. I also don't need him hearing what I have to say. He's heard more than enough." Her voice caught at the end. Enoch knew that sound. His mother was crying. Again.

Fabrizio

(novel excerpt)

GUILLERMO REYES

217

CHAPTER 1 (excerpt)

I went looking for the mother, but I also met the son. I became useful to them both, so they weren't exactly blameless in all this. I am convinced after all these years that our deeply conflicted love was mutual—and yes, the word "mutual" accommodates more than two people. It's versatile that way.

But I've really gotten ahead of myself.

These are just my sins. Don't judge humanity by them.

Her sweet breath closed in on my fat lips. I sensed her fingers on the back of my neck. I waited patiently for her lips to meet mine, but that didn't happen. She continued to smile. She was then using my own whiskers to scratch the back of her hand, as if she got a relief out of it. My eyes stole a glance down at her crotch where I imagined all the mysteries of creation were hidden and would reveal themselves to me, when suddenly, the door blasted open, and that's when he blazed in, sweaty and out of breath, bringing the warm air of the Santa Anas inside with him.

"Shit, that was awesome!" he said, catching his breath. His mother and I pulled apart, rather brusquely, noticeably.

Fabrizio stood all moist, shirtless, with red shorts covering a lean set of buttocks that absorbed the sweat that ran down his torso. His nipples glowed firm and upturned. He was a young man, seventeen at the time, and his face immediately showed off his mother's symmetry, that Italian-Chilean con-coction of genes, dark almond-shaped eyes with thick black eyelashes, and longish messy hair almost down to his shoul-ders, giving him the look of a flat-chested girl. His nose was pointy and menacing just like his mother's. All the beauty of the female transferred well onto the young man.

218

I was struck by the strange dynamic, as if a double vi-sion of Eros were playing tricks upon me. Mother and son stood as reflections on a mirror. My eyes strayed from one to the other. I became tense with a pulsating energy that ran through me. At any other time, I might have told my friends, I met a woman who changed my life. I didn't realize it then that I was also being transfigured by the sight of them to-gether, by their similarity, their incredible energy of male and female rolled into one.

I met a woman and her son and something in me awak-ened to a feverish high. I became the man I am today in those few seconds, the man who has plenty to account for, not that I'm entirely ashamed, just perplexed that my body reacted in that manner. It was a physical sensation that en-raptured me and stirred me to act upon all sorts of biological necessities.

Fabrizio barely acknowledged me as he ran quickly toward the fridge and got himself some bottled water.

"No Kool-Aid? Who do I have to fuck around here to get some real sugar into this house?!" he shouted.

"Fabrizio!" His mother was already scolding him in that mix of English and Italian and Spanish that I found so charming upon hearing for the first time. "*Non essere* un maleducado. *Vieni qua.* Say hello to Mister—oh, what was your name again?"

"Sal. Sal Senzaluna."

"Hello, Sal!" The kid chimed in with a clownish smirk on his face. His legs jutted forward, almost touching me, as he patted my back. I noticed they were athletic and lightly muscular and the sweat from his torso sprayed my face in passing. He headed for the TV set to turn it on—he said he had an *I Dream of Jeannie* episode to catch.

"Fabrizio, this is rude! *Sei uno stronzo, vieni qua!*"

"Come on now! I ran from Sunset and La Brea all the way to Griffith Park and back. That's like a half marathon right there, mommy, and I did it in under two hours, too—a personal best. I'm almost as good as you now—I'll be catching up with you and leaving you in the dust one day."

"Not quite yet." She looked unimpressed. "You still need upper body workout. All that running will give you a skeletal look and you know I'm not fond of that."

What on earth was she talking about? The kid was in perfect shape. No, he didn't have a Mr. Universe type of muscularity, but he looked like a fairly tight and lean vessel of flesh. Heavy weightlifting would have thrown off the symmetry of the shape, I figured, but I didn't get a vote on this—not yet.

"Mom!" he said, looking annoyed. "I'm a runner, not a bodybuilder! It's my shape and if you don't like, *se ne frega!*"

"Don't you say that to your mama! *Stronzo!* Y mal educado más encima."

"Too bad! Now I'm watching Jeannie. This is the episode where she finally gets to marry Major Nelson—or Captain Nelson, I forget. It's so romantic!" He gave us both a girlish, pouty little smile.

"*No, piccolo figlio*, you take a shower first," she said. *Figlio?* The Italian word for son still sounded like a babying tactic coming from her. That had to go and I was eager for a vote. "You're going to stink up the place, *figlio*, and get sweat all over the couch!"

"All right, all right!" he finally consented. He ran toward the bathroom, and after a few seconds behind the door, threw out his skimpy shorts for good measure.

"*Ma che schifo!*" she said. *How disgusting!*

220 She threw the dirty shorts into the laundry basket in the hallway that led to her bedroom. Then she plopped down on the chair next to me with a look that meant to suddenly move the conversation beyond anything we had touched upon.

"He's been running way too much in my opinion. And at school he's taking dance lessons. Dance lessons! I never approved of them! He faked my signature. He's after that lean look that is much too girly for my taste. Now he thinks he's going to UCLA to be a theater and dance double major, when I'm pushing for him to get an athletic scholarship. But no, he'll only run for exercise and he dropped the track team. He was on it for almost three years and he could have competed, maybe even in the Olympics. You got any kids, Senzaluna?"

"Oh no, not me," I said. I was turning thirty-three that year and was still on the run from the relationship squad.

"Well, I tell you, it's a constant battle every day," she rattled on about her favorite darling. "I mean, did you hear that remark about soft drinks?" Her face looked sullen, as if she stood ready to wipe away a tear. "I want to protect my son from processed sugar."

"There, there," I had to console her. Was this woman really going to cry over processed sugar? "Other boys in the neighborhood join gangs," I added.

"I know, but sugar's just as destructive as gangs. My friend Hugo Talca drove us and his kids to a baseball game in Anaheim, and I told Hugo that his kids can eat whatever they want, but I didn't want Fabrizio buying hot dogs, pizza or cola, and they all looked at me like I was the wicked witch. American parents want to poison their children with corporate swill and I'm the bad guy in all this? It's not fair. I need to keep track of his glycemic index. If that goes, it's the first step to high blood pressure, strokes and heart attacks at twenty. I'm losing control of this whole parenting ordeal. Oh, and he even auditioned for *Cabaret* at his high school and got cast!"

221

Now we were getting into other areas of even greater vulnerability.

"What? *Cabaret*?" I imagined Little Fabrizio as one of the drag performers playing German girls or something else in that androgynous, decadent musical. I'd seen the Bob Fosse film starring Liza Minnelli and found it perverse in the best possible sense of the word, because it went well with a hit of pot.

"He's playing the Christopher Isherwood part, or Clifford Bradshaw, as he's called in the play," she said, shattering my fantasy. This was the sexually repressed, less flashy male part. Our Fabrizio deserved a better, more bodacious part.

"Can he do a British accent?" I asked. It seemed reasonable, but she corrected me.

"In the musical he's American. I mean, Isherwood was British, but in the musical they wanted to appeal to American audiences and they kept Sally as the British character. In the movie they made him British and Sally's the American. Her dad's an American ambassador. But whatever—Fabrizio's wrong for the part. He should have been the Host, the Joel Grey part. That director, some high school drama teacher, should be sent back to Tel Aviv where he's from. But really now, forget high school musicals! We have to be ready to go back to Chile and fight for the revolution."

"The revolution doesn't include musicals?"

"I don't know! But it's my son, *il mio figlio*. I sense that he's growing up too fast in this society. Just down the street, you have porno shops and male and female prostitutes walking the streets of Santa Monica! I don't know what on Earth to think." I sensed sadness in her voice, even moisture in her eyes. "He needs a male role model," she added. "Fabrizio's father wouldn't have helped, he was a homo."

"Excuse me?"

Too much information or not enough? I was fidgeting in my seat, yearning to take notes, but it all came at me too fast—and besides—she stopped me from reaching for my notebook.

"This doesn't go in the story you're writing," she warned.

"Not a problem."

Once reassured, she leaped into the story with revolutionary fervor. "His father was a Communist and a homosexual and went to Cuba to fight for the cause. Except the Cubans sent him to a concentration camp that Fidel Castro used to turn queers into real men—los campamentos UMAPs. The poor man tried to escape on a boat and drowned. We never saw him again. I got a letter from the Cuban Ministry in Havana informing me of his death and a death certificate. I'm left to care for my son alone. And my parents are big right-wing types. They're shocked that I'm having the child of some Communist homosexual and…..you're probably not interested."

"I'm fascinated."

"Still, I'm just trying to parent him in a difficult environ-ment, that's all I can say." She hid her expression in the palm of her right hand. There, there, I comforted her. For a few seconds we sat there in that position, my arm thrown around her for good measure, until Fabrizio surprised us by pour-ing out of the bathroom wearing a large, white towel around him. He rushed over toward me and gave me the strangest look.

"Sal Senzaluna!" he shouted with a sense of accusation. Then he broke into the biggest smile. "Dude, it's you! Dude! I knew the name sounded familiar. Just wait right there, don't move. Don't go anywhere."

He ran back into his room and Elena and I stared at each with great bemusement. In no time the kid was back. He was holding a clipping of my article, "Fairfax Teenager Survives Adversity and Runs the Marathon." It was the Richard D'Arcy story that was quickly establishing itself as my most recognized oeuvre.

"You wrote this," he said. "That's you! I kept it, dude! I read it in the paper and then told my mom, didn't I *carissima mamma*? Told her how inspiring—dude! Inspiring!"

"And he cried, too. My Fabrizio had tears in his eyes. The story of a boy who survives cancer and runs the marathon."

"Yes, I'm familiar with how it turned out," I said cattily. But they were too ecstatic to notice my double-faced append-age known as sarcasm.

"And I know the fucker, too!" said Fabrizio. "I ran against him during a school meet, when Fairfax beat Hollywood High, which means he beat me pretty badly and I was pissed off. I didn't realize it then—I didn't know he had survived cancer. Damn! If I'd known I wouldn't have called him a fucker to his face. I feel bad about that now because I was really a sore loser, but when I read this, I finally understood. Dude, you're the man."

223

He patted my back; the towel barely hid his thin runner's body.

"Okay, you go get dressed now!" his mother told him.

And soon he was back in some skimpy shorts and tank top; he continued to stare at me in awe, installing himself in front of the TV to watch Barbara Eden blink a marriage ceremony into existence. "Come and watch it with me," he bid the two of us, and something drew us to him—the need for Elena and me to sit next to each other and do as the kid asked.

"I still don't know why Jeannie has to call Captain Nelson her 'master,'" said Elena. "Women don't have masters."

"Mother, please!" shouted the boy. "She's a genie in a bottle, not a modern woman."

"Even if she were a man, I'd find the word offensive." She had reached for my hand as if begging for support. I pressed on her hand, but didn't say anything. I smiled through the argument. "Nobody should be calling anyone 'master.'"

"I'm not going to miss the wedding episode." Fabrizio turned up the volume by walking up to the TV and turning the knob. They didn't have a remote.

We sat down to watch and Elena placed my arm around her. Fabrizio smiled at the sight, and then put his entire attention on the TV set. Something kept me watching for an entire episode, mostly the strange sensation that when three people can stare at a TV set in silence, something intimate among them is being taken for granted. I was already beginning to feel absorbed into their lives, and cast into the role that fit me best—I as daddy, Elena naturally as hot momma, and son as destiny.

Michael Moves to Faile Street

CHARLES RICE-GONZÁLEZ

Rosanna was watching him. At first, Michael didn't notice because he was concerned with the "Brute with a Van" he'd hired to move his stuff from Long Island to the Bronx. But then he felt her stare and that of the neighborhood—from the children playing jump rope, the women sitting on beach chairs in the shade of the building, and the teenage boys walking up and down the block teasing young, pretty girls. Everyone went about their business, but stole glances at the white man moving into their neighborhood. Michael wondered if any of the adolescents eyeing him would be in his class in the fall.

"You sure you know what you're doin' mister?" The van man looked around. Michael too saw the rundown brownstones across the street; the cluster of tough looking young men on the corner in front of the bodega, a tall black guy with dreadlocks tied high on his head, two men working on an old car, the trash in the gutter. Black and Latino people sat on steps, on parked cars and on fire escapes. A car sped down the street with hip hop pounding out its speakers setting off car alarms.

The van man shook his head. "It don't make no sense to me. I know the papers say the South Bronx is up and coming, but I don't see it."

"That's all you got?" The super of the building, Don Willie, looked into the empty moving van. "I was gonna get my son Enrique to help, but I don't need to."

There wasn't much to move after Raul left. Michael got rid of everything except a Keith Haring painting, an old lamp he bought from an antique dealer in New Hope, ten knee-high bundles of books tied with rough twine, his chair—one Queen Anne wing chair from a set they'd bought—and a picture of Raul taken in Mallory Square, Key West. Raul was shirtless and strong. He wore a straw hat and his brown skin radiated as if he'd been sprinkled with glitter.

Michael looked up at the open window. The old woman was a motionless shadow behind the lace curtains that waved slowly in the slight breeze.

"¡Vieja loca!" Don Willie winked at Michael. "She a little cuckoo. But she no trouble." He carried two book bundles into the building.

"You don't have to carry that, Mr. Willie."

"Call me Don Willie, por favor. And it's no problem. You waste your money on the van man. Most of your stuff coulda fit in your car. Qué desperdicio—I coulda go get this for you and charge you half." He vanished into the building.

Michael heard screams. In the middle of the block a jet stream of water from a fire hydrant sprayed excited brown and olive kids. Shirtless boys glistened as rushing water threatened to push their baggy shorts past their slim hips, and young girls squealed in delight as gelid drops rained down on them.

"Good thing you ain't got much, mister." The van man emerged from the building. "You didn't tell me it was a walk-up."

The old building had three floors with two apartments on each floor. Michael was moving into the apartment on the third floor across from the old woman.

The van man struggled with six bundles of books, leaving the last two behind. "You gonna bring those up?" Then he was swallowed into the building's entrance.

Don Willie emerged from the building. "Let that lazy bum take those up. What are you paying him for?"

The sound of books tumbling down the stairs was followed by a gruff, "Fuck!"

Don Willie shook his head. "Where you get this guy, huh? I woulda done it for half and you don't lift one finger."

Michael went to pick up the last bundles of books.

"Oye, leave that for him. You got stuff in your car?"

"Just my laptop and a garbage bag with some clothes."

"I bring that up for you and then I introduce you to Rosanna Maria Gonzalez."

Michael looked up but she was gone. He could hear Ravel's *Bolero*, quiet and distant.

"That's Rosanna. She plays esa música clásica a lot. But you lika that stuff, no?"

Michael smiled. "No."

Don Willie led the van man into the building with the last of Michael's things.

"Hey mister," the van man turned to Michael. "Could you watch the van until I get back down? I want to make sure I make it out of here."

"Nobody gonna touch your van," Don Willie called from inside the building.

"Could ya do me the favor?"

"Sure." Michael leaned on the van and checked his cell phone to see if there were any messages. Even though a year had gone by since Raul had left, Michael still hoped that he'd at least call for holidays, his birthday, or maybe because he'd heard that Michael had rented out their home and moved away. But Raul had vanished. He never called and asked their mutual friends not to share his whereabouts with Michael.

When the van man emerged from the building, Michael handed him his payment. Don Willie shook his head and sat on the building's stoop.

The van man spit on the ground. "I hope you got yourself some protection." He shot at Michael, flicked his thumb, blew the tip of his index finger, and got in the van. "You got my number in the event that you should need my services. It would be my pleasure to oblige." He laughed and then sped away. As he reached the hydrant, a young man sprayed water on the van using an empty can with both ends removed. Michael could see the van man give the boy a finger through his rolled up window. Then he was gone. Michael felt alone.

Don Willie knocked on Rosanna's door. "Come meet your new neighbor, Michael."

Michael stood in his doorway. Ravel's *Bolero* had reached its climax and the horns wailed. Don Willie smiled at Michael. "She okay once she get to know you. I'll send you up some arroz con pollo to welcome you to Faile Street, Michael Gringo," Don Willie laughed. "I playing wi' choo. You drink beer?"

Michael nodded.

"I put beer in my arroz con pollo to give it sabrosura, eh? I send you some to drink, too. Let me know if you need anything, okay? And don't worry about your car. Faile Street is safe and you a tenant in Don Willie's building. Nobody gonna mess with your car."

228

"¡Embustero!" Rosanna appeared in her doorway. She was short, less than five feet tall and had her grey hair in a tight bun. She was thin and wore a dark blue dress with a white collar. Her earrings were white gum drops and her lipstick was florescent pink. The scent of rose and Florida water filled the space between the two apartments.

"Buenas tardes, Doña Rosanna. This is your new neighbor, Michael O'Reilly."

"I'm not blind, Don Willie." She hobbled toward Michael and extended her delicate knobby hand. "I'm sorry it took me a while to answer the door. When I sit in a certain position my legs fall asleep and it takes me a while to get up. I'm eighty-three. Un placer, Mr. O'Reilly."

"Pleasure to meet you, too. And my full name is Michael O'Reilly Green. I keep my mother's name to honor her."

Rosanna narrowed her eyes and searched Michael's face. "Is that an Irish thing or a Jewish thing?"

"A Latino thing, no?"

"Sí." She folded her arms across her chest.

Don Willie continued down the stairs. "I'll send you some arroz con pollo, too, Doña Rosanna."

She wrinkled her nose and turned back to go to her apartment. "Your car has an alarm?"

"No."

"Get one. I've lived here for sixty-five years and I've seen some abominations on that street." And she closed her door behind her.

Faile Street begins on the Bronx River, stretches across the Hunts Point peninsula, is interrupted by the Bruckner Expressway, and continues on the other side, slicing its way through the South Bronx. From the expressway to the river, there are eleven blocks and only three are residential. Michael's family used to own a small building on Faile Street.

229

He looked out the window and wondered what the neighborhood must have been like when his parents lived there.

"You're moving where?" Michael's aunt, Helen, stood up from her easy chair.

"Faile Street."

"Michael, for God's sake, what do you want to prove by moving back there?"

"Nothing. The neighborhood is changing and I'm going to teach in a public school. I'm sure I could do a lot more good there than at the St. Paul's school."

"You're taking this Raul thing too far."

"This has nothing to do with Raul leaving me."

Helen sat back down and cried. He knelt before her.

"Your mother died there."

"She died in a hospital, not on Faile Street—and it's changed."

Helen held Michael's head in her hands. "You're not cut out for that kind of life."

"Aunt Helen…" Michael couldn't complete his sentence. The tears were coming, again. He stepped away from his aunt. "I've rented the house and sold most everything in it. I just didn't want to go without letting you know."

"You don't give me a choice."

"I'm forty years old. I want this change."

"I'll die if anything happens to you."

Michael wanted to hold his Aunt Helen. He wanted to tell her that he couldn't bear seeing Raul's shadow in every corner of their house. He wanted to tell her that his leaving had everything to do with Raul. "I'll be fine."

Michael plugged his cell phone in to charge it up. He would call Aunt Helen to let her know that he was safe. He looked around the empty apartment. The hardwood floors gleamed and there was a faint smell of new paint. The apartment was a railroad flat with high ceilings, spacious rooms all in a row. From the entrance, there was a narrow hallway that ran the length of the apartment. The rooms could be entered from the hallway or through doorways that connected one room to the other. The living room windows faced the street and French doors opposite them led to the dining room which led to the kitchen, then the bathroom and the bedroom; there was a small porch in the back of the house that could be reached only by the bedroom.

231

The wing chair was arbitrarily placed in the living room. Michael moved the lamp next to it and plugged it in. He tried the light. It worked. He took the framed picture of Raul and settled into the wing chair.

The empty rooms were fresh and ready. Michael thought about getting new furniture. New paintings. New clothes. New everything.

"Raul would love this place." Michael was surprised to hear his own voice. There was no one to hear him. "But he's not here. I am." Michael continued to speak out loud. "I've got to take chances, try new things, meet new people." He started doing jumping jacks and running in place. He shook his hands repeatedly and felt a shiver go through his body. "I'm gonna put shelves over there, all along that wall. *What do you think, Michael?* I think that works. *What kind of shelves?* Oh, something built into the walls, but definitely not boxes." Michael laughed, out of breath. He fell back in the wing chair and panted.

With all the doors open, he could see the sunset through the bedroom windows. The light stretched across the entire apartment and Michael closed his eyes to feel its fading warmth on his face.

He remembered taking the photo of Raul. They both loved the ritual of going to Mallory Square. The dock overlooked the water and there was a clear view of the setting sun. There was a reverent joy as locals and tourists came to bid farewell to the day and welcome the night. Raul didn't want to miss one sunset. He brought champagne and they shared it with anyone near them until they ran out. As the sun slipped past the horizon, the crowd cheered and applauded. Sometimes musicians came and played music or a poet would recite work. One evening a group of dancers did an interpretive dance and Raul and Michael took home a curly-haired blond dancer and slurped champagne from his golden pubes.

232

A sharp rap on the door woke Michael. The room was dark. The pink glow from the street light below his window made the stacks of books around the room look like mini skyscrapers. He turned on the old lamp, got up, and the framed picture of Raul fell to the floor, shattering the glass. "Shit!" Michael stumbled to the door, knocked over a bundle of books, looked through the peep hole, and saw a young man standing away from the door as if he expected to be inspected. He held a small pot with a lid.

"Yo, wassup? My pops told me to bring this to you."

Michael opened the door and the young man looked into the dim apartment.

"And these." He handed Michael two beers.

"Thanks." Michael noticed a similar small pot on the floor in front of Rosanna's apartment.

"She didn't answer. I'll check by in a coupla hours and see wassup. If she don't bother, I'll take it back down. No sense in feeding the rats." A sly smile spread across his face. He had perfectly straight white teeth. "I'm Enrique, my peeps call me Reek. You Michael, right?"

Michael nodded. He watched Enrique's every move as he held the pot up to him. His arms were long and slim with big hands he had yet to grow into. His lean torso was hugged by a white ribbed, tank top and his loose shorts hung precariously on his hips. He wore flip flops exposing neatly manicured bare feet; the tiny hairs on his toes seemed drawn on.

"Well my pops serves it in the little pots in case you want to heat it up later, besides he serves enough for like six people. Know what I mean?"

"Thanks. You want to come in? I don't have anything to offer, except what you just brought."

"Sure." Enrique stepped into the apartment. "You gonna drink both of those?"

"How old are you?"

Enrique took a beer out of Michael's hand. "Old enough." He twisted the lid off the beer and gulped. "Eat if you want, I already had me some of that. It's fuckin' good. You like Puerto Rican food?" Enrique rubbed his hand over his flat stomach and winked.

Michael nodded and opened the pot. "I don't even have utensils."

"Oh, I almost forgot." Enrique reached into his back pocket, pulled out a napkin wrapped around a knife and fork and handed it over.

"Your father thinks of everything."

"He's cool like that. Damn, you ain't got shit up in here."

Michael ate and watched Enrique inspect the walls, the French doors, the moulding. "I painted this place, got it all ready for you."

"Good job. You work with your father?"

"Slave labor is more like it."

Michael laughed.

"I'm serious. May I?" Enrique pointed to a spot on the floor next to Michael in the small circle of light from the

233

old lamp. He sat with his legs crossed. Long fingers resting on the slippery beer bottle. "Oh shit, is that real?" Enrique jumped up and examined the Keith Haring painting leaning against the wall, dimly lit from the streetlight.

"I bought it at a silent auction."

"That shit is pretty big. It's probably worth a lot."

"Well, not what you might think."

"Fuck. An original Keith Haring is big cheddar. I dig 'im and understand what he was about, but this is not my style. I'm into the classics. Rembrandt and shit."

"You paint more than apartments?"

"Fuck yeah. I did the whole graffiti-class-at-the-community-center-thing, but the classic shit with the cracked paint in the Metropolitan is dope. I paint dudes like me in those old school styles. I got a little studio in a storage room down in the basement. I help my pops out with the building and he let's me have the storage space. You wanna see it?"

"Yeah, I'd like that a lot."

Enrique smiled. "Just let me know when. I'm always around. The slave master keeps me on a short leash."

Michael scooped tasty chunks of chicken seasoned with garlic and nestled in moist rice. The aroma filled the apartment. "I didn't realize how hungry I was. You sure you don't want some?"

"It's good, but too much of that shit will make a nigga pudgy like my dad."

"You two get along?"

"We all we got. My moms bounced about three years ago. She was too smart for all this ghetto shit and she couldn't take my dad's drinking. He ain't a mean drunk, but a sad one. First he starts with the, *I love you, papito* and the slob-berin' all over me—then he gets to crying. Now he's passed out." Enrique unscrewed the second beer and handed it to Michael.

"Thanks."

"Drink up, bro. The night is young and hot."

They clinked bottles and drank deeply.

"Me, I'm like my mom. I know there is a bigger world out there and I'm a get mine. As soon as I turn eighteen…"

"You're not eighteen?"

"Nah, but soon."

Michael pointed to the beer in Enrique's hand.

"My dad lets me. I had one with him earlier. It's cool." Enrique leaned back on the floor and a thin line of his flat belly was exposed. "So who's the guy in the broken picture? Your man? Your reason for starting over?"

Michael set the pot of food on the floor next to the beer and picked up the picture. "I don't even have a trash bag to get rid of the glass."

235

"I'll get you one." He rolled back on his shoulders, then rolled forward and jumped up. "We got tons."

"Wait." Michael knew that he should let Enrique go. There was no reason to ask him to wait. "How old are you?"

"What do you care? Unless you thinkin' of fuckin' me and I'm still tryin'a figure out if it's gonna be worth the drama." Then he winked and headed toward the door. "Eighteen on August 14th, in two weeks. I'm a Leo." Then he roared. When Enrique opened the door Rosanna was standing outside poised as if she were about to knock. "Damn, Doña Rosanna. You scared me."

"Ay perdon, m'ijo. But you don't have anything to be afraid of with a little viejita like me." She looked past Enrique into the dark apartment. "Are you already bothering the new tenant?"

Michael wondered how long she had been standing outside the door. He got up and stumbled, knocking over another bundle of books. "He was going to get me a trash bag to clean up the glass."

"Be right back." Enrique scrammed down the stairs.

"¿Qué pasa, Doña Rosanna?"

"So, you speak Spanish? The accent is not bad."

"My boyfriend was Puerto Rican."

And she wrinkled her nose. "I see. O'Reilly Green, right? I knew your family." She turned, went into her apartment, and locked the door behind her.

Michael O'Reilly Green was born in the old Lincoln Hospital in the South Bronx in 1967. His mother, Gail, died while giving birth to him. The hospital was not equipped to deal with her heavy hemorrhaging. His father, Devlin O'Reilly, grew up in Norwood, a working-class Irish enclave in the Northwest Bronx. Gail and Devlin had met in high school, got married right after graduation, and moved into Gail's father's six-family apartment building on Faile Street to manage it. Devlin was good with his hands and was fearless of the South Bronx neighborhood changing from Jewish to Puerto Rican.

Aunt Helen and Uncle Simon came for newborn Michael at the hospital and took him to live with them in Great Neck, Long Island and raised him as their own.

Enrique came up the stairs taking two at a time and stood in Michael's doorway. "Here you go."

Pachelbel's *Canon* played from Rosanna's apartment.

Enrique looked at her door. "Good. She took her food. I ain't got to wash her pot. You can leave yours outside your door when you're done."

"I'll wash mine, too. When I get some dishwashing liquid."

"You pitiful. Just leave it here outside your door."

"What about feeding the rats?"

"I was just messing with you. We ain't got a rat problem up in here. You want to see my studio? It ain't all that, but it's cool."

Michael heard the metal scrape of Rosanna's peephole cover closing. "Some other time, perhaps."

"Whatever." Enrique turned to Doña Rosanna's door. "Did you eat the arroz con pollo yet, Doña Rosanna?"

She opened her door and clutched her pink robe. "It's a little greasy, but se deja comer."

"You a trip." Enrique disappeared down the stairs. "Check you later, Michael."

"He's an artist." Rosanna shook her head sadly. "Pobrecito." Then she laughed loudly and closed her door.

Michael shook the shards of glass into the industrial-strength garbage bag. He put the pot of food in the refrigerator and sipped his beer. He settled in the chair, turned off the old lamp, and by the time he finished his beer he was riding Pachelbel's *Canon* into dreams of passion.

237

Michael quietly watched Enrique unfold a cot and dress it—fitted sheet, cover sheet and pillow.

"Did you let yourself in?"

"Your door was open, bro. My dad told me to bring this up for you."

"Thanks, but I didn't ask him for it."

Enrique smiled. "Fresh clean sheets? How you gonna say no?" Then he sat on it and bounced up and down. "It's not so bad for a couple of nights." Then he stretched out on it, folded his hands behind his back and slipped off his flip flops which made soft, dull thumps when they hit the floor. He removed one hand from behind his head and invited Michael over to join him. Michael didn't move from the chair.

"C'mon. I see the way you look at me and I think you got it going on so why play a game?"

"I could get in trouble. I'm trying to start anew."

Enrique dropped his arm. "Papa, I am new. Nobody's gonna find out. What's the big deal? You into me, right?"

Michael nodded. His throat was dry and his mouth wet. He swallowed.

Enrique smiled. "Relax, pa."

"You should go."

"You are so fine." Enrique bit his lower lip. "I want to be all over your pretty green eyes and that curly blond hair." Enrique pulled off his tank top and propped himself up on his elbows. "I want you, Mikey. What's it gonna be?"

238　　Michael remained seated. He thought, *Enrique is the age of the students I'll be teaching Hamlet to in a few weeks.*

Enrique swung his feet around and sat up on the cot. The pinkish light from the street made his face glow in the darkness. As he stood he became more illuminated by the streetlight. "I may be young, but I'm no kid." He loosened one of Michael's fingers that were gripping the arms of the Queen Anne chair. Michael stood. They were almost eye-to-eye. Enrique pressed his forehead to Michael's. They looked in each other's eyes; Enrique placed Michael's hand on his crotch and they slowly began to kiss.

Enrique sat on the cot and extended his hand. Michael accepted it.

Michael awoke to Yul Brynner's "Et cetera, Et cetera, Et cetera." His watch read 3:10 in the morning. His nakedness was covered by the thin sheet and he was alone. He heard Anna challenging the King of Siam and he moved to the wall that his apartment shared with Rosanna's. As Anna began to sing, Rosanna sang along.

Michael pressed his ear against the cool wall that Enrique had painted and listened to Rosanna sing.

In the morning, Michael rose from the cot. He could still smell Enrique. He rinsed out his mouth and looked at himself in the bathroom mirror, at the small wrinkles around his eyes and the lines that looked like parentheses around his mouth. "I must still have it." He ate a few cold chunks of arroz con pollo, stepped out of his door and locked it behind him. Rosanna opened hers.

"Going to the store?"

"Sí, yo hablo español Doña Rosanna, remember?"

"And I speak English. Can you buy me a pound of Bustelo coffee, Italian bread, a pound of queso de papa, and a half gallon of milk?"

239

"Sure."

She reached into her bra and pulled out a satin change purse from which she removed a neatly folded twenty dollar bill. "Your groceries are my treat." She held out the bill.

He accepted it.

She nodded, asking, "Why are you here, Michael?"

"My family used to own a small building on this street."

"I know. O'Reilly Green. They burned it for the insurance money. Why are you here, now?"

His face reddened. "I'm coming to teach…"

"Go to the store and you can tell me the truth when you come back."

She toasted the bread in the oven and served sweet hot coffee to Michael. She dropped lumps of the cheddar cheese into their coffee mugs.

"Let it melt a little and then scoop it out and spread it on the bread. Delicious. I got it from my husband, he was a campesino. So why are you back?"

He had thought about her question on the way to the store, on the way up the stairs, and as he sat before her. He stirred his coffee.

"You're attractive, you're young, you're educated and you're white. You could go anywhere, no?"

"I suppose."

"Suppose? No me venga con esa mierda. White people come here for two reasons, because they want to take something away or they want to hide. I know the blanquitos are gonna wanna buy this building from me. I read the papers. The Bronx is next they say. But I don't think you're here to buy—so I guess you here to hide. "

Michael sipped the coffee. It was so sweet it stung his teeth. It was just how Raul liked it. "My boyfriend, Raul, left me after almost twenty years."

"Twenty years?"

Michael nodded.

"Raul? ¿El puertorriqueño? What happened?"

Michael sipped his coffee to push away the lump that had formed in his throat. He'd asked himself the same question over and over, but no one had ever asked him.

"I'm not completely sure. We met in college on Long Island. I was a freshman and Raul worked in the cafeteria."

"He wasn't a student?"

"No. After I graduated and started working I moved into his apartment in Queens. It wasn't the safest neighborhood, but everybody knew each other and everybody knew Raul. His family knew that he was gay, so when I moved in with him it was no big deal to them that we were a couple. When I came out to my aunt and uncle—that was a big deal. I lied to them and said that Raul had graduated with me, but he served me three meals a day while I studied." Michael sipped the coffee and looked away.

Rosanna's chair scraped across the linoleum as she got up then she placed a hand on Michael's back. "Why are you crying, lindo?"

"He had it tough and I loved him and I wanted to make life easier for him, for us. But years after we moved to Long Island he wanted to leave. He missed his Queens neighborhood. He said Long Island was too white for him."

Rosanna laughed. "When I moved to this neighborhood it was almost all Jewish people and blancos. But we moved here, because we were trying to move up in the world and living with white people was moving up. But nobody wanted us here. Do you know what that feels like?"

"I'm gay. I know what it feels like to not be wanted. But you lived here when you weren't wanted."

241

"I chose to be here. The people that lived here took me a little because I'm blanquita, but my husband was as black as espresso." Rosanna let out a hearty laugh.

"What's so funny?"

"He used to tell me 'make a cafecito, strong and black like me.'"

Michael laughed, too.

"My husband never forgot that he was black, and if he did, he was reminded of it every day. You're white and your family has money. And m'ijo, when someone leaves a relationship after twenty years, it's because they stop putting up with something they'd been putting up with for a long time." Rosanna finished her coffee and she patted Michael's hand. "I know." She put her plate and coffee cup in the sink.

"So you stayed in Long Island." She shook her head. "Well m'ijo, you won the fight, but you lost Raul." Rosanna dusted off her hands. "You think moving to Faile Street is going to bring him back?"

Michael stared at the cheese at the bottom of his coffee cup. "How did you get so wise?"

"How could you think that I wouldn't be?" She chuckled. "So are you here to teach our children or are you checking out the property for your family? They want to come back now that things are getting better? Buy the building and burn it down!"

"No."

"Hmph," she sat down and looked tiny amongst all the kitchen clutter. "I'm gonna die and I have no family. I love this building and this block. I want to make sure it's in good hands when I go."

"I can't buy it." Michael sat down across from her.

"I don't want to sell it. What am I going to do with money after I'm dead? I'll leave the building to somebody, but someone who will love it and take care of it. Don Willie, he's not good with money and he'll lose it. Enrique loves it here, but he's just a kid. They need to be protected." Rosanna hobbled over to the sink and turned on the water. "I made breakfast so you wash the dishes."

Michael washed the cups, saucers, teaspoons and dessert plates.

"I hope you love it here, Michael."

"I hope so, too. The kids here need me more than those privileged kids in Garden City, Long Island."

"They really do. Enrique does, too."

Michael stared at her blankly and his face reddened.

"You haven't told me why you're here, Michael?"

"For the children."

"Don't you dare disrespect me!"

"Miss Rosanna…"

"You're not here for them, but for yourself. You can't be honest with me, a little Puerto Rican woman from Faile Street? Don't fuck up our kids, carajo. What can you give to them?"

Michael knew he was there because he wanted to prove to Raul that he could live in the Bronx among black and Latino people. He wanted word to get back to him. To prove to him that he cared enough to teach in their schools. And if that didn't work Michael knew that he could find another Raul a lot easier in Hunts Point than in Garden City, Long Island. He knew that he would not be under the scrutinizing eyes of his aunt and uncle, and that he could do whatever he wanted. And in less than twenty-four hours of being back on Faile Street, he already had.

His heart knocked at his chest. "I'm a good teacher. I can give them that."

"Then teach, por dios." Rosanna turned off the water.

Michael stepped out into the hall separating their apartments. He put on sweats, a t-shirt and running shoes. He ran past the bodega, past the auto glass shops on Garrison Avenue, and ran until he reached the high school where he'd be teaching. The thick black gates surrounding it were locked and there was debris on the front steps. He imagined that if he'd grown up on Faile Street, that he might have attended this school. He knew Raul attended a school very much like this in Queens.

He'd made the choice to be on Faile Street and he knew that in order to be a good teacher he had put his preoccupation with himself aside. As he ran back to Faile Street he looked at the teenagers and wondered to which of those students would he give what he had? Would he grade papers for the young woman with the large hoop earrings and speak of Shakespeare, García Márquez and Baldwin to the young black man wearing the baseball cap turned to the side? He also saw about ten Rauls. They were sitting in front of bodegas, playing handball, fixing cars or walking arm in arm with lovely women.

As he climbed the stairs and opened the door to his new apartment he decided that he would be the best teacher he could be. He arranged the stacks of books neatly against his living room wall. Then, he looked out his window at Faile Street, watched as Enrique took out large black bags of trash and listened to Vivaldi's *Spring* play from Rosanna's apartment. Then, Michael smiled.

The Unheard Border Story

BRYAN PACHECO

"Por fin, Alejandro!" I'm relieved to see my best friend. I need his ears, so he can help me understand why I could possibly be sad about a dad I never knew. I want to tell him I still hope and pray my mom is alive and how...

Now is not the time. Alejandro has another black eye; his dad beat him again. But he has new jeans, so that means he was at the bar. Anytime he has anything new, he paid for it himself. Then his dad boils into a rage because he's heard all the whispers of Alejandro moaning through the motel walls and getting paid for it. And everyone knows, only men pay for sex.

"Me voy—te juro, te juro Dorian, me voy." His watery hazel eyes buried in his hands.

I hate hugs, but I hug him, partially because I need one too. I get ice and slide it over his eye. This is our usual routine every time his dad hits him. Next, he will calm down; we'll stay silent and then laugh. He'll go back home to that devil and I'll walk alone trying to find motivation for each next step. I'll fall into a daydream about Mami returning or calling me from up North. Then, I'll buy a soda, an orange one, from the guy across the counter who I can't face, who makes my pulse sweat. Happens. Every. Time.

"¡Dorian, vente ya—tenemos órdenes!" my boss, El Gordo, is yelling again.

My break is over. All he does is yell. Maybe he'd shut up if he knew I now have two dead parents. I've worked here for two years and, so I yell, and everyone yells, and all we do is yell—or just not listen and say nothing. More food to make, I'll have to console Alejandro later.

246

"¡No, no te vayas!" Alejandro points to a bag. Why does he have a bag? He shows me a bulky white envelope; there is a lot of American money inside. Oh shit!

We were supposed to leave in three months, but he wants to leave tonight. Right now.

Alejandro is like my brother and his eyes stare at me with desperation; he needs to be far away, where his father's fist can no longer force his smile away. I have my own reasons for leaving, but I let his motivate me. I rush home to pack a bag. Alejandro gives me two hours, the bus leaves in three. There's no time to consider if what I'm doing is absolutely stupid, but I pack for an adventure.

As I sort through clothes, I think that where I'm from, Guatemala, little boys usually go without fathers, and I find some old photos of Mami, some with notes in her handwriting, "para mi hijo Dorian, Mami te quiere tanto." When she left to cross borders, my angry tears stained her white sweater. I was fourteen, but her motherly embrace always made me feel like a two-year-old. We sat on my childhood bed and I stayed under her arms for hours. When she finally

shut the door on me—abandoning me—my bright blue bedroom walls faded and darkness choked me. There were no
thoughts. No smiles. No vigor. Loneliness wrapped around
and closed me in.

I enter lost through a creaking motel lobby door. Alejandro
told me to meet him here. My eyes scan around. I don't see
him. I walk over to the clerk to ask if he's seen a spunky
average height boy, except I'll ask in plain terms. A pair of
skinny smooth arms embraces me from behind my broad
back and I turn around and see just who I am looking for.
Alejandro always has to make an entrance and I like to let
him.

A short, stocky, not-to-be-trusted kind of thug motions
us to a corner of the lobby. He is Paco, a Mexican "coyote"
from Veracruz. *How he's in Guatemala?* I don't know, but I'm
not sure I want to. Alejandro slides him $4,000 American
for himself and me, an agreed upon amount. He guarantees
freedom across both borders and to the North.

Paco gives us a threatening glare, "No digas nada de mí…,"
warning us that no mention of him can escape our lips once
we are on the bus into Mexico. If he gets caught, he promises
we'll go down with him.

Alejandro calls for my attention, "¡Dorian! ¿Estás listo
vos?" I'm not sure I am ready, but I pinch myself and manage to board the bus, committing to the thoughtless impulse
I had just acted on hours prior. I tuck my black book bag
under my seat. I've packed my favorite black t-shirt and my
dark denim jeans that make my butt look nice. I like a lot of
black. I playfully fight with Alejandro for the window seat.
I'm not only taller and more muscular, but very convincing,
so I get what I want. I stare at the window trying to keep
every moment that passes. Soon the vistas become mun-
dane, like my life. I rest my head on the glass and drift off
to sleep.

The motors make exhausting pitiful noises and I can feel
the momentum slow. My half open eyes see dust consume
the air around the bus. My heart rises in beats, like a dark
samba. The wheels trickle to a violent stop. We're stuck. The
doors open slowly and dusty smoke fills the inside of the bus.
Through it, I can only see faint images of men stampeding
aboard, charging in and ordering everyone out.

Outside, a border patrol agent targets me: "¿A dónde vas?"
Ufff, where am I going? I have to think fast.

I invent a story about a sick grandmother in Mexico,
clamped on the edge of death in a hospital bed. Abuela was
frail, with perhaps only minutes left of her relentless pulse. I
let tears burst from my swollen eyes. There was a fierce ur-
gency for the bus to continue and this officer has the power
to reunite a dying grandmother with her beloved grand-
child. I hand fate over to him, let it rest on his hands, and
confront him dead in his eyes. He has a choice: be an agent
or be human.

And just like that, I, Dorian the Great, am back on the
bus ready to cross the first border from Guatemala into
Mexico.

My accomplishment fades and my heart speeds. Alejandro
is not next to me. I look out my window and see him being
bullied by two agents. I'm worried because Alejandro is a
terrible liar. He told me once he had a girlfriend and I never
believed him. I can see him sweat as I see more agents approach him. Paco knows what I am about to do: "No vayas,"
he threatens with a begging tone—if I get caught, so does
he.

I push his hand. I can see the situation getting more urgent,
"¡Muévense!" I suffer the anxiety of others coming back on
the bus, making my trek to the exit an obstacle. My eyes jolt
from side to side; no one is in the seat in front. I'll jump! And
I do. The bus stairs seem like a pyramid, but I scale them

in seconds. Border agents are blocking me from reaching Alejandro, but impulse pushes them aside. And hard.

"Tus papeles. ¡Muéstrame tus papeles!" Neither Alejandro nor I have papers to allow us into Mexico. I kick the dust from the dirt. It's over. They caught him. They caught us.

"Esperen, esperen," Alejandro begs for their attention. He moves his hand toward his jeans pocket. Like me, he's heard stories of being able to bribe border patrol to get across. How much would it take? A few hundred American dollars? Maybe a thousand? One agent draws a pistol. I thought only real cops carried guns. As Alejandro reaches further down his pocket, the pistol rises higher. I'm in a nightmare; my hands are over my head, "No, no, no."

Alejandro retracts his hands as the agent violates his jeans pocket. "¿Qué es esto?" He knows exactly what it is, but wants to play tough cop. He opens the envelope flap before Alejandro can tell another bad lie to try and save some of the money. With a sly grin, the agent pulls the green out. He pushes Alejandro forward and the dust from the dirt road rises as he crashes. The agents—and our money—vanish, but the bus door is open and the driver honks.

After the border ordeal, the bus drops us at the very first town on the outskirts of the Guatemala-Mexico border. We're illegal now. Paco rushes us into a small cherry red car that takes us seven miles north to another bus. I've heard terrible stories of people getting caught, getting deported before they even have a chance to get to the desert. We're lucky. We have a smooth ride and get to the north of Mexico in two days.

We arrive during the sun kissed morning and are immediately taken to a safe house. This "house" is nothing more than a glorified motel, with six-foot tall broken fencing attempting, and doing a bad job, to hide the premises. There is a scent on the air that hints to the many border crossers who have stepped on these grounds before us.

With my book bag over my large shoulders, Alejandro and I walk at Paco's every command. Paco talks to some other sneaky looking thugs and I can maybe spot one who looks half decent. Alejandro quickly realizes they are the other coyotes. We walk past them without being introduced or locking eyes. Paco brings us over to a group, mostly farmers from Mexico. I can see their lost and confused faces mimicking my own, obviously other border crossers.

I become overwhelmed by the fury of incoming handshakes pressuring me to be cordial and awake. "Hola, soy Dorian." My accent tells them I'm not from Mexico. I introduce myself as Paco pushes us through everyone else making the journey north: some women, some old, some young, one child—but mostly men.

Seconds ago, the sun was hiding, but dusk has awakened it to its fullest potential and it's irritating my large eyes. Girls always told me I had beautiful big coffee eyes with a hint of dulce caramelo and I'd tell those girls they were beautiful, but I never meant it. The heat glues my wavy brown hair to my forehead as I brush my hand over it to wipe the dripping sweat. Not too far away, Alejandro is off being the people person that he is. Maybe I'll join him? As everyone waits for instructions from Paco and the other coyotes, the sun shines a spotlight on each person who takes a turn telling their story.

A man with a burden so large fights back his crackling voice as he tells the story of his three young children. Children are naïve creatures who can only understand what they want. His brown lip quivers and his black eyes sink low. His children could not understand why he'd left; all they knew was that he did. But to be a man and give his family life he had no choice but to be right where he was. Not his first time crossing the border; he warns us all that of the fifteen people here, only two or three may make it across. My eyes open wide at Alejandro.

Would we?

Others step forward with deep wounds that have also forced them to this moment. In the order of things, we all shift our attention to the girl with the gorgeous face. She looks like a shorter version of the women in the Miss Universe pageants that Mami loved to watch. She keeps her head down, but shifts her rare blue eyes toward the sky. She's left two younger brothers at home for whom neither of her parents can care for.

A motherly figure rises. I could tell she was unsure why she was here, but somehow she was. Her jet-black hair hides her face and the visible features hint toward what was once a happy life. Each line around her small black eyes shows the pain and stress her husband's abandonment had put on her. In hopes of providing more she has left behind four children, one a thirteen-year-old son. I was fourteen when Mami left. I can't listen anymore.

Leaning his head forward in the way I've grown accustomed, a gesture so inviting, Alejandro gives each story sincere attention. He's always there for anyone who needs an ear and he does it well. Now, I need him to listen to me. I grab his arm and yank him to the side.

I harshly whisper, "¿Por qué cruzamos?" I need reassurance that our lives were bad enough that crossing makes enough sense. Guatemala is only a bus away; it's now or never if we are going to realize our foolishness and return. Besides, those corrupt agents robbed us of our money. I only have some that I saved of my own and I'm not sure it will sustain us.

"Cállate Dorian, ya estamos acá."

So what, being already here is not enough for me. I fight back, "No seas idiota." Sometimes his passion and stubbornness lock him into situations where bad decisions become irreversible. But me? I need to be sure this is right.

He stares at my unsure face with a look so intense and angry that I'm speechless—say something damn it, say something. Silence makes me uncomfortable.

"¿Dorian, lo ves? ¿Lo ves?" He points to the scar above his hazel eye. "¿Y esto?" He points to the cut on his left arm, "¿Y esto?" He alerts my eyes to the bruise on his abs, there are two. "¿Y esto?" His right leg is black from the knee down.

Okay, I get it.

Going to motels was the only way Alejandro could be with men. Having them pay for it was just a gratuity for his time. While he sang those sweet sounds of ecstasy, from the pleasure—none of it meant more to him than just being able to look over and explore who he was. He'd usually find them at bars. That's how he found me.

Now that the sun is on him, and I am his audience, the words struggle to leave his shaking lips. He tells me going back is not an option because of his father and people like his father, which are most people in Guatemala.

Why am I leaving? I realize it is not him I need to ask, but myself. It's a question I can't answer, so as his eyes penetrate mine, I decide to stay, not only with Alejandro, but for him.

Paco and the other coyotes order us all into a room. There is no life here, just white walls and one TV for noise. Five beds are pushed together so all fifteen of us can strive for comfort. The three pillows and spread out sheets have been used previously, probably recently. I drop my bag to the floor and everyone follows my lead, placing down their small bags packed with essential things like water and pictures to get them across the border.

We are told two things: There will be two meals a day and we cannot leave without telling a coyote. Paco warns us that we are not a family, we are strangers, and anyone will be left behind who is not where they have to be when they have to be there. Today we're allowed a break, but we'll leave tomorrow night. He tells us to lay low, eat and save our energy, because the desert will be the worst thing we will ever experience.

We all stare at each other; no one speaks. I spit my chewed nails onto the wood floor and keep my head down and away from Alejandro. He did not force me here, but I want to make him feel guilt for making me care so much about him. With a cold attitude I walk to the bathroom, a sharp turn away from Alejandro for effect.

253

When I decide to be an adult again, I peacefully walk back in and suddenly lock eyes with someone who stops my breath. I have not seen him before and I've met everyone. He takes over the room as everyone else miraculously drifts away. I focus in, my breath is still. He's growing ever tanner as my red drains to pale. I float over to the bed, my eyes on this creature so marvellous. He glides over as images of splendor pierce my thoughts and I imagine all sorts of scandalous acts. His hand is reaching closer and closer and closer. It's firm.

"¿Qué tal? Soy Javier." He's going to make this journey much more exciting.

I squeeze his manly grip and yelp, "Soy Dorian."

He smiles and I try again, my face more serious. I'm ready. "Soy Dorian." That's much better, a deep tone that projects what a man should be.

When I don't know what to say, I say everything, but Javier has kept me silent. I want to go and he doesn't want to leave. He stands and mutters that he's left his wife behind in order to provide her a better life. *He's chained in marriage?* Taken.

I don't care. Javier has given me my own reason for staying here. And his wife is the reason he's here, so she only has herself to blame for us meeting. But I suspect that he had other reasons for leaving. The hours sped by as I lost myself in Javier.

I rush to Alejandro in a giddy little prance—the kind of annoying dance one does when happiness has infected them. He gives me an odd look, "¿Dorian, estás bien?"

Of course. I don't tell him why, but I'm pretty okay. Actually, I'm great!

Life is F-A-N-T-Á-S-T-I-C-O and I get a wild idea. "¡Tomamos algo!" I expect this journey will get difficult and sipping tequila will mark our celebration of our new lives. I look at Alejandro's empty pockets and remember we were robbed, my high is falling. Dying. Fate intervenes and the girl with the gorgeous face, the one that looks like she is from the Miss Universe pageant, overhears us and wants to tag along. I know why she's coming and it's obvious, if not to her, it is to me. I'll even play along, because we need her. I move a lock of hair away from her brow. She tells me I have beautiful big coffee eyes, with a hint of dulce caramelo and I tell her she's beautiful. I even ask her name. She's María. I'm happy because pretty girls get free drinks. I want to invite Javier, but that would seem too obvious.

Los jovenes—as adults call us—my generation, acts on impulse, because only stupid kids would go to a bar with the journey ahead of us and risk being seen and getting caught, but we're stupid and young and I guess that means the same thing. We climb out of the bathroom window, as to not be seen by the coyotes or the rest of the group, and because it's fun to escape from a small window that only opens halfway. Alejandro is flexible and makes it look easy.

And María? All young girls have experience sneaking out. I am the one who gets stuck, one muscular leg out and one in. Once the soft laughter dies, and it does not easily, María and Alejandro yank my leg hard, causing me to crash onto the hard ground below. The muffled laughter finds life again, but I make a successful escape.

María, Alejandro and I didn't really think our outing through, but I have not been thinking anything through since I decided to cross, so why start now? I'm not sure how we found the bar, La Cantina, but we have. It's a small bar in a whole strip of small bars with the exciting scent of all things liquor and lime. The music is cheery and the voices boisterous.

"Dorian," María calls and her hair falls to one side, as she disappears in the desperation of the men looking for an escape through a woman's body. She emerges victorious, drinks in hand.

"¡Arriba, abajo, al centro y adentro!" And we drink; drink the night to a fuzzy blur. Alejandro is doing what he does at bars and I know he'll get what he wants and today what he wants I don't like. Had I had two tequilas less, maybe I could warn him. María is laughing at everything, even when there is little to laugh at, and I know she'll be my responsibility tonight. Seven shot glasses over a puddle of tequila and my eyes open large and close swiftly, my mind in a foggy glaze. The only image with sharp resilience is Javier and he won't exit my thoughts.

María spins me to the dance-floor. Unlike most Guatemalans, I'm not very good at cumbia. I spin and spin and spin and she twirls. The music is loud, the lights are flashing. I can feel the sway of the wood floor as the stomps of proud feet cause bodies to spin and spin. Men are supposed to take the lead, but I'm clueless, so María takes charge. She guides me under her arms and into another spin; seductively she comes under my bicep into an embrace and twirls herself free. I'm enjoying this. She puts her flirty hand over

255

my large neck and tours us around the dimly-lit room in a dance, with all eyes on us. She kept her head down when I first met her, but now her smile is bright and she's projecting it to the world. The beat changes, people sway from side to side, and we hug.

María is doing her own tequila-inspired cumbia and I know it's time to get her home, though we have no home. I throw her on my back; by her embrace I can tell she likes it there, protected and safe. Alejandro wants to stay. I forget to warn him.

Only someone foolish would leave his best friend at a bar in an unfamiliar town, but I'm tequila foolish. With María still on my back, I arrive at that half opened window, an easy exit, but an impossible entrance. I kneel down and cradle her softly onto the rocky earth. I peer over, the front entrance in sight, no Paco, no coyotes. I scoop María up and sneak over. I softly turn the doorknob. It's locked.

I can see a blue old pickup truck pull in; its lights shining closer toward me. I feel like a fugitive. My heartbeat speeds up like Brazilian drums and my mind panics for ideas. María sleeps on the dirt ground unaware of the impending chaos. I see a glimmer of light from inside. I hear a familiar voice that I have recently met. Javier with bleary eyes and tired body picks María up and motions me into the room where everyone else is asleep.

Luckily for me, she doesn't awaken. I use drunk to my advantage and collapse on Javier. He doesn't resist or move me. I think about Alejandro briefly, but shift my attention back to Javier who is making a space for him and me to lie on.

I can feel that Alejandro is not okay, but my trembling hands explore Javier's chest, who feels like such a man. I can't stop the nervous shivers that overtake my body. I feel wrong, but I like it. I dare to run my hands down his stomach's trail and pursue his zipper. He wants it. The air changes and I seize the moment. I've never felt one but my own.

Life fills me and drains from Alejandro, two oppressed hands tightening around his neck. My tongue rolls in sin and Alejandro is at peace, his vision blurring. Night falls silent and my eyes shut, my body stills.

It feels like a dream, Paco poking my bare chest. My eyes open and it's not a dream at all; Paco is above me, his brown worried face looking into mine. I slowly rise and wobble straight. I can still feel the tequila in my blood and struggle to make my face neutral, square and alert. *Maybe he saw me escape from the window? Or carrying María?* I don't want to hear his words, because no one wakes you late at night for anything good.

For the first time, and I never expected it, Paco sounds human, "¡Dorian—tu amigo, tu amigo!" It all rushes to me, pierces me, my heart bleeds a terrible horrible color; the worst in the world. My ears mute and Paco's lips just move; I'm too scared so I choose deafness.

When I first met Alejandro, I knew he was the best person in the world. He was in a bar and he had a glow. It was then I decided he would be my friend; I just didn't know he'd become my brother. Paco's lips are still moving and my arms shove him to the floor. I trip on those sleeping in front, startlingly them awake. I freeze at the door, not knowing what to think. I hear my breath, it's slow and tense and rising. I reach and my hands shake a painful guilty tremble. For once, I'm not sure what truth will be on the other side. I close my eyes and open the door to the night sky.

The breeze hits my face and it's cool. I hear the honk of the lone truck passing by, like a silver bullet in the glimmer of the full moon.

257

I can hear songs in my head and allow my eyelids to rise and I can see. The coyotes are hovered around him. He's just there, on the dirt road, no movement.

Paco and the other coyotes help me carry Alejandro inside the safe house. Their helpfulness surprises me. They let me stay in a small common area with him passed out on the floor. It was depressing until I start singing Juan Gabriel and heard his muffled voice trying to sing along.

I feel guilt in my chest and I sit and stare at Alejandro, cuddled up like a baby in the corner. He's still singing "Así es," at least it sounds like that, and I know he's trying to make me feel better. He's half asleep; his face is lowered, trying to hide his bruised neck, stained with those hateful hands that tried to steal his life.

I can sense his embarrassment too, because he was on his knees, doing what guys do on their knees to get money, to replace what was stolen from him—but that guy had no intention of paying. Alejandro managed to break free and run, but not without a chase, and I know he's not even sure how he got here, how he knew where to run to, but he ran and ran, until he collapsed.

Alejandro, with his glazed over eyes, stares at me. Tequila, because we are both still very drunk, makes you admit everything. And he says he has something to tell me. His voice is numb, words falling from his mouth. He's been going to motels since he was twelve and he has something that up North they have medicine for, medicine they don't have in Guatemala or Mexico, especially for someone poor like him.

I know what he has, but I ask anyway, hoping maybe I'm wrong—but I'm not. He has that disease with no cure. I'm curious and I ask him how? He did not get it from someone in the bars or the motels; he got it from the only guy he ever loved. An older guy who promised the world and to never hurt him, and to a boy with an abusive father those words mean everything. That's why he knows love does not exist and life is no fairytale. That's why he never loved again, because it was safer in the motels and at least he'd have something to show for it: money. All love gave him was the harsh truth about life and a disease that would hasten death.

As much as it hurts, and I so badly want to help, this is his life and my eyes have no right to tear. I want to hug him, but I'm paralyzed. A hug can do nothing for him now except pity him and what good is pity? He speaks and I listen. I want him to stop, because I can't understand how one person can experience all of this, and I feel lucky in comparison, lucky to never have had a father and that Mami leaving was my only heartache. I stare at my long fingers, because if I look at Alejandro, I'll break. And as the cold bitter night rocks him to sleep, I vow to myself to get him up North and to the other side.

259

"Hoy cruzamos," Paco tells; the time is right, today we'll confront the desert. We have our last meal.

I save Alejandro a plate and put it to the side; I know he needs sleep right now, not food. We circle around the table and say a prayer, for ourselves, our families—and friends— for safety on this hard journey ahead. Amen.

"Cruzar es más difícil que antes," I hear. There are more fences now, more border patrol, even the people up north, on the other side, the gringos; they don't like us and they volunteer to make sure we fail. I hear stories of people getting caught along the way, dying, turning back, and giving up. Fear creeps in again in, but I think of Alejandro and I know we have to make it.

My eggs turn black.

Javier walks in, his eyes refusing to meet mine, only to look when I'm turned away, nodding at the other men, looking at me, accusing me. Last night we were kind of sloppy, didn't clear our tracks. It only took one eye to see, two ears to hear, and suddenly everyone knew, except they got to Javier first and he denied wanting it, saying I forced him. I didn't.

They want the truth. I can see Paco and María. I see me. They ask me that question I have not asked myself, "¿Dorian, eres gay?"

My hands are melting. My fever is rising and sweat floods my face. I look at Javier and I hate him. "No, no soy pato—no soy hueco." I'm not a faggot.

They don't ask anything else; just leave me and my beating heart. María stays and I can't confront her eyes. She felt protected in my arms last night; I told her she was beautiful. How stupid she feels. She touches my face, tells me it's okay. I shake my head wildly, I deny it. I have to protect myself, but she knows the truth—even if I won't admit it to myself.

It's time.

It passes in snapshots: men on their phones crying to their mothers, begging for their blessing. I can taste fear in the air. Alejandro cannot recover anymore; I pack his bag and yell for him to awaken. I throw his food in front of him; he either eats now or starves. The coyotes tell us all we need to throw our clothes away and can only keep the clothes we have on. Extra clothes are extra weight.

I motivate myself and motivate Alejandro; it's just me and him now. Life is a risk anyway and we choose to risk it all. Paco and the other coyotes throw jugs at us and we must fill them with water, it is all we will have to drink in the parched desert.

One small car drives in on the dirt road to the safe house and all fifteen of us must fit in. In this car, we will drive to the desert and start our journey to the border. The coyotes choose comfort and lounge up front and force all of us to find seats in the back. The women are petite, smaller than us, so we lock them in the trunk, with our bags, and food, and water. I feel bad, but it's the only way, and only a dead man would allow his feelings to mean anything right now.

The guys, we squeeze in the backseat, air-sealed tight, like sardines. I feel feet, faces, bodies, and I don't know whose hand I'm grabbing, but I grab it tight and pray to a God I never prayed to before.

After a two-hour ride, the car sneaks into the silent desert and the men pour out. I try to stand, but collapse. How quickly the body forgets movement when it's deprived of any. The men try to regain strength after the suffocation of the car, gasping for air and taking a quick rest. I force my blood to flow and open the trunk, helping the women out, taking the water, the food. The coyotes rush us—we have to be invisible and I pull on her arm, but she won't move.

"Muévete, por favor—muévete vos." I'm desperate, but she won't move, her body is motionless in the trunk of the car. "¡Muévete! ¡Levántate!" Alejandro rushes over. He sees my tears. She won't move. Alejandro's mouth is open wide, words collapse as they hit the air. No sound. Our eyes shatter open. "¡Muévete!" I beg, but María won't move.

That guy was right, we won't all make it.

I can hear the song of the lady mountains, the chatter of the trees, and feel the death of the sun. Paco knows what happened all too well, he's seen this scene before. "Dorian, la tenemos que dejar allí." He tells me to walk away.

I have to find the passion to move my legs, to continue on. I don't know where I am, where I'm going. One feels desperate not knowing where he belongs. Out of anxiety, I've swallowed half my gallon of water, a dumb mistake. We stop for a meal, tortillas and apples, and that'll be our meal every time we sit to eat. No one says a word and I certainly don't want to hear their voices. Orange paints the blue sky into dawn and black becomes night.

The moon illuminates the desert and I can see the yellow vicious snake eyes patrolling the dark skies. I want to sleep, forget I'm alive. But I listen to every command from the coyotes and we have to move on, the best time to move is at night. So we walk down the rocky roads, down the blind paths, my eyes can't see anything so my feet tell me where to go. I hear the buzzing of an approaching river and think of the warm beaches of my childhood, with Mami, when life was at its best and I believed, like any dumb child, it would only get better.

The only way to save time is to cross the thirsty river. I remove my shoes and let my feet explore the water. Alejandro grabs my hand and we share a breath. I hear the crunch of others grabbing their bags, trying to float. Everyone is in, but no one is moving. The river is warning us and no one dares to challenge it. The current is too strong; we have no choice but to cross another day. My wet feet crust with mud. Defeated, Paco allows us to sleep. Closed eyes will bring renewed hope.

The night hums a vile lullaby.

The unfriendly sun burns my eyes awake. There's a delicious breakfast of tortillas and apples, but I only eat a little. I'm thirsty, but know I must save my water. I maybe have enough for one more day and that's if I only drink once. So my lips will have to crack and bleed before I can drink again.

The river is friendly today, calm, and we cross. The water, on our bodies, feels cool, but the sun robs it quickly. We walk up a hill, filled with dead dreams. I can see Alejandro focus on everything around him and not at what is ahead. I see it too, old things, discarded things, dirty bottles, bones. We are not the first to tour these grounds and I allow myself to think it—that thing I've tried to reject from allowing to float in my mind. *I wonder if those bones belong to Mami? Did she cross this path, too?* I step extra hard, stomp, spit on the evil desert—it's the only revenge I have.

"Dorian, vente aquí." Paco calls me over, tells me to step hard and force it down. I feel the barbwire cut into my shoe and tease my skin. The group hurries along. Alejandro goes last, makes sure I get across. As I sneak under the wire, it slices my arm, sends a firm warning to me and a drop of blood drips and splatters on the dry dusty terrain. I've left my mark.

We have to lay low and be extra cautious. In front of us lies a big obstacle; where border crossers frequently meet their end. It's an active road. American border patrol keeps close watch here. Paco sneaks out first, checks it out, and his hand is urgent. We have to move!

263

We run and run until we feel we're safe. My body begins to tremble. I've noticed one of the tire marks on the ground, on that active road. It was fresh, no more than a few minutes old.

The wind finds its strength and blows in our direction. A woman begins to weep; she can feel it, too. Paco seems nervous. Alejandro looks back at me and I have no answers. I look up and see the day becoming brighter, the brightness hovering in. The wind is blowing harder, scratching my face, restricting my vision.

"It's approaching!" Paco roars.

I see flashes of black, of white, of fear, of defeat. The scenes splice together, everyone is running, looking to hide. I feel someone snatch me from behind, force me in their embrace. Alejandro pulls me with him. It's just me and him—just us—and we run!

I hold his hand tight and don't ever want to let go. I can feel we are wanted, they are after us. As we're running, holding on to our hopes and dreams, the sirens of the agents' cars wail. I know I have to let go. Only one of us will make it.

I feel a warm puddle bust from my lips and I can taste the dirt. Only my eyes can move, and I look ahead, my face on the ground. I feel a knee pressured over my head, forcing me still and I look at Alejandro. His eyes salute mine and we see each other. I see him. He sees me. We don't want to let go, but I know that he won't make it unless I do. My eyes, they tell him a story. They say goodbye and they close.

Orchard Beach, Section Nine

ROBERT VÁZQUEZ-PACHECO

We went to Orchard Beach in the Bronx: Joey, Gladys, Tony and I. We brought arroz y habichuelas, pollo frito, la Miller, potato salad, potato chips, (not a culture afraid of carbs) and the ghetto-blaster. You know, bien Bronx Puerto Rican picnic. Actually, that's not true because a true Puerto Rican picnic would've been the entire family including primos y vecinos.

So we were at Orchard Beach which—in case you didn't know—had various terms of endearment such as Horseshit Beach, the Puerto Rican Riviera, Chocha Beach, La Playa de los Mojones, etc. Anyway, so there we were at Orchard.

Now La Joey, or more formally, José Donato, was my cousin, one of the Bronx's true reigning cha-cha queens, a fierce reigning diva—you know what I'm saying. Gladys was this rubia a la fuerza (you know, what I call Aretha Franklin blond) dyke friend of ours, bien femme. You know, the type that kept her makeup in the cooler. Tony was Gladys's cousin, adorable and at the time, my obsession. We were sprawled out on our blankets, carrying on, checking out all the hebos and hebas (meat on the hoof) who were promenading up and down the boardwalk.

Well, there was this fine, fine Puerto Rican brother who was just a few blankets away from us with his girlfriend. Coño, qué santo macho. This boy was fine—*fine*—you know what I'm saying? So Joey started carrying on, bien loca, bien cafre, bien loud, hissing at him, calling him his huzzz-band, papi chulo, and singing "Come to Me" by France Joli—remember that song?

Well, this macho—what he could do with us and what we would do to him—was the subject of endless discussion that hot summer afternoon. We pointed him out to visitors. Actually, La Joey pointed him out as the future father of his children. Nene, we took him apart and put him back together again. You know?

And the brother knew we were talking about him—damn, the whole goddamn section knew we were talking about him. After we exhausted the topic, after we were roasted and toasted (if you know what I mean) we decided to take our asses home so we could shower, moisturize, take a disco nap, and go out dancing, dressed in white, working our tans and looking fabulous.

Pues mira, on the way back to the bus, doesn't this straight boy go right up to Joey—*très* butch as La Joey would've said—and start calling him faggot all up in his face, getting all loud and shit. You know, like straight men do when they have to prove they're straight. Actually, it's when they need to convince their girlfriends that they are. Straight.

¿Nena, pa'qué fue eso? La Josephine, que nunca tenía pelo en la lengua got loud right back at this asshole. So the boy swung at Joey y Miss Thing gritó a to' boca, "Wait! Not in

266

the face!" Then she proceeded to take off all her jewelry. You know, like the Puerto Rican girls did in high school before they got into a fight. You know, screaming at the girl they were gonna fight, "Wait! Wait! Bitch, I'm going to fuck you up, bitch!" and then they'd turn to their girlfriend saying, "Hold my earrings!" and they'd take all their shit off.

Honey, La Joey—once all the joyas were off—le dio una santa escarpesa a ese nene. La Joey jumped on that straight boy and proceeded to kick his ass up and down the Orchard Beach promenade. Miss Thing beat the *shit* out of him.

And his girlfriend, who slowly realized her piece might not survive this encounter, tried to jump in. ¿Pa'qué fue eso? Gladys dropped her bag and yelled, "Oh no, bitch!" and proceeded to tear her apart. Meanwhile, Tony and I just stood there, holding the ghetto-blaster (which was still playing music) and the bags and Miss Thing's jewelry yelling, "Go 'head, Miss Rocky! Kick his ass!"

When Miss Thing was done there wasn't a scratch on him. Darling, that straight boy was a mess; cuando Joito was finished she walked away fixing her hair like white girls do—even though Miss Thing had an Afro. Turning back, she drew herself up to her full five-nine height (in flats) and looked down at the formerly cute straight boy, declaring in bien dramática, in true Bronx diva fashion, "Remember. I was a man before I was a lady."

267

About the Authors

DAVID CALEB ACEVEDO was born in San Juan, PR and grew up in Hartford, CT. He has a bachelor's degree in Visual Arts-Painting and another in Foreign Languages, both from the University of Puerto Rico in Río Piedras. His work has been published in literary magazines such as: *The Caribbean Writer, Poui* (from Barbados), *Tonguas, Contornos, Pastiche, L'Antesala, Hostos Revew* (Open Mic/ Micrófono abierto), *El Sótano 00931* and *La Secta de los Perros,* among others. He's also been featured in cyberspace in Alberto Martínez's Letras Salvajes and En la Orilla.net. His work is also featured in the anthologies *Cuentos de Oficio* edited by Mayra Santos-Febres and *Nueva Poesía Hispanoamericana* edited by Leo Zelada and *Los otros cuerpos: Antología de temática gay, lésbica y queer desde Puerto Rico y su diáspora* edited by Moisés Agosto-Rosario, Luis Negrón and himself. He's won several awards and received an honorable mention in the Certamen de cuento para jóvenes from *El Nuevo Día* for his short story "Ébola." His first book, a poetry collection *Bestiario en nomenclatura binomial* was published in 2009 by Editorial Aventis. He's finishing his memoirs of sex, *Diario de una puta humilde,* via facebook.com.

MIGUEL ÁNGEL ÁNGELES is a queer Xican@ migrant born and raised in Lindsay, a small agricultural town in California's Central Valley. The youngest child of a migrant farm working family, he has been fascinated by the word from a young age. A voracious reader, Miguel has been inspired by the works of Greco-Roman as well as contemporary writers, especially Gloria Anzaldúa, Cherríe Moraga, Arturo Islas, Michael Nava, and Manuel Muñoz. He studied Classical Studies at the University of California at Riverside and has been transplanted in New York since 2005 where he currently works with immigrants in adult education.

RICARDO BRACHO is a playwright whose work has been produced at Brava Theater Center, Theatre Rhinoceros and INTAR and has been stage read at Pregones Theater, Intersection for the Arts, Brown University and Stanford University. A former participant in the NEA/TCG Residency Program for Playwrights, Bracho has received two commissions from the Latino Theater Initiative of the Mark Taper Forum. His plays include *The Sweetest Hangover*, *A to B*, *Sissy*, and *Querido*. Beyond his career as an artist Bracho has a long history of community involvement and education and has worked closely with lesbian and gay youth of color, Latina/o HIV services, incarcerated men and the harm reduction movement.

C. ADÁN CABRERA is the queer son of Salvadoran refugees. He was born and raised in Los Angeles. His work has appeared in *Switchback*, *Westwind*, and numerous other anthologies, and he has also served as a freelance reporter with *El Tecolote*. Carlos holds a bachelor's degree in English from UCLA and recently earned his MFA in writing from the University of San Francisco.

BRONCO CASTRO was born in Río Grande, Puerto Rico, grew up primarily in the New York/New Jersey area, and completed his undergraduate degree in Spanish Literature in New York City. "That Chilly Night in Old San Juan" is his second published, gay-themed story. He's presently working on his first queer anthology and novel. As a fiction writer, his focus is on the dichotomy of bilingual (English-Spanish) gay/queer life.

JOHNATHAN CEDANO was born in La Romana, Dominican Republic to a Dominican mother and Mexican father, which makes him "Mexinicano." He lives in Harlem, NYC with his guitars, his dreams and the voices in his head. Some of which found their way into this story.

BOOH EDOUARDO received a BFA and MFA from California Institute of the Arts (CalArts), and his visual artwork has been featured at many private and public venues and in several publications. He is an MA candidate in the English Composition Program and works with students who wish to improve their reading and writing skills at Learning Assistance Center at San Francisco State University. More of his writing is featured in the anthologies *Kicked Out* (Homofactus Press, 2010) and *Why Are Faggots so Afraid of Faggots?: Flaming Challenges to Masculinity, Objectification and the Desire to Conform* (AK Press, 2012).

BEN FRANCISCO'S short stories have been published in *Realms of Fantasy, Lady Churchill's Rosebud Wristlet, Wilde Stories, Podcastle,* and other anthologies and magazines. His current long-term projects include a set of interconnected surrealist stories taking place in the fictional setting of Gay City and a young adult novel about a Puerto Rican high school student who is surprised to discover that she's been drafted to serve as the (secret) ambassador of Earth in an interstellar confederation of planets. Visit Ben's intermittent blog at www.benfran- 271 cisco.net.

DANNY GONZÁLES was born in Brooklyn, New York. The eldest of four brothers, he was leader-by-birthright of that brat pack. His artistic ability was recognized early, evolving as it did from the simple drawings placed on the family refrigerator. A product of the New York City Public School system, he was blessed with teachers who exposed him to various art movements and fashion trends that otherwise would not have been accessible to a food stamp Brooklyn kid. A graduate of Parsons School of Design, Danny's formal training includes fashion and interior design. He developed a love for theater that led to his producing, directing and writing works in the tri-state area. His comedy troupe, Nuyorican Rule, eventually toured the college circuit, was featured repeatedly on *Good Day, New York,* and had its own variety hour on Metro TV. Danny was also a staff writer for the *The Big Gay Sketch Comedy Show* on LOGO and is a co-creator and co-producer of the *A-List* on LOGO. Currently, Danny is bi-coastal.

RIGOBERTO GONZÁLEZ is the author of eight books of poetry and prose including the memoir *Butterfly Boy: Memories of a Chicano Mariposa* winner of the American Book Award from the Before Columbus Foundation. He is also the recipient of a Guggenheim Fellowship, a National Endowment for the Arts fellowship, The Poetry Center Book Award from San Francisco State University, and of various international artist residencies and was named the 2009 Poet-in-Residence by the Board of Trustees of The Frost Place, the farm house of Robert Frost located in New Hampshire. He writes a monthly Chicano/Latino book review column, now entering its ninth year, for the *El Paso Times* of Texas and is also contributing editor for *Poets & Writers Magazine*. He is an executive board member of the National Book Critics Circle, a contributing writer for *Lambda Literary* and the *Los Angeles Review of Books*, and is on the Advisory Circle of Con Tinta, a collective of Chicano/Latino activist-writers. He curates and hosts The Quetzal Quill, a reading series in Manhattan, and is Associate Professor of English at Rutgers—Newark, State University of New Jersey.

ANTHONY HARO was born in Zacatecas Mexico. Arrived in the U.S. in 1976. Soaked up his surroundings like a sponge. Has lived in Southern California all his life. Loves to travel, and make new friends. Hates television but loves music, art and photography. He isn't afraid to tell you what's on his mind, but welcomes your opinion and points of view.

W. BRANDON LACY CAMPOS is a queer, poz, Afro-Boricua, African-American, and Ojibwe blogger, poet, playwright, and novelist. MyLatinoVoice.com named him the #2 Queer Latino Blogger in 2009. His work has been published broadly including in *Mariposas: A Queer Latino Poetry Anthology*, edited by Emanuel Xavier. His work has also been published in *Ganymede Journal #6*, *Under What Bandera* by Calaca Press, *Zona Rosa Magazine*, and a half dozen other journals, magazines, and anthologies. His performance poetry has been performed at colleges and universities across the country, and his play, *Dividing Lines* was taught as part of the theater curriculum at Macalester College. He is a recipient of two Many Voices Fellowships from the Jerome Foundation, and he was awarded a Minnesota State Arts Board Cultural Community Partnership Grant in playwriting. Brandon's first book, a collection of poetry, *It Ain't Truth If It Doesn't Hurt* will be published in 2011 by Summerfolk Press, and *Eden Lost* will be published by Rebel Sartori Press in 2011.

LAWRENCE LA FOUNTAIN-STOKES is a Puerto Rican writer, performer, and scholar. Born and raised in San Juan, Puerto Rico, he received his bachelor's degree from Harvard in 1991 and a doctorate in Spanish from Columbia University in 1999. He is currently an Associate Professor of American Culture and Romance Languages and Literatures at the University of Michigan, Ann Arbor, where he specializes in Latina/o, Puerto Rican and Hispanic Caribbean studies, with additional interests in women's, gender, and sexuality studies; lesbian, gay, and queer studies; and theater and performance. He is author of *Queer Ricans: Cultures and Sexualities in the Diaspora* (University of

Minnesota Press, 2009), which focuses on Puerto Rican LGBT migration and culture, and of a book of short stories called *Uñas pintadas de azul/Blue Fingernails* (Bilingual Press/Editorial Bilingüe, Arizona, 2009). He was one of the co-editors of a special issue of *CENTRO: Journal of the Center for Puerto Rican Studies* on Puerto Rican Queer Sexualities (2007). He regularly teaches courses on Latina/o literature, culture, and cinema.

J IMMY LAM is Dominican by birth, Caribbean by choice and Gringa by accident. He writes poetry, short stories, memoirs, political and cultural analysis and essays. He studied at the Universidad Autónoma de Santo Domingo school of Humanities and obtained a BA in English and French. Recently he completed an MA in International Relations at City College. His writing has appeared in English and "Dominicanish" in the Dominican Republic, New York and on the web in *El Listin Diario, El Nuevo Diario, Antologia de la Literatura Gay Dominicana, Colour Life Magazine, Vanity Fair, The Village Voice, Siempre, Dominican Today* and Cielonaranja.com. Jimmy's essay, "In Defense of Pleasure: Sensuality and Eroticism in Dominican Women 273 Writers in the US," appeared in the anthology *Mujeres de Palabra*. Most recently his poetry was featured in *Mary, a Literary Quarterly*, and *The Best of PANIC!* His book *Sexiles* is scheduled for release in the fall of 2011. He lives in Jersey City with his paitner, Oskar, and continues to write the interminable memoirs, *Neurosis of My Own.*

M IGUEL M. MORALES is a student, an employee, and a diversity fellow at Johnson County Community College in Overland Park, Kansas. Originally from Plainview, Texas, Morales began working as a migrant farm worker at the age of 10 helping his three older sisters support the family. Morales has always loved libraries and admits being one of those kids who repeatedly walked past the gay section hoping no one would notice. After finding his big gay voice, Morales became an active member of ACT-UP/KC. After finding his big gay Latino voice, he served as the first youth board member for the Latino/a Lesbian & Gay Organization (LLEGO). He also worked as an HIV educator and coordinator. In addition, Morales is an award-winning journalist. In 2006, Morales earned the Society of Professional Journalists' First Amendment Award. The Kansas Associated Collegiate Press has honored him with several first place awards including Journalist of the Year. Morales is a member of the National Lesbian & Gay Journalists Association (NLGJA) and the National Association of Hispanic Journalists (NAHJ). Currently, Morales serves as a board member for the Latino Writers Collective and is featured in their latest offering, *Cuentos del Centro: Stories from the Latino Heartland.*

BRYAN PACHECO is a native from the Lower East Side of NYC. This is his 2nd time being published—his first being an essay about the Queer image in pro wrestling. He attended Middlebury College where he majored in Spanish literature and taught education and on his spare time produced documentaries about Vermont Mexican migrant workers. "The Untold Border Story" is a tale inspired by a dear friend who shared his plight about being gay and crossing the Mexico/U.S. border. From that came an idea to share the "untold" stories and struggles of not just being an immigrant, but what it can mean to be gay in Latin America.

ALFONSO RAMÍREZ, originally from Los Angeles, attended the University of Southern California. He's lived in New York City for over 34 years. He came out of the closet when he was twelve years old, which annoyed his older brother very much. His plays have been performed at the Puerto Rican Traveling Theatre, Public Theatre, Circle Rep. and Repertorio Español in NYC; Nosotros Theatre and Ford Theatre in Los Angeles; and Teatro Esperanza in San Franciso. He has won several awards for his plays, including NYFA grant, Arizona Theatre National Hispanic Playwrights Award, the Isadora Aguirre Playwriting Award (twice), finalist in MetLife Nuestras Voces Competition and South Coast Rep's Hispanic Playwrights Project. His play, *The Watermelon Factory* was published in an anthology in 2002. In 2001 he was one of three writers invited by the Mexican government Arts Commission to spend the summer in Coyoacán as part of its first exchange program with the USA, where he started his first novel. He completed an MFA in Creative Writing at Goddard College, and is editing his first novel. He's also an accomplished director and ac-tor/dancer and he has several Off-Broadway, film and television credits to his name.

GUILLERMO REYES is a Chilean-born U.S. citizen, and is as-sociate professor of theater and film and head of the MFA Dramatic Writing program at Arizona State University. He is the au-thor of *Men on the Verge of a His-Panic Breakdown* and other plays. His autobiographical book, *Madre and I: A Memoir of Our Immigrant Lives*, was recently published by the University of Wisconsin Press.

CHARLES RICE-GONZÁLEZ, born in Puerto Rico and reared in the Bronx, is a writer, long-time community and LGBT activist and Executive Director of BAAD! The Bronx Academy of Arts and Dance. He received an MFA in Creative Writing from Goddard College. His debut novel, *Chulito*, will be published by Magnus Books in the fall 2011. His work's been published in *The Pitkin Review, Los Otros Cuerpos*—the first anthology of Puerto Rican queer work, *Best*

Gay Stories 2008, The Best of PANIC!: En Vivo from the East Village and in the upcoming *Ambientes: New Queer Latino Writing* edited by Lázaro Limas and Felice Picano. He co-edited, with Charlie Vázquez, *From Macho to Mariposa: New Gay Latino Fiction*. He's working on his second novel, *Hunts Point*, a look at a South Bronx neighborhood through a queer Latino lens. Mr. Rice-Gonzalez has written several plays including *Pink Jesus, Los Nutcrackers: A Christmas Carajo* and *I Just Love Andy Gibb* which won Pregones Theater's 2005 ASUNCION Play Reading Series and received a workshop production in May 2007. He's attended Bread Loaf Writers' Conference, VONA, Voices of Our Nation, Lambda Literary Writers' Retreat and Macondo, and has done residencies at the Woodstock Byrdcliffe Guild and the Virginia Center for Creative Arts.

ALEX G. ROMERO was born in New Mexico, has lived there most of his life and enjoys writing about some of its cultural aspects. An ordinary pilgrim and Veteran of the U.S. Army, he is presently at work on a novel about exile and the paternal drive childless gay men often experience, the compulsion to nurture someone in some capacity and at all cost.

CHUY SÁNCHEZ is a first generation son of guanajuatense Mexican immigrant parents who grew up in the Chicago area. At the age of 7 his first short story "El conejito" was published in the Gale Community Academy Student Journal. He has participated in INTAR's one year Hispanic Playwrights Residence Lab in New York City. His play *god's creatures* was the winner of Pregones Theatres' Asunción Playwrights Project. His plays have been featured in the Hemispheric Institute of Performance and Politics, UCSB Chicano Playwright's Competition and the Spanish Repertory Theatre's MetLife Playwrights Competition. His writings have appeared in *La Opinión*, *El Diario/La Prensa*, *Ambiente Magazine*, glaadblog.org & the *New England Blade*. He collaborated on the WW Norton & Co. publication titled *Crossing the BLVD: strangers, neighbors, aliens in a new America*. Chuy was a producer on the Telemundo morning talk show *Las Comadres con Gloria B* with MapiTV where he also worked as screenwriter for the Mexican movie project titled *El sueño mexicano*. He is currently the Marketing & Communications Manager at In The Life Media, producers of the public television show *In The Life*. Sánchez is a graduate of Antioch College, NYU's Performance Studies and the Actors Studio Drama School.

EDWIN SÁNCHEZ's recent productions include *Trafficking In Broken Hearts* at the Celebration Theatre in Los Angeles as well as the world premiere of his romantic comedy *I'll Take Romance* at the Evolution Theatre in Ohio. His newest play *La Bella Familia* will be produced by Teatro Vista in Chicago in 2011. Other productions include, *Diosa*, produced by Hartford Stage after a successful workshop by New York Stage and Film, *Trafficking In Broken Hearts* at the Atlantic Theater in New York, *Unmerciful Good Fortune* at the Intar Theater in New York, among others. Mr. Sanchez's work has been produced regionally throughout the United States as well as Brazil and Switzerland. Among his awards are the Kennedy Center Fund for New American Plays (*Clean*), three New York Foundation for the Arts Playwriting/ Screenwriting Fellowships, the Princess Grace Playwriting Fellowship (*Unmerciful Good Fortune*), the Daryl Roth Creative Spirit Award and the AT&T On Stage New Play Award (*Unmerciful Good Fortune*). Mr. Sanchez lives in upstate New York where he continues to write as well as teach and mentors playwrights.

RICK J. SANTOS is a feminist-human rights activist and scholar currently living in Long Island, NY. He earned his Ph.D. in Comparative Literature from SUNY-Binghamton with a specialization on feminist and translation theories in 2000. Dr. Santos has published numerous essays, translations, and poems in the U.S., Brazil, and Europe. He has lectured extensively on issues of contemporary Brazilian women's writings, Queer theory, post-colonial translation theories. Last year he gave lectures at Yale University, the University of Illinois Urbana-Champaign and University of Sao Paulo. Dr. Santos was the second NEH/Sophia Libman Professor of Humanities (2005-08) at Hood College, and the recipient of two additional NEH Summer Research Seminars Fellowships. He currently teaches English, Women's Studies, and Latin American Studies at SUNY-Nassau Community College.

JESUS SUAREZ lives in Miami and travels regularly to Cuba. He is a priest of Yemaya and is a certified member of the Church of the Lucumi Baba-lu-Aye and is a local, national and international activist in matters regarding Santeria, Lucumi and Yoruba religion and culture. He workS in his family business running Botanica La Caridad. This is his first publication and he plans to continue proudly contributing his experience to our gay Latino community. He was born in the Bronx to Cuban refugee parents who arrived in the U.S. in 1962. He attended Florida International University and he's participated in dozens of interviews both on local radio and TV. The piece that he contributed to this anthology will be a part of a full book and is a tribute to his lover Abel who was murdered 25 years ago and who truly was and always will be his hero.

DAVID ANDREW TALAMANTES is a gay Piscean fronterizo (borderlander) born and raised by an awesome family in El Paso, Texas. He earned a BA in Creative Writing from University of Texas-El Paso where he began his career as a freelance hardcore eroticist, publishing in magazines like *Playguy, Honcho,* and *Inches.* His poetry (a rare happening) has appeared online and in the *Rio Grande Review.* Currently, David resides in Albuquerque, NM where he complains, teaches, writes, and is finishing his MFA in fiction. David lives with Lola and Frida, two feline Divas, who try very hard to keep him writing, dancing, and loving life.

JUSTIN TORRES is author of the novel, *We the Animals* (Houghton Mifflin Harcourt). A graduate of the Iowa Writers Workshop, and currently a Stegner Fellow at Stanford, his stories have been published in *Granta, Tin House,* and *Glimmer Train.* He is the recipient of a United States Artists Rolón Fellowship in Literature.. 277

BENNY VÁSQUEZ is a native of Brooklyn, New York and graduated from Wesleyan University with BA's in African American Studies and Sociology, and then later from Columbia University with a MA in Education. He has a strong passion for peace and justice, activism and the arts. He currently works with children and is working on creating a book of short stories. This is Benny's first published piece!

CHARLIE VÁZQUEZ is a radical Bronx-bred writer of Cuban and Puerto Rican descent. His fiction, articles, and essays have been published in various anthologies, magazines and newspapers and he hosts a monthly reading series called HISPANIC PANIC! (in the East Village), which focuses on original queer Latino literature. His second novel *Contraband,* was published in 2010, and his third, *Corazón,* is wrapping up for future publication. Charlie Vázquez has lectured and participated on panels relating to gay and/or Latino literature and culture at Fordham University, New York University, Hunter College, the CUNY Graduate Center, Portland State University, Barnes and Noble, and cultural institutions. He has also been interviewed by NPR, CNN and New York's *Daily News* and has appeared on New York's WNYW Channel 5 show *Good Day Street Talk* and is the New York coordinator for Festival de la Palabra, an international literary conference held in San Juan, Puerto Rico and New York City.

ROBERT VÁZQUEZ-PACHECO is a native Nuyorican gay writer currently residing in Brooklyn. He is a writer, a poet, a painter and a former community activist, agitator, organizer and general agent provocateur. His work has been published in a variety of venues including scientific journals and fiction anthologies. He is a member of the AIDS artists collective "Gran Fury."

278

CPSIA information can be obtained
at www.ICGtesting.com
Printed in the USA
BVHW071215230821
614883BV00003B/139